THE KING TRIALS

---◆---

CHRONICLES OF WEHLMIR BOOK ONE

BY: D.L. SIMS

This book is dedicated to anyone, young and old, who had ever wished of living in fantastical lands. We are the dreamers. We are the world.

The King Trials. Copyright 2020 by Diondra Sims. All rights reserved.

This story is a work of fiction. All names, companies, events, organizations, etc are the imagination of the author or are used fictitiously. No portion of this book should be used or distributed without direct permission from the author.

Cover by: RebecaCovers
Edited by: Charmaine Tan

Map by: Frostwindz

Chapter One

Men and women dressed in immaculate fashion bustled around Khett as he stood in the middle of the ornate train station. They wore the conservative fashions of Rivland: coats and dresses with high collars. Men wore trousers with gold or silver chains dangling from the pocket watches hanging at their hips and shiny leather boots, which clicked against the marble floor. Women held purses made of fine fabric with beaded designs threaded into the front, and had their hair twisted at the nape of their necks, not a strand out of place. They wore little makeup. Only rouge on their cheeks, but nothing more.

"The train's late," his steward, Dallin--a much too skinny man with a large mole on his right cheek--said. He was older than Khett by five years and found displeasure in most things Khett enjoyed. Dallin wore his displeasure now as Khett leaned on a post with one leg crossed over the other and pulled an apple from a pocket inside his coat.

"The train's always late," Khett replied, peeling the apple with a small jeweled knife he kept tucked in his belt.

Khett's presence in the station had not gone unnoticed. A circle gathered around him and his steward. People clambered over each other to be close to the Prince. Khett remained indifferent to the scene and let his apple peel fall to the marble floor in front of him, catching Dallin's sharp frown out of the corner of his eye as the steward picked the peel up and threw it in the trash can.

Khett ate in silence and discreetly looked at the sea of women around him. Some he had already bedded once or twice, but there were a few that caught his attention, like the young woman with brown hair and ample breasts to his left and a red-haired beauty in the front.

"Rivland women are educated. One would make a perfect bride."

Khett snorted at the memory of his mother trying to push him to find a wife. He had no desire to seek a bride from Rivland. He believed them to be bland creatures who loved nothing more than discussing philosophy and dead writers. Khett got enough of that with his tutors. Rivland women were great for sex, but dull for conversation.

Somewhere in the station, a bell rang to signal a train's arrival. Khett stood straighter and lobbed his half-eaten apple at the nearby trash can. Dallin's frown grew deeper as the apple core bounced off the rim of the can, and he chased it as it rolled away. Khett chuckled when Dallin came back with the core covered in dirt and hair. His steward hated that Khett didn't act like a proper prince; he hated it even more when he had to clean up Khett's messes.

"How's my hair?" Khett asked, looking at the oak-colored strands in the reflection of a gold statue a few feet away. "Too much oil?"

"Just the right amount, Your Grace."

He chuckled. "Good answer, Dallin."

His steward bowed his head, and Khett swore he heard the man sigh.

Somewhere nearby a train whistled, and Khett readjusted his burgundy velvet tunic. The crowd waited in silence to see who Prince Khett could possibly be meeting at the train station.

The train pulled in with a hiss and a plume of steam. Khett stood with a cool, but feigned confidence. He checked his hair in the reflection of the statue again as passengers began disembarking. He scanned the crowd, his eyes glancing over the train's passengers until Andalen's wild, black curls came into view.

He stepped forward, gliding through the throng of people like a god. He smiled when his eyes met Andalen's, and only grew bigger when Arlen came into view, followed by Lord Halon Amadon, and Andalen's handmaiden, Nixema Maldreen.

Khett extended his hand toward Halon, who followed behind his children with a purposeful gait. He shook Khett's hand with an iron grip that had the prince grimacing, but he kept his smile in place. "Father will be so pleased to see you, Lord Amadon."

"I'm sure he will," Lord Amadon replied in his frigid, clipped tone. Lord Amadon was tall and skinny like his children, but he had pale skin, much unlike Arlen and Andalen's darker complexions. "How has he been?"

Khett stiffened. "The Illness is aggressive. Sadly, I believe you came just in time to say goodbye."

Lord Amadon bowed his head, his face solemn.

Uncomfortable with the man's display of emotion, Khett turned his attention to Andalen's handmaiden. "Good afternoon, Nix."

She smiled wide, making her round cheeks puff out. "Khett."

Dallin frowned. "You should call him 'Your Grace.'"

Khett pulled Nixema into a hug. "She isn't required to, Dallin. Nix is a friend."

Dallin grumbled, and Nixema giggled. Khett released her and turned his attention to Arlen, who was running a hand over his short, black curls. Blush tinged his cheeks.

"Why are you so nervous, my friend?" Khett laughed.

"I'm not nervous." Arlen protested, but his posture suggested otherwise. He stepped forward and clapped Khett on the back. "It's been too long."

Khett turned to his last visitor. Andalen stood tall and noble in a green dress with a large hoop skirt. Her curls were long and wild, barely contained by a small ornate hat. She wore light makeup that made her brown eyes appear larger and brighter.

"Andalen," he breathed out.

She smiled, showing a row of perfect white teeth. "Hello, Khett."

He held an elbow out for her to wrap her delicate, but deadly hands around, then led the party forward with Andalen at his side. Whispers followed them out of the train station.

Khett stood tall and proud. A devilish smirk curved on his handsome face.

The sun reflected off the pristine marble buildings, casting glittering light over the gray cobbled streets as the glossy black carriage with gold trimmings bumped over the pristine cobbled streets in a gentle rhythm as Khett's visitors marveled at the beautiful buildings. He had seen the same architecture more than a thousand times before, so he sat back with one leg crossed over the other, observing Andalen and her wide-eyed wonder of the shimmering structures. She had been to Rivland many times, but whenever she visited she acted as if it was her first time seeing the white and gold city.

"That is the university," Dallin provided, directing the Amadons' attention to the window on the right of the carriage. "It spans the length of two miles."

Halon yawned.

"Do they have an artist program?" Arlen wondered.

Khett looked curiously at his friend. Arlen had been an amazing artist, but an eye disorder had left him unable to paint. Or so Khett thought, but he wouldn't embarrass his oldest friend by bringing it up.

"Hmm?" Dallin asked, distracted. Khett looked out the window to see what had caught the steward's attention. Dallin's wife, one of the professors at the university, had taken her students outside. "Oh, no. Rivland's schools focus on relevant subjects such as science, arithmetic, the study of nature, and literature."

Arlen frowned. "That--"

"Are you saying art is irrelevant?" Andalen challenged. "Arlen is a great artist. Is his work not relevant?"

"N-n-not in Rivland," Dallin stammered, looking to Khett for help, but the young prince sat back. It brought him immense enjoyment to see his steward floundering under Andalen's fierce stare. "It just isn't taught here...at this school." Dallin swallowed, and Andalen raised an eyebrow. "The...um...university in Palamar teaches art."

Andalen rolled her eyes. "So, is it relevant to you? Art?"

"Y-yes, Lady Andalen."

Arlen patted Andalen's hand with an amused smile. "Sister, stop torturing the poor man."

Andalen looked at the steward as he sweat beneath his collar. "I apologize, Dallin."

Khett chuckled. "Serves you right, Dallin. Everyone knows the Amadon twins stand up for one another."

"Yes, Your Grace."

Halon cleared his throat. "It doesn't matter if art is relevant or not. Arlen--"

His voice cut off as he realized what he was about to say. The Amadons had kept Arlen's disorder a secret; only Khett and a few others knew of the diagnosis.

The passengers fell into a tense silence until the castle came into view.

The carriage pulled up to the golden gates of the castle, which were molded to look like leafy vines. The castle itself was constructed of white bricks forged from marble and Opal Stone, with large veins of ivy climbing up the side walls. Tall turrets pierced the sky, and stained glass windows glittered in the summer sun with a rainbow of colors. The Royal Guard stood sentry every few feet along the castle walls, each donned in their burgundy and charcoal uniforms with Opal Stone swords at their belts.

Khett jumped out of the carriage before it came to a stop.

His mother stood at the top of the steps, wearing an elegant dress with her brown and gray hair twisted back from her face. Beside her--in his wheelchair--sat King Jalinan with his hands clasped in his lap. He was older than his queen by four years but looked even older than that. The Black Illness had turned the strong man frail, leaving him skinny and pale. The golden, ruby and onyx jeweled crown laid slightly askew on his head.

It had been three years since his father had contracted the Illness. King Jalinan had deteriorated slowly. First, he had lost the ability to walk, then his heart became weak, and he sometimes found it hard to breathe on his own. Over the last six months, the Illness had become more aggressive, rapidly taking what was left of his vitality. He could no longer eat solid food and had begun to cough up blood. A black, tar-like substance also leaked from his nose and ears.

No one outside the castle walls had seen the King in months. Khett had been the face of the Crown since his father had taken a turn for the worse.

But the Eltharian people knew of the King's illness. Khett had heard the rumors. He had heard that the guards at the Round Tower were placing bets on his father's passing.

"How was...the journey...my son?" King Jalinan asked as Khett approached.

"Well, Father. We brought you a surprise."

The door to the carriage opened, and out stepped the Amadons, followed by Dallin and Nixema.

The King's laugh was brittle. "Halon Amadon...as I live...and breathe." He coughed into a handkerchief, and black and red stained the white cloth.

Halon's eyes softened, but he didn't draw attention to the King's disease. "Two years and three months by my calculations."

"Aye." The King motioned for one of the servants to wheel him back inside. "The staff will...show you to...your rooms," he said to Andalen and Arlen as he pulled back and turned to Halon. "Come."

The party followed the King and Halon inside, but Khett stopped Arlen with a hand to his shoulder. Arlen turned, his gaze questioning and an eyebrow raised, reminding Khett of Andalen.

"Come to the gardens with me. We must catch up. I haven't seen you in nearly a year."

Arlen nodded, and they started down the path that led to the front gardens. The gardens were a maze of flowers and bushes, and the smell of roses and tulips hung in the air. Gardeners tended to the plants and grass, greeting the Prince and the young Lord as they passed.

Arlen remained quiet, but then again, Arlen was always quiet.

"What has been going on with you, my friend? Bedded anyone?"

Arlen shot him a look, causing Khett to chuckle.

"Right. Still a virgin, then."

"Not all of us bed whoever we like, Khett."

"But those that do are happier because of it." Khett laughed boisterously. "Why did you ask about the Art program? You planning to go to school?"

Arlen nodded. "It's a dream. With my sight going, I want to experience university before I can no longer see."

"The Doctors said you were only losing it in one eye, correct?"

"For now," Arlen mumbled. "I can still read and paint, but they don't know much else."

"You could study Literature at the Rivland University," Khett suggested. He would love to have Arlen closer.

"Books are a great escape, but art--art is my life, Khett. I live and breathe color and canvas."

Khett pursed his lips, thinking. "Well, Palamar isn't that bad," he offered. "The people are wild, but still educated, unlike the dregs in Oszerack." Khett plucked a flower from the soil without touching it, relishing the feeling of his powers surging through him as the flower left the dirt and floated into his hand. "Do you think Oszerackians are born with those sad looks on their faces or do they develop over time?"

"You shouldn't poke fun, Khett." Arlen frowned. "Tell me about yourself. Have you found a wife? I'm sure your mother is already planning the wedding even if you haven't found a woman you desire for more than a night in bed."

"Mother's been wanting me to marry since I came of age. I turn twenty-five next year, and according to Mother, I should be married and have a child on the way. You know how much my mother loves tradition."

"Especially for us nobles," Arlen continued Khett's unspoken thought. "That way, there are heirs for the Trials."

"No. I haven't found a wife."

Arlen stopped, studying his old friend. "Are you still waiting for my sister?"

Khett ignored his question. "She ended things with me when we were eighteen. We're only friends, Arlen."

"And yet, six years later, you're still in love with her."

Khett scoffed and continued down the path. He would not admit that Arlen was right.

Khett, Arlen and Andalen spent the night reminiscing about old times. Arlen teased Khett for being enamored with Andalen after all these years, but how could he not still love her? Her laughter was like music echoing through the white halls of the castle; she was strong and beautiful. He valued her mind and would love her always. When they turned in for the night, Khett found it hard to sleep, and when he did sleep, he dreamed of her. He dreamed of her light sepia skin, her curly hair, and her deep brown eyes. He dreamed of kissing her again, of pressing into her warm body, and the familiarity of her hands on his skin.

He woke in the morning with a smile and headed down to breakfast after getting dressed, only to find that the Amadons had left before the sun rose due to urgent business Lord Amadon had in Odenmal. Khett's smile quickly turned to a frown.

He didn't get to say goodbye.

"Is my father up?" he asked one of the servants while buttering his toast. He then tossed the knife on the table instead of on the plate, smearing butter and jam on the tablecloth.

"No one has seen him this morning, Your Grace," the servant answered as he stood against the wall with a pot of tea in his hand. "Nolan was just going to check on him."

Khett waved his answer off and stood from his chair, placing his toast between his teeth. "No need," he said around the bread. "I will go."

He walked through the white halls as he ate. Adorning the walls were tapestries in the Pedgram colors stitched with a hawk and roses, and others depicting events of Elthare's past, such as the Elf Wars of 1539 and the invention of the Steam Train. Just before the hall on the fourth floor branched off into his father's wing, the family tree hung, dating all the way back to the first King of Elthare, King Valnar Pedgram I. Khett's little branch was at the bottom, his name stitched into the burgundy fabric with gold thread.

He turned, intending to head to his father's bedchambers, but the door to his study stood open, the tip of his father's boot visible from the hall. Khett pushed the door open further to enter the room.

"Father--"

His words stuck in his throat. His father was huddled in his wheelchair, his face a pale ghost white. Crimson dotted his lips and chin. His eyes were wide and gray with death. Khett inched closer. The room smelled of something so foul Khett couldn't put a name to it. The black oozing from his father's ears and nose had dried to tar-colored rivers on his ghostly skin.

He touched his father's hand. It was stiff and cold.

He pulled back. Everything in him--his mind, his heart, his breathing-- stuttered to a halt. He was too shocked to move, to make a sound. An odd croaking sound escaped his parted lips.

He sank to his knees. His brain seemed to jolt to a start, and internally, he screamed. His thoughts were nothing more than a stormy mess of grief and devastation.

A scream ripped up from his throat, turning to a loud sob. His heart pounded against his ribs, almost painful as it clenched with sorrow, beating too fast and too hard in his chest. His breaths came in rapid, unsteady bursts as tears streamed down his face.

The servants came running. Nolan was first to enter the room, but Khett paid no attention to the young man until he spoke.

"Prince Khett." He heard the servant's voice as if he were underwater; the man sounded garbled, far away. "Prince Khett, let go."

He hadn't realized he still held on to his father's hand. He released his fingers and could swear he heard his joints creak as if he had been holding on forever. The hand fell into the King's lap with a small, dull thunk.

Nolan steered him away, and his eyes focused on the other servants. All were in a state of shock, hands covering their mouths, tears streaming down their cheeks.

Khett's mother entered with a look of confusion on her face until she saw her husband in the chair.

"No! Jalinan!" His mother screeched. She flew into the room, only to be pulled back by her handmaid. She reached for her husband, her eyes wide with horror. "*Jalinan!*"

"Mother." Khett went to her, and she sank into his arms.

He held her as she cried.

Chapter Two

Andalen raised her arm, sniffing the sleeve of her tunic. She turned her nose away, repulsed by the rancid odor clinging to the dull fabric. She smelled of fish and the Azuken Sea--to be fair, all of Odenmal smelled like fish--but *she* smelled like it, and her father would not be happy that she had spent her morning down at the docks again, helping the fishermen lug in their nets and gut their catch.

She looked down at her fingernails. There were scales and innards underneath, staining her nail beds black and red. She made a face at them and then wiped her hands on her trousers.

"Oi, Andi!" One of the fishermen called. She looked back over her shoulder to see Kelmen Stocke trudging up the path after her.

She waited for Kelmen to reach the top of the hill, the line that separated the small eastern village into its distinctive parts. The bottom of the hill was where the fishermen lived and worked, and on the top were wheat and corn farms. On the other side of the hill stood the main village, and just beyond that was the Amadon estate.

"Oi, Kel. Ya alright there?" She needed to make sure she swallowed this fishermen speak before she got back to the estate. Andalen found it easy to slip into fishermen speak because it was free, rough and not strangled by rules.

Again, her father would not be pleased.

Kelmen was only nineteen with hair as black as night, warm brown eyes, and a crooked smile.

"Ya left this down by tha docks." He held up her bow and quiver, and she smiled.

How could she have forgotten about her most prized possession? It was easy to get lost in the rhythm of the sea, pulling nets and gutting fish. She had no need for her bow at the docks, and she couldn't believe she had nearly forgotten about it.

"Thanks, Kel. Ya need a hand ta'morrow?"

"I'll be fine, there, Andi," he replied and turned to trek back down the hill. "Thanks fer yer help!" he called.

Andalen looped the bow and quiver over each shoulder, and stood at the top of the hill, watching Kelmen disappear. After she could no longer make out his silhouette when he reached the docks, Andalen turned and continued to the other side of town.

Silent, imposing guards opened the gates of the Amadon estate as she approached, and she walked past them without a word to see Nixema and Arlen on the steps of the manor. Nix's beautiful face pinched into a frown as if she had just sucked on a lemon. Her brother stood behind her handmaiden, eating an apple with a book tucked under his arm and paint smudged on the front of his tunic.

"*Andalen,*" Nixema clucked at her as Andi got closer. Her petite nose wrinkled. "You smell!"

Andalen smiled at her. "That's so nice of you, Nix."

"You really do smell, Andi. Were you down at the docks again?" her twin brother asked.

"I'm always down at the docks, Ari."

He smiled. "My sister, the fish whisperer."

Nixema huffed at the twins, gathered up the skirts of her servant's uniform, and turned, leading them into the manor.

As the trio walked, they lost Arlen somewhere along the way. He ducked into the library without so much as a goodbye.

"Playing with the fishermen again?" Nix asked as she quickly ducked around a corner.

"Wha' did ya think I was doin'?" Andi replied as she followed.

The servants they passed wrinkled their noses at the smell emanating from her clothes.

Andalen saw Nix's shoulders bunch up before her. "You better lose that fishermen speak. Lord Amadon won't like it."

Andalen rolled her eyes, despite having that similar thought earlier in the day.

They scurried through the gray halls, which were decorated with suits of armor emblazoned with the Amadon insignia, a fox head in a field of lilies. Sometimes when it rained the water seeped in through the dark, cool stones, filling the manor with moisture and a slight smell of mildew. It was a nightmare on Andalen's curls.

"Your mother has set up a dinner with a suitor." Nix's voice strained with jealousy. Andalen couldn't help but smile; jealousy looked good on her handmaiden.

"Gods, I hate those dinners," Andalen complained, annoyed that she was to be paraded around like a show pony yet again.

She dreamed to one day be queen, but she had no desire to marry any of the men her mother presented to her. They were always too narcissistic, too dull to hold her attention. Besides, what would she do about Nix if she were to marry one of those men? They would not take kindly to her bedding her handmaiden.

"And who am I supposed to be falling madly in love with tonight?"

"Prince Hektor of Soldare."

"Gods, help me." The Soldaren prince was known to be spoiled and insufferable.

Nixema led her into her chambers where a tub had been dragged in, the perfumed water making the room warm and heavy with humidity. Rose petals floated on the surface of the water. Despite her love for roses, Andalen made a face at the tub; the perfume smell overwhelming. Someone had dumped the entire bottle into the water.

"In," Nix directed.

She caught a glimpse of herself in the mirror nailed to the stone wall as she slid her smelly trousers from her legs and pulled her equally smelly tunic over her shoulders. Her curls were in disarray, coming loose from the plait down her back, and a large dry spot on her arm itched from where the sun had beaten down on her throughout the day. The muscles in her arms and legs burned from hauling in fishnets, and grime smeared on nearly every inch of her umber skin. Andi grimaced at herself in the mirror before turning towards the bath where Nix waited with the sponge and soap made from beeswax and goat's milk.

"In."

Andalen made a face at Nix, but got in. The hot water released the tension in her bound muscles. She tipped her head back against the lip of the tub and closed her eyes as Nix set to washing her.

"You know," Andalen said, her words coming out lazy in her stupor. "You could strip and do that while you're in here with me."

"I see you've lost your fishermen's speak," Nixema replied. "Thank the Gods I was able to find the perfume oils. This smell seems to be clinging to your skin."

"Even if I smelled like I fell into the ocean and didn't bathe for weeks you would still come to my room at night. I'm like the air you breathe, Nixema," Andi repeated the words Nixema had said to her weeks ago.

Nixema snorted at Andalen's statement, but said nothing.

"You're like the air I breathe, Andi. Loving you is a constant need that keeps me alive." Andi smiled at the memory of Nix's words.

Nixema was a rare rose in a field of thorns, one that Andalen held close to her heart.

I should have told her I love her, she thought as Nixema washed her back. She hadn't, and even now the words clung to her lips. But she couldn't say them, not when she knew her relationship with Nix could not last. If she were ever to become queen she would have to marry a prince and stop bedding Nix.

She had never meant to fall in love with her handmaiden.

Nix finished scrubbing her and then laid out a dress on her bed. She turned back to Andalen as she relaxed in the bath, and placed her fists on her plump hips, fixing Andi with a stern look. "Your mother wants you dressed and in the dining room in a half-hour. I will return in ten minutes to do your hair and paint your face."

"Not makeup, Nix. You know I detest it."

Nixema huffed again. "I follow the orders of your mother and father, Andi. You will wear the kohl and rouge, and you will wear the dress your mother picked out for the evening."

Her tone made Andalen smile with affection. She reached out, pulling Nixema close by her hips.

"We have no time for this, Andi," she said with a laugh, pulling herself from Andalen's grasp. Nix swatted her hands away. "Hurry up. The Prince waits."

The door closed behind Nix, and Andalen climbed out of the bath to dress. In an act of rebellion, she left the emerald-colored dress on her bed and donned her brother's old clothes to meet the pompous prince of Soldare.

Andalen, dressed in a tunic and trousers, smiled at the exasperated look on her parents' faces as she entered the dining room. And though Nix had fought valiantly, her face remained devoid of makeup. Her curls were pinned with one springy tendril falling over her left temple, and the only reason she had let Nix style her hair was because the handmaiden had started cursing her to the Gods.

She sat next to Arlen, who greeted her with a broad smile. She turned to the Prince of Soldare with a practiced smile. "Welcome, Prince Hektor."

Prince Hektor, an average looking man with a large nose, which he constantly looked down the tip of when he addressed people, had light brown hair and olive skin. It was known throughout the three western kingdoms that he had a fondness for all things shiny and opulent.

"Lady Andalen, you look lovely," the Prince said in a heavy Soldaren accent. His smile was arrogant, and Andi resisted the urge to scoff at him as he turned his attention back to her father. "Thank you so much for inviting me into your home, Lord Amadon," he drawled, but his words felt wooden, as if he were reading from a script. "These goblets are exquisite. We have some just like them in Soldare, but those are made from real gold, of course."

"As are these," Andalen snapped under her breath as she picked through her food and leaned heavily on the table with her head in her hand.

Prince Hektor moved closer.

"If you ever visit Soldare I will show you the golden goblets. We mine the gold right from underground."

"In Elthare we have Opal Stone," she shot back and looked up at the prince with a sneer. "Opal Stone is much more valuable than gold."

"Andalen!" her mother admonished. Andi looked over at her mother. Lady Amadon's thin eyebrows were up in her dark hair and her full lips pulled down in a scowl. "I apologize for my daughter, Your Grace. She's been feeling under the weather."

Andalen rolled her eyes. "I feel fine," she muttered.

"It's quite alright, Lady Amadon." The prince turned to Andalen. "Is it your womanly time, my lady?"

Andalen jerked back in her seat, and her head shot to the side. She stared wide eyed at the prince, her mouth hanging open in a wide 'O'. Her brain stuttered for something to say. Her father coughed into his napkin, and her mother made a small squeaking sound in her throat. Then, the table fell into silence.

"E-excuse me?"

"Is it your womanly time? My sister always acts insane around her time."

"The Gods," Andalen whispered under her breath. She pushed up from her seat and looked at her parents' shocked faces, her brother trying to hold his laughter in with a hand over his mouth to keep from spitting out wine. "I'm going out to the garden."

No one tried to stop her.

Andalen shook her head at the Prince's idiocy. She walked down the corridor of her home to the main door; the two guards at the entrance barely glanced up as she passed. She descended the outside steps, inhaling the salty tang of the air, her mind still reeling at the buffoonery of the Soldaren Prince.

The estate gardens were not as grand as the ones in Rivland's castle. They held a smaller variety of flowers, and there were no fountains, but it was still beautiful in its simplicity. Andalen sat on the bench in the middle of the garden and scuffed her boots back and forth on the stone paver at her feet, losing herself in the stillness and tranquility of the evening.

Hours later, Andalen finally made her way back inside. Dinner had finished, but she could hear the prince's loud voice traveling through the estate from the sitting room. She hovered in the main hall, contemplating whether she should rejoin the party or be rude and retire to her chambers. Instead, she went to the kitchen to find the dessert she had missed out on.

Isa, the estate's cook, was still in the kitchen. Her frizzy hair stood on end, and her apron smeared with grease and chocolate. She smiled at Andi as she entered, but did not slow down in preparing for the Amadons' breakfast the next morning.

"Dessert's under that dome, love," Isa said, pointing to the silver lid. "Chocolate cake with caramel frosting. Your favorite."

"Thank you." Andi pulled a plate and a knife towards her and cut off a large slice. She leaned over the counter to eat before she had to face her family and the Prince again. Isa disappeared into the large storeroom for something.

"We were wondering where you had gone off to," the Prince said from behind her.

Andalen sighed and turned to look at him. "Well, you know, my womanly time and all that."

"Did I offend you when I said that?" he asked, leaning too close to her, his hot breath fanning the side of her face.

She inched away from him. "I do not offend easily."

He moved closer. "I still feel like I should apologize." His hand trailed her arm before crawling down her back and cupping her ass. "Allow me to apologize properly, Lady Andalen. I meant no offense."

Andi leaned away from him, but his hand followed her movements. She narrowed her gaze at him. Her returning smile was false and sweet. "The only thing offending me is the location of your hand."

The prince smiled and leaned closer until they were almost nose to nose. "Is it now?"

She dropped her fork on her plate and took his wrist with her hand. His skin felt feverous to the touch and smoother than her own skin. She let her powers flow through her.

The prince screamed out in pain, gasping for breath and clawing at his throat with his free hand. Isa came out of the storeroom, clutching a small bag of something to her chest with her eyes wide and mouth agape, but she said nothing. The prince fell to his knees, still trying to draw air into his lungs.

"You feel that, Prince Hektor? You finding it hard to breathe?" He had started to turn blue. "Touch me again and I will afflict you with something worse." She let him go, and he fell to all fours, taking in huge, shaky gulps of air. "Do you understand me?"

His eyes watered, but his face slowly returned to a normal color. "You bitch! Wait until my father hears about this!"

Andalen resisted the urge to punch him and turned on her heel. She exited the kitchen with the prince shouting threats at her from behind.

"I'll have your head on a pike!" he yelled. "And to think I considered marrying you! All the coin in the world couldn't persuade any man in his right mind to marry you!"

"Making friends with the prince?" Her brother's voice came from her left. She turned to see him leaning against the stone wall, a book in one hand, a letter in the other. He smiled at her. "So, I take it you won't be the new princess of Soldare any time soon?"

Andi laughed and went to Arlen. "I feel sorry for any woman that marries him." She looked down at the letter in her twin's hand. "What is that?"

"It just arrived. It is addressed to both of us. From Khett."

Andalen took the letter and opened it.

Andi and Arlen,
Kurem has taken my father. He had passed sometime before you left Rivland, but no one is sure when. The Illness has finally taken him.

I don't know what else to write in this letter. I cannot focus on the words I need to say to you both. The funeral will be two days after you receive this letter. The entire kingdom will show up, but it would mean the world to me if you both were there. Please. I can't do this without the two of you.

You know what this means, Arlen? We will have to compete against each other in the King Trials. You are like my brother. I do not wish to compete against you, but fate has always been a cruel mistress.

I will see you at the funeral,
Khett

Tears burned in Andalen's eyes. "He's right," Andalen said, reading through the letter again. "Another King Trials is going to happen soon. Father is going to make you enter."

"Please, Andi." Arlen looked at her with sad, fearful eyes. "I can't--I don't want--I can't enter the Trials. Not with this." He waved vaguely at his right eye, the one he was going blind in.

Unfortunately, Andalen didn't think Arlen's disorder would stop their father from making Arlen enter. Lord Amadon's dream was to see one of his blood take the Elthare throne.

She pulled her brother into a hug. "I know, Ari. I know. We'll find a way to get you out of it. I promise you won't have to enter."

His arms wrapped around her, and she held him as he shook with silent sobs.

Chapter Three

The sun hung high in the sky as Grantham Sinero walked down the cobbled streets of Oszerack. It was market day--his favorite day of the week. The streets bustled with people buying or selling food, wine, old books, prayer candles and other commodities. The smell of cooking meat, perfume oils and fruit hung heavy in the air. A group of children knocked into Grant as they ran for the table holding wooden toys and children's books. Multiple conversations fluttered around him; the buzzing of so many different voices reminded him of a colony of bees.

Grantham and his brother, Mikhial, were dressed in simple Oszerackian fashion: vests over linen shirts with trousers. Their vests were made of a soft, rich fabric dyed blue and red, and had the Sinero emblem stitched over the left breast: a crow carrying a single poppy flower in its beak. Silk lined their pockets, and their boots were made of supple leather advertising their status as descendants of one of the five founding families of Elthare.

Their sister's fashion mirrored the other women in Oszerack--clean, simple dresses dyed natural colors--except it had been made by a seamstress in Rivland. Ralsair's dress was linen and dyed soft pink. Her brown-black hair was plaited with ribbons; Mikhial had gotten good at braiding Ral's hair after their mother was killed. Her sandals slapped against the cobbled street in a happy rhythm.

"I'm going to buy sweet dough!" Ralsair exclaimed. She was the youngest of the three Sinero siblings with almond shaped brown eyes. Ralsair held out her small hand, showing her brothers the two silver pieces in her palm. "Father gave me money!"

"Don't flash your coin around, Ral," Mikhial instructed. "You never know who might try and snatch it." He swiped at her hand, pretending to steal the two silver pieces. Ralsair squealed and laughed, closing her fist over her money. Mikhial looked over at Grant. "What are you going to get with your money, Grantham?"

His brother had eyes and hair the color of tree bark like their father, and though he was only three years older than Grant, he acted as if he were older than his twenty-six years.

"I don't know. Possibly a pint of ale from the tavern." Grant answered, looping an arm over Ralsair's shoulder as they walked.

Mikhial frowned. "I wish you wouldn't waste your coin on drink, Grant."

"And you plan to spend your coin at the Night House again, older brother?"

Mikhial blushed, and Ralsair giggled, jabbing Grant in the ribs with her elbow.

"I haven't been to the Night House in ages," he mumbled.

The Sinero siblings entered the main part of the market, where most of the sellers' carts and tables were congregated. The merchants called out their products, trying to get people to spend money on their goods instead of the person's next to them.

"Apples! Fresh picked apples!"

"Bread! Baked just this morning!"

"Daggers! Pottery! Jewels!"

"Wine! Only three gold pieces a bottle!"

The siblings wove their way through the crowded streets. Ralsair wanted to stop at each booth and look at everything, but Mikhial dragged her along as if he had a destination in mind. Grant trailed behind, not really looking at the booths, but at the people.

Lovers held onto each other as they looked through the goods on the carts and tables. Children ran through the streets, laughing and calling after one another while families huddled together, trying not to lose each other in the masses. Grantham watched a young mother with her two children. Her dress had a mysterious stain on the front and strands of hair were coming out of her braid. Her children were pulling her in different directions, all vying for her attention.

Grant thought of his own mother. She had been beautiful. Her hair had been a shade darker than his, but she had the same emerald colored eyes. As a child she would sing him to sleep, and had called him her 'sweet one'. She had died seven years before, two months after Ralsair's sixth birthday.

She had died at the hands of thieves on the Main Road on her way back from the Temple in Rivland. She had been a priestess, and visited the Temple often to commune with the other men and women in her profession. She had overseen the Temple in Oszerack, holding weekly sermons that inspired the Oszerackian people.

"Grant!" Ralsair's voice brought him back to the present. "Look at this!"

He turned to see that Mikhial and Ralsair had stopped at a table full of jewelry and perfume oils. Ralsair held up a necklace with a stone butterfly pendant at the end. At first glance, Grant thought the pendant to be Opal Stone--the most expensive and most coveted natural material in Elthare--but then decided it was either pearl or ivory. Grant took the necklace from her and held it up.

"It is beautiful, sister. Is this what you want to spend your two silver on?"

"It's six silver," the seller said.

Grant ignored him. "I thought you wanted sweet dough."

"I do," she groaned, "but it's *so-o* pretty."

"You have to choose one or the other, Ral," Mikhial interjected. "I can give you the rest of the coin for the necklace, but that means you won't get any sweet dough."

"But--"

"I'll buy it for you, Ral," Grant offered.

Mikhial frowned. Grantham spoiled Ralsair, partly to spite Mikhial, but also because he wanted to give Ral anything she had ever wanted.

"I'm trying to teach her the value of money, Grantham. Just because we're rich doesn't mean we have to spend our coin on everything we see."

He chuckled and patted Mikhial on the shoulder. "Maybe I should buy *you* a pint of ale, Mik. You need it more than I." Grant turned his attention back to his sister. "Would you like me to buy this for you, Ral?"

"Really?" Ralsair's eyes grew big and a broad smile split her face. Grant laughed when her arms flew around his middle. "Oh, thank you. Thank you!"

He pulled back and looked down at her. "On one condition."

Her face fell. "What?"

"Tell me I'm your favorite brother."

Ralsair giggled. "You already made me tell you that this morning!"

"I want to hear it again."

Mikhial's frown had become so severe Grant worried his brother was doing permanent damage to his face.

She glanced at Mikhial before kissing Grant's cheek and saying, "You're my favorite brother."

Smug, Grant smiled at his older brother.

Mikhial shook his head. "You're a child, Grantham."

"Smile, Mik. The day is young. I could still find something to buy for you."

He turned away. Grant paid the seller for the necklace and handed it to Ralsair, who fastened it behind her neck before they followed Mikhial through the crowd. As they reached their eldest brother, he came to a stop and pinned Grantham with a look after telling Ral to go look at some books on a nearby table.

"You shouldn't spoil her, Grant."

"It's harmless, Mik," Grant countered. He bought a loaf of bread from the baker's table they stood near. "Are you mad that I buy her whatever she wants or that I never buy you anything?"

He huffed and turned away, but didn't answer the question. Grant wondered what his brother's answer would have been, but didn't press.

Mikhial was quiet as he began to move through the crowd again. He stopped at a vintner's table to buy a bottle of the famous Oszerakian wine and said something to the woman selling the wine that made her blush and giggle. Despite the fact that his brother had been courting the young woman for six months, Grantham had trouble remembering her name.

"Should we leave him here?" Grant asked his sister. "We can go on the hunt for sweet dough."

"Aye. I think this could take a while."

Grant followed her to a cart that sold sweet treats, including sweet dough, honey candy and a drink made from lemon, honey and cinnamon. The woman behind the cart smiled at them pleasantly, revealing a gap between her two front teeth.

"Lord Grantham, Lady Ralsair, what can I do for you today?"

"Sweet dough for my sister and a bag of honey candy," Grant replied with a smile, pulling coins from the pouch at his hip.

Ralsair took the plate of sweet dough from the woman. "You hate honey candy."

"It's for Lonis."

"I should have known," she said with a knowing smile that had Grant rolling his eyes.

Grant took the candy from the woman and paid for everything, including Ralsair's sweet dough. They turned and found their brother still talking to the vintner's daughter. Ralsair made a face when Mikhial and the woman kissed.

"What do you say we go home?"

Ralsair nodded. "Can I take the candy to Lonis?"

Grant laughed. "You're not going to sneak off with it, are you?"

"No! I promise."

"Then you may take it to him."

They started their walk through the village. Ralsair hummed a song as she ate her treat, dirtying her hands with sticky syrup and fried dough.

"When did you meet Lonis, Grant? I don't remember."

"When we were four."

"Would you say he's your dearest friend?"

Grant stumbled slightly on the road. "I would," he replied as he corrected his footing.

She was quiet as they turned the corner between two stores onto a smaller street. "Kal and I have been friends since we were five. Is he my dearest friend?"

"He could be. That's your decision to make."

She went quiet again. It had always amazed Grant how much she contemplated the smallest things, like how she wrote her name or what her favorite color was, or in this instance--trying to decide if Kal was truly her closest friend. Grant looked at her out of the corner of his eye, noticing the sweet dough syrup that stained the front of her dress. *Her governess won't be pleased.*

Ralsair nodded in resolution. "He's my dearest friend."

"Congratulations!" he exclaimed, clapping and laughing. "Would you like me to make you a cake?"

Ralsair rolled her eyes in such a spectacular fashion, he was surprised they remained in her head. "You don't know how to bake."

"For you, my dear sister, I could learn."

Ralsair laughed loudly and with her whole heart, bringing a grin to Grant's face.

The Sinero estate, a stone manor at the end of the main village, stood at the end of the road. The gates were closed, and a guard stood sentry in front of them. Flowers bloomed in the pristine lawn and along a wall topped with iron rails. The guard watched as Ralsair and Grantham approached, his eyes scanning the area behind them

"At ease," Grant teased the older man. "It's only us."

He didn't laugh or move a muscle, except to open the gate to let them through. Grant and Ralsair continued up the pathway and climbed the stairs to let themselves into the manor. The light stone walls were lined with torches and silver framed portraits of past Sineros, dating back hundreds and hundreds of years. Lush cobalt blue rugs covered the floors, and servants bustled through the rooms, completing their daily tasks. Guards stood at their posts, armed and protected by swords and breastplates made of Opal Stone, a white stone that glittered when the sun caught it, was sharper than steel, and unbreakable.

"Where do you think Lonis is?" Ralsair asked.

"The armory. That's where he always is."

Ralsair followed behind her brother as he led her through the halls and down the stone steps to where the servants' quarters and the armory were in the underbelly of the estate.

The door to the armory was ajar, a scraping sound coming from within. Grant pushed the door open, revealing the swords, arrows, and daggers that lined the walls. The steel of each weapon reflected light from the dim oil lamps around the room. Lonis didn't look up as the siblings entered. He sat on the stone floor, dressed in a simple Oszerakian tunic and vest, the color faded from navy to a light blue. One of his legs pulled up, and his elbow rested on the brown fabric of his trousers as he worked a blade over the whetstone.

"Is that my dagger?" Grant asked, walking towards him. He slid to the floor in front of Lonis, watching his friend's long fingers work the steel blade of his grandfather's dagger over the stone.

His father had given it to him after his mother's death, along with a letter she had written only weeks before she passed. Grant held both items close. He usually kept the letter tucked into a pocket and the dagger at his belt. He had left the dagger that morning out of fear that someone would nab it in the busy market.

He had missed the dagger's weight at his hip, but had taken the letter in his pocket. He had read it so many times over the years the parchment had yellow and frayed. He had memorized the words and repeated them to himself whenever he needed to feel close to his mother.

My sweet one,
In all my years I had not known what love was until I laid eyes upon you, Mik and Ral. You had been a difficult birth--nearly killed me as you clawed your way out into the world, but I would have died happily knowing that you survived. Keep that tenacious spirit, my sweet one, it is the only thing that is going to get you through this life.
Never forget who you are and where you come from. You are a Sinero. Our family motto is Strong will. Strong mind. Strong heart. *Follow the Sinero motto, and you will survive anything.*
All my love,
Ma

"Don't you have anything better to do than hang out in here? You turned down my invitation to come with us to the market for this," Grant huffed. "You're becoming a recluse, Lonnie."

"I went to the sparring field." Lonis had eyes the color of honey candy and a bump on his nose from when he had broken it four years prior. His inky black hair curled away from his angular face, showcasing his sharp cheekbones. His warm tawny skin was darker than usual since he spent most of his days training in the summer sun. He smiled at

Grant, revealing a row of slightly crooked teeth. "You've been letting it get dull, Sin."

Grantham smiled, as he always did, at the old nickname Lonis had given to him when they were children.

"We got you honey candy!" Ralsair exclaimed, pulling the bag from her brother's hands and thrusting it at Lonis.

Lonis withdrew his intense gaze from Grant and turned towards her. He dropped the stone and dagger to his lap, took the bag from Ralsair and popped a large piece of candy into his mouth. "Mmm. Thank you, Ral."

She beamed and ran from the room, calling, "You're welcome!" as she went.

Grant laughed and shuffled to settle in next to Lonis with his back against the stone wall. "I think my sister is sweet on you."

Lonis rolled his eyes at his friend's statement and went back to sharpening Grant's blade. "Are you going to the festival in Palamar tomorrow?"

"I am. I'm taking the train at eleven. And I'm disappointed you're not coming with me," Grant added, nudging Lonis with his elbow. "The festivals are fun, Lonnie. There will be dancing and singing. Food--you love food." Grant sighed wistfully. He had a soft spot for the colorful city.

"Your disappointment is noted," Lonis replied with a small smile. "I have to train."

"You're always training lately. You never have time to have fun with me anymore. When is the last time you left the armory or the sparring field?"

Lonis made a noise in his throat, but otherwise ignored Grant's whining.

Grant leaned his head against the wall and sighed as they sat in companionable silence. The sound of Lonis working the dagger over the stone lulled him to a near sleep.

"Your father got a letter today." The shift in Lonis' mood was as swift as a rushing river. The room felt heavy and sticky against Grant's skin with tension when moments before it had been light as air.

"And? My father gets a lot of letters."

"The King is dead." His voice did nothing to ripple the silence of the room.

"Hm," Grant replied and looked over at him. He had met the King once. He had been kind, but had not made a lasting impression on Grant. He supposed he should be sadder about the death of his king, but despite the pang in his gut about the upcoming invitations to the Trials, Grant felt nothing more than a small sadness for a life lost.

"Are you going to enter the Trials?" Lonis asked, his voice smaller than before, just a breath above a whisper.

"I don't know. I have never really thought about it."

Lonis' returning silence drove Grant mad. Lonis was reticent by nature, but Grant couldn't handle his friend's tense brooding. He itched to bring a smile to Lonis' face.

"Do you want me to enter?"

Lonis shrugged.

"Well, you're a lot of help." Grant leaned back again, and they fell into silence again.

"Your birthday is coming soon." Lonis shifted beside him, his arm brushing against Grant's. "You're going to be twenty-three."

"And you'll be twenty-four three weeks later. So what?" Grant was still annoyed they were talking about such heavy topics. He cracked an eyelid to look at his friend, seeing nothing but Lonis' profile, his raven hair falling in his eyes.

"It's different," he said carefully. Grant shifted against the wall and cleared his throat. Lonis wouldn't look him in the eye as he continued, "When you are in your twenties you are expected to have a wife--"

"I don't want a wife."

Lonis ignored him. "--but you haven't been with anyone since Milden." Grant frowned at the mention of his former lover. "Your father is already grooming you to take over as Lord, or possibly king if you decide to enter the Trials. I'm supposed to join the Guard under my father's command. I'm going to become a soldier."

Grant's heart stopped. He had always known that this was expected of them, but the deep emotion in Lonis' voice filled Grant with dread. "You're saying this like it's going to be the end of our lives, Lonnie."

"It could be, and I--" He shook his head. "Things are going to change, Sin."

Grant blew out a breath that did nothing to release his tension. "You remember when we were children and nothing was expected of us?"

Lonis' chuckle held no humor. "I remember."

"I want to go back to that."

Ikar's boots slapped against the snow eroded stones of the Alithane streets. He tucked his face into the shoulder of his heavy cloak to keep his cheeks from blistering due to the evening winds. A lantern swung from his gloved hand, bathing the near dark stones in yellow light. *At least it's not winter.* In the colder months the sun rarely shone on Alithane, and the wind pricked against the skin, icy and sharp, like shards of glass.

Someone shouted his name from somewhere to the left. He raised his hand in a half-hearted wave as the wind blew too strong to greet anyone properly, and even if it didn't, the person would have still gotten the same greeting.

Somewhere in the distance he heard a lute, the sound carried from some other part of the village on the winds. It took him a moment to figure out the tune--an old song about Kurem, the god of death, winter, hunting, wisdom and so many other things Ikar couldn't remember half of them. Kurem was the god that Althanens favored; Ikar had named his horse after him.

Ikar Dominikov was the son of a Lord. He had learned how to hunt like all the Althanen kids, how to skin animals, how to dry those skins out to make blankets and cloaks and whatever else they were needed for. Their cook, Vanya, had taught him how to boil the meat into stew when he was nine. But, unlike other Althanen children, Ikar was also educated in arithmetic, literature, politics and history. Skills and knowledge he didn't need to hunt, skin or--if he were a poor man--work in the coal mines or as a logger, but they would help him if he were ever invited to compete in the King Trials, and if he ever took over the Dominikov estate.

Ikar opened the heavy wood door to the tavern. Heat hit his body, and he lowered his shoulders and his lantern. The warmth in the tavern wasn't created by any fire, but rather by the amount of people all pressed together inside.

The atmosphere of the tavern, loud and overwhelming, irked Ikar, but this was where Briar had wanted to meet. Ikar had learned not to argue over such small matters; despite his size, his friend could be a stubborn mule.

Briar's vibrant red hair caught Ikar's attention. He sat at a table in the back of the room, clapping along with the music. Ikar was surprised that he wasn't singing and dancing with the rest of the bar's patrons. That type of wild abandonment was the type of thing his friend enjoyed.

He wove his way through bodies as someone started singing a chorus of 'This Fair Maiden'.

"This fair maiden with skin like pearls
With hair like sun and plenty of curls"

The rest of the tavern's patrons joined in, even the barkeep sang along as he filled glasses.

"Lips like roses, eyes like moss

My fair maiden in the woods, lost"

It really was a terrible song.

Was that his tutor dancing a jig on the table?

Gods. It is. Ikar averted his eyes, shaking his head.

The depravity already caused a sharp pain to start behind his eyes. He squeezed between the people who were dancing and clapping, cheering his tutor on. A woman squealed as a man scooped her up and began twirling her around the room. The town butcher spotted him and clapped his shoulder with a meaty hand and a loud, slurred, "Ikar, my boy!"

Finally, blessedly, he made it to Briar.

"There you are!" Briar exclaimed, sipping on a mug of ale. "What took you so long?"

"It was quite the adventure getting through that," Ikar replied in a flat tone, pointing at what seemed like half the town dancing, laughing and singing. "Why did you want to meet here, Bri? You know I hate this place."

"You hate most places!"

That was true. Ikar's fondness did not extend to most people.

Someone started a new song. This one slow and melancholy, about a love lost. Briar frowned at the sudden change in tempo.

"Ale? Wine?" his friend asked, already standing up from the table and going around the bar to fill a mug of ale before Ikar answered.

This was allowed, considering Briar worked as a...barmaid? *What were they called if they were male?* Ikar wondered.

Briar appeared with two pints of ale.

"So, tell me, Ikar, what have you done today?"

"Well, I took lessons from the tutor." At this Ikar looked over to see that his tutor had lost his tunic; his flabby belly and hairy chest on full display. Ikar made a face. "I shot a rabbit with an arrow. The ladies in the kitchens at home are turning it to stew. I read about Lysic. Did you know they have a school dedicated to making soldiers?"

"Everyone knows that!" Briar sipped his ale. "And dragons!"

"Of course all you care about is the dragons." Ikar paused and drank his ale before continuing. "I read poetry by some dead Eltharian. It was rather boring, so I'm sure you would have enjoyed it."

Briar smiled at that. He enjoyed poetry, especially poetry about men finding love, but not losing it, not like the man in the song the tavern's patrons were singing. Again.

"I brushed Kurem."

"The god or the horse?"

"Funny," he said dryly, which made Briar shrug and smile. "And your day?"

"You're looking at it!" Briar waved at the debauchery happening behind them.

Ikar nodded. "You got the town drunk."

Briar's brows knit together. "The town got itself drunk!"

Ikar shrugged, but didn't smile.

The door to the tavern opened again, and a small statured, but stocky man entered. The man's brown hair swept around his head as if he had stepped out of a tornado. His face grim and his eyes bloodshot as if he had already had more than enough to drink.

"Wylon," the barkeep raised his voice to be heard over the loud singing. "Why do you look so glum?"

Wylon sank against the door after struggling to close it against the wind. The room fell silent, each entranced by the gloomy man who had interrupted their fun. "The King..." the man's voice rose an octave above a whisper, but Ikar heard him clearly. "The King is dead."

A collective gasp sounded throughout the tavern, but Ikar just shook his head. He met the news with nothing more than apathy.

"I can't believe it," Briar said, his voice already thick with tears. "Our poor King."

Ikar scoffed. "He was old, Briar."

"He wasn't that old, Ikar."

Ikar conceded. The King had only been forty-six. "He was sick."

The patrons consoled each other, crying onto their neighbor's shoulder, and sharing drinks in the king's name. The jovial fun of only moments ago had turned into a drunken memorial.

His tutor came forward, his flabby belly bouncing as he walked. "That's a shame about the King," he slurred. His ale spilled all over the floor. "The Trials will be happening soon, my boy. Keep that in mind."

Oh, he was. The Trials would serve as the perfect opportunity to make a name for himself. For twenty-two years he had been living in the shadow of his parent's great heroics during the War of Wars.

His brother had been the greatest wolf hunter in the north for five years in a row. He wanted a title for himself, and what better than being the first Dominikov to sit on the Elthare throne?

"I plan on entering, Quill."

His tutor beamed. "That a boy! Such good news deserves a drink, especially following such tragedy." He gulped down the rest of his ale.

Ikar raised his glass, clinking his pint against Briar's.

"To the King," Briar said in a solemn voice.

To being king, Ikar thought with pride.

Chapter Four

Andalen woke up to the sun streaming in her face and her bed still warm from Nixema's body.

Once dressed, she ventured out into the manor in search of Gellen, the games master and groundskeeper. He was an elderly man that had been in the Amadons employ since his thirties.

The chatter of the servants filled the warm halls as they completed their morning duties. Andalen said hello to a few as she walked by on her way to the front hall, where she knew Gellen would be preparing for the hunt.

Andalen was so lost in her thoughts of the king's death and the upcoming Trials that she almost didn't notice her brother sitting on a bench under a window, just before the corridor that led to the kitchens. His nose was tucked in a book like always, with a quill stuck behind his ear, partially hidden by his short curly hair.

"Morning, Ari."

He waved at her, distracted by whatever he was reading.

She stepped into the main hall to find Gellen waiting with two soldiers and her father. He smiled as Andalen approached, while the soldiers gave no expression, and her father frowned.

"No, Andalen," her father commanded. His white bald head glistened under the lights of the candelabra above as he fixed the lapel of his elaborate black-green coat. "You have a needlepoint lesson."

Andalen snorted. Needlepoint was such a tedious task, and she often pictured jabbing her needles into the thigh of her unbearable instructor, a haughty creature with breath that stank of rotting fish.

Andalen came to a stop in front of him, looking up until her brown eyes met his. "Please, Father. I promise to double my time at needlepoint tomorrow." She laid on the charm; her father was a stern man, but he rarely refused Andalen.

Lord Amadon's face didn't soften, but he conceded. "Fine, but you will wear a dress for the entire day tomorrow as well as triple your time at needlepoint. I do not want to see any trousers or tunics."

Andalen readily agreed; a dress was worth a day's trip into the Eltharian Forest.

"Come," Gellen said, ushering the party forward and out of the castle.

Outside, a cart and horses had been prepared for the hunt. Andalen went to the black steed in the back. Her horse, Nomir, greeted her with a soft nuzzle to her hand; her sword and scabbard had been attached to his saddle. She pulled the blade from the sheath and admired it.

The sword had been a gift from Gellen for her twenty-second birthday. The handle was simple, made of black stone melted together with the steel. The blade itself was thin, sharp and sleek. It was nothing like the expensive and beautiful Opal Stone weapons the soldiers in their noble guard and her father carried, but she treasured it just the same.

Andalen felt Gellen come up to her side. She placed the sword back into its sheath before turning toward the wizened man. His hair was white and thinning in more places than not, and when he smiled, it was apparent that he was missing a majority of his teeth; the ones that remained were rotted and brown.

"How many ducks?" he asked.

Andalen smiled at the old game. Ever since she was a little girl, Gellen would ask her how many ducks she thought they would bring back from the hunt. If she guessed correctly, he would give her his dessert at dinner that night, but if she was wrong, she would have to give him hers.

"Ten."

Gellen let out a small laugh. "Ten? You must have high faith in us, my lady. Last time we only caught five."

"Last time you didn't have me."

Gellen laughed again. "You have always been so modest, my dear."

Andalen laughed along with him.

Her father came near, wiping the smiles from their faces. "We need to go. I would like to return before the sun sets."

"Yes, My Lord," Gellen said, bowing low.

He departed and took his spot on the bench of the cart. The cart held weapons and rope to tie the ducks together, and large spears in case the hunting party came across a boar. Andalen took her place on the back of Nomir, and her father climbed on his steed while the two soldiers on their horses took their place on either side of the Amadons.

They set off down the road that led to the Roaming River and the forest.

"Did you see your brother this morning?" her father asked.

"Aye."

"He did not want to join the hunt?"

"Does he ever?"

Her father fell silent, but she could feel him seething.

It was an ongoing battle between her father and brother to get the other to understand their position. Their father wanted a 'proper' Lord to take over the family title, but all Arlen wanted to do was go to university and paint. With Arlen's eyes going, he had been more adamant about fulfilling his dreams. Lord Amadon wanted him to pretend to be as healthy as every other Lord in Elthare. In those moments Andalen was happy that her father ignored her daily activities. As long as Andalen married a prince or a noble born from one of the other villages or neighboring kingdoms, Halon cared very little about what his daughter did with her time. It was her mother who harped about her acting like a proper lady.

The road outside the village was empty but shaded by the branches of the trees that lined it on either side. They rode in silence with Gellen quietly singing a song about a maiden in a tavern.

They traveled for a little over two hours until they came to a bank on the Roaming River, a large body of water that bisected Elthare from Alithane to Oszerack until it opened up into the Azuken Sea. Several ducks lazed on the river's banks nearly a couple hundred meters down.

"Come, Lady Andalen, let's see your skill," one of the soldiers teased.

Andalen scoffed, but had to forgive the man his ignorance. He was new to the estate guard and had never been on a hunt Andalen attended. With a false sweet smile, she slid from the back of her horse, picked a bow and quiver from the cart Gellen drove, and nocked an arrow.

"We're too far away," the soldier protested. "You'll never hit it."

She ignored him and aimed for a lone duck that was getting ready to take flight from the bank of the river.

She breathed in and then let the arrow fly. It pierced the duck straight through the body.

The soldier whistled through his teeth. "I've heard stories..."

Gellen's large hand came down on Andalen's shoulder with pride. She shot the soldier a smug look. "You might want to watch your tongue, soldier. Our lady here could hit a fly at fifty feet."

Andalen smiled at Gellen's praise and then went to retrieve her kill. Behind her, the soldiers and Gellen were still discussing her skill. Her father remained silent.

Surrounded by brambles and winter flowers, the Dominikov estate was made of black stone and wood--a dark silhouette in the northern tip of Elthare. There were four servants and a cook, and the halls were always cold, even when a fire roared in the crate of every room.

Lord Dominikov sat at the head of the table in the dining room. He was not a good looking man; there had been times where he had been compared to a troll. He was bald with many scars on his face and torso, and an eyepatch covered the gaping hole where his left eye should have been. Lady Dominikov was no less battle-worn than her husband. She had hair the color and texture of straw and a scar that pulled the corner of her mouth into a scowl. Despite their wealth, Lady Dominikov wore the plain dress of a common Althanen woman: a thick, black material lined with the fur of a fox.

Ikar sat in stony silence, poking at his rabbit stew and tearing his dark millet bread to pieces. His brother sat across from him, covered in scratches. The bite on his left shoulder had been bandaged, but blood still seeped through the white fabric. Yvney smiled.

"You're not still mad at me, are you, brother?"

Ikar huffed as he wiped at the scratch on his forearm that began to bleed again. "That was *my* wolf, Yvney. You took my kill."

"I saved you from being eaten." Yvney smiled again.

Ikar grumbled. In three days, he would turn twenty-two. He had to kill a wolf by the time the clock struck midnight on his name day. It was an old Althanen tradition, and if he failed to complete the task, he would be branded a failure, both literally and figuratively. Even now, he could smell the flesh of Briar's Branding from a year before. Ikar had yet to kill a wolf, and all because his fucking brother kept stealing his kills.

"Yvney, stop bullying your brother," their mother commanded in her heavy Lysin accent.

It had been their mother who had trained them in the ways of battle. She had taught her sons how to hold a sword and shoot an arrow while their father had been off at war, aiding their allies, the Lysins, against the Soldarens. And then, she too had been called to war, leaving Ikar to endure his brother's torment alone.

Their mother's voice sounded as chilly as Althanen winds and as sharp as an Opal Stone blade when she continued speaking, "Leave Ikar alone, Yvney, or you be sleeping in stables."

Yvney made a crude gesture in Ikar's direction. Lady Dominikov cursed in Lysinic, rose from the table, and left the dining room.

"One of these days, brother," Yvney hissed across the table in a low tone, "you are going to learn how to stop suckling at our mother's teat and stand up for yourself."

Their father, nearly deaf and blind, continued to eat, oblivious to Yvney's words.

Ikar felt a fiery rage start somewhere deep in his belly. He clamped his hands around the edge of the table as it consumed him. He ground his teeth together as a surge of power rolled through him, deep, dark, and alluring as it prickled under his skin. His breath came out hot and shallow as he tried with everything within him to not attack Yvney with the sharp blade of his dinner knife.

His brother smiled.

"Still haven't learned how to control your powers, brother?" Yvney's black hair turned red, strong features softening to match Briar's. "It's fairly easy, brother," he continued in Briar's voice. It sent chills down Ikar's spine to see his friend wearing his brother's cold smirk. Ikar hated when Yvney used his powers to distort the people he loved as a way to torment him. "But you are too weak, too *childish* to learn how to control your power." The mask slipped, and Yvney was himself again.

Still, power flowed through Ikar, but nothing happened. He didn't change, and the power died in his veins as quickly as it had came.

"Defective little shit," his brother spat before rising from the table and disappearing through one of the many closed doors just off the dining hall.

Lord Dominikov looked up from his dinner to the two empty chairs. "Is dinner over?" he asked, peering at Ikar with his one good eye.

Ikar stared blankly at his father and then burst into laughter at the absurd timing of his father's words. He stood and walked out of the dining room, and out of the manor, leaving his father at the table by himself.

The night air slapped against his skin, stinging against his fair cheeks. He had grabbed the wrong cloak, this one was too thin for the night and not lined with fur, but at least his boots were keeping his feet warm.

He came to the Shaden cottage, a small structure made of wood on the edge of the forest, close to the village, but not in it. He could hear laughter coming from inside and smelled something cooking in the small hearth as he knocked on the flimsy wooden door.

The door opened, revealing a young woman with long red hair, a petite round face, and freckles that dotted the bridge of her nose. Her blue eyes, the same color as a cloudless sky, twinkled with a joke that had yet to be told. Her plump, pink lips turned up into a smile.

"Ikar!"

She flew into his arms, and he wrapped her warm body against his, inhaling her scent, and reveling in the way her slender frame molded to fit into him. He twirled her, and her giggle warmed his chilled blood. A smile curved on his lips.

He set her on her feet and took her face in his hands. "Let me look at you, Roz. It's been too long since I have seen your face."

Roslen giggled. "It's only been six hours."

"Six hours too long."

Roslen tugged him into the small cottage. Her family gathered around the fire, each of them with their sunny smiles and bright red hair. Mrs. Shaden, a plump figure with the same mirth in her brown eyes as her children's, welcomed him into their home. Ever since he had met Briar at the age of twelve, he felt that the Shaden cottage was his true home; Briar was the brother he had always longed for, but never got from Yvney. The overflowing affection from both Mr. and Mrs. Shaden brought tears to his eyes, making him long for something of the sort from his own parents.

A pang twinged his heart for a different life and family dynamic.

"Sit, love, I've just put the food on," Mrs. Shaden commanded in her kind voice. "Have you eaten?"

"Unfortunately, dinner was ruined by Yvney." Ikar accepted a cup of hot tea from Mr. Shaden. "Again."

Roslen sat at Ikar's side. Her hand tightened in his as her pretty mouth pulled into a severe frown. Ikar soothed her by rubbing the back of her hand with his thumb while looking at Briar. His friend sipped at his tea. Dark storm clouds swirled in his usually bright gaze.

"Briar, are you alright? I didn't think you had it in you to be angry."

His friend huffed at his joke. "Your brother is a snake."

Roslen made a noise of agreement. "Eventually someone will chop his head off, and he will no longer be here to fill you with his poison," she said. Ikar kissed the back of her hand. "I have half a mind to do it myself."

"Roslen Shaden, defender of impassive lords everywhere," Ikar said with a smirk, pulling her to him. "I can fight my own battles, my love." He felt

Roslen's body shake in his hands. He pulled back to see tears brimming her eyes. He wiped one away from her cheek with the pad of his thumb. "Why are you crying?"

"Don't mind me," she replied.

Ikar raised an eyebrow in Briar's direction. His strong Roslen didn't cry over something so trivial as his brother giving him grief. Usually, she fought fire with fire. His Roslen was a warrior.

Briar shook his head in confusion and dug into the stew his mother handed him.

Chapter Five

The sun shone down on the castle with a false jovial light; Khett cursed it and continued getting dressed in his family's colors. A patch shaped like a black rose rested on the left side of his chest, a symbol of respect and remembrance for the fallen king. His cape seemed to be choking him; it felt too heavy, and the fabric irritated his skin.

His eyes burned with unshed tears.

"Are you ready?" his mother's voice sounded behind him.

He turned to see her in the doorway, dressed in her burgundy and charcoal dress, a black rose attached to the high collar. Her brown hair was tied up at the nape of her neck, and her face looked haunted, sallow. Khett couldn't remember the last time he had seen his mother eat in the last week; he couldn't remember the last time *he* had eaten.

Khett nodded and followed his mother through the castle. The staff bustled around them, greeting them with their heartfelt condolences, and tales of how much they had loved the king. Khett ignored them all. He couldn't bear to listen to it. He trudged along, pulling his mother gently by the elbow beside him.

Outside the castle, a carriage had been brought around for them. The interior smelled of leather and wealth. Normally, Khett would have loved the smell of a new carriage, but not that day; his brain was too muddled to enjoy anything.

They rode in silence, with his mother tapping her nails lightly on the wood of the door as she stared out at the silent city. As Khett expected, most of the shops had been closed, the streets were empty of carriages and pedestrians, and the college looked barren and ghostly.

Khett sat, stock still, hands folded in his lap.

He tried to think of his father. He knew he had many fond memories of the king, but in that moment, he seemed to be failing to come up with anything specific. He could see Jalinan's straight nose, his dark eyes and hair in his mind, and he could remember his father's strong voice and boisterous laugh, but for some reason he couldn't picture anything beyond the frail man of the last three years. He didn't want to remember his father as the sick man; he wanted to remember the healthy, strong man of his childhood, and it frustrated him that none of those memories entered his mind.

The carriage came to a stop in front of the Temple where people were overflowing out onto the street. Khett shook his head. The people were early--too early. He had wanted time alone with his feelings, with his thoughts. With his father.

Khett climbed out of the carriage, and a hush fell over the crowd. Hundreds of eyes stared at him, into him, but he looked up at the temple, a grand building made of marble with statues of Nomir and

Kurem on either side of the golden doors: Nomir, bearded, holding a dove and a branch full of leaves; and Kurem, clean-shaven, holding a trident and a scale.

Khett had never put much stock in prayer and religion, but he had been known to look to the Gods when he needed their divine guidance. He hadn't prayed to the Gods since his father died. What would he pray for? His mother swore by religion. She believed the Gods had a reason for taking the King weeks before his forty-seventh birthday. Khett wished he could have that same belief.

No one spoke as Khett and his mother passed. Bodies pressed in on him, and he recoiled from the touch.

Inside the temple was stifling hot. Every pew filled with villagers from every far corner of Elthare. Only one pew in the front stood empty. The glass coffin had already been brought out, and Khett could see his father inside, surrounded by roses, and dressed in the family colors with two Opal Stones over his eyes--an offering for Kurem to guide him safely through the Afterworld. A gold plaque with the Pedgram crest above the coffin read:

Honor, truth, and heart--long may they reign.

Khett let out a breath when he saw Andalen and Arlen sitting in the pew behind the one reserved for Khett and the former queen. Andalen offered him a supportive smile, but he offered nothing in return. Next to her sat two men Khett had only seen in passing: Grantham Sinero and Phinn Monneaire. He nodded at them, and they gave a responding, solemn nod.

A man in white robes took the podium just as Khett and his mother sat.

"Let us begin," the priest said in a crisp, clear voice that sounded slightly too cheerful for a somber occasion. "Bow your heads in prayer."

Father would not want us to pray to the Gods for him, Khett thought as he bowed his head and clasped his hands in his lap. His father had not believed in the Eltharian religion.

Through the prayer and speech the priest gave, Khett's mind remained blank, unable to retain any words the man spoke until he said: "Now, Lord Khett would like to say a few words."

Khett jerked at the title 'Lord Khett.' For his entire life he had been Prince Khett or 'Your Grace'. The title of Lord felt like he had lost his footing in the world.

Khett stood and walked to the podium. He was overly aware of the sharp clack-clack sound his boots made on the marble floor. He turned and looked out at the sea of people and swallowed a lump that had formed in his throat.

"My father was a great man," he began. "H-he taught me how to swing a sword and skin a rabbit. I remember when I was younger he would bounce me on his knee." The memories that had eluded him earlier flooded his mind. One after another, they blinked into focus, bringing a small smile to his face. "Many of you know him as the Great King Jalinan, the man who brought an end to the War of Wars, but I know him as the man who would sing when I was sick and read by candlelight every night." He paused and cleared his throat. "I loved my father, and I *will* make him proud in the upcoming Trials."

His words were met with silence, everyone lost in their own grief, and he descended the podium and found his seat again. Andalen reached over the back of the pew and squeezed his shoulder. His hand came up and captured hers.

The cemetery in Rivland was filled with past kings, members of the noble families and soldiers who had died in battle. The Golden Tomb, where all Elthare's past kings were buried was a grand spectacle of a mausoleum filled with numerous plaques made of gold and rare jewels depicting the king's name, the date of his birth and death, and the years of his reign. The tomb carried centuries of history. And Khett stood in the middle of it all, staring blankly into the large black hole in the east wall where his father was to be put to rest later that day.

He had left his father's funeral after his mother had given her eulogy. He couldn't bear to be in the Temple anymore with the entire kingdom looking at him, pitying him. Somehow, he ended up in the Golden Tomb, staring at that blank hole in the wall.

"Your mother's looking for you," Andalen's voice came from behind him.

He turned to see her and Arlen standing just at the entrance to the mausoleum, identical figures in their house colors: emerald and gold. Together, his oldest friends came into the mausoleum, settling at his side. Andalen's arm went around his shoulder, and he leaned into her while Arlen stood on Khett's other side, hands in the pockets of his simple coat.

"The Dominikovs have been entertaining your mother with tales from the north."

Khett let out the first genuine laugh he'd had in days. "I'm sure my mother is loving that. She had always found the Dominikovs to be brutish."

"Perhaps we should go rescue her," Arlen suggested, putting his arm around Khett's other shoulder, over his sister's. The nearness of them seeped into Khett, warming his chilled bones. "The funeral ended. Everyone's heading back to the castle for the feast."

"My father would hate that he's missing a feast," Khett said sadly. "Especially one being thrown in his honor."

As one, the trio turned and made to head out of the tomb. Khett cast one more look at the hole that would be his father's tomb.

I will make you proud, Father.

Chapter Six

"You seem distracted today, Sin."

Grant rubbed tenderly at his bruising ribs as he looked at his friend. Lonis' bronze chest shimmered in the summer sun and his ink-colored hair dripped with sweat.

Grant smiled at him. "Not distracted, Lonnie. Thinking about how I am going to beat you."

Lonis laughed. "I think the scoreboard favors me."

Grant adjusted his stance and delivered a combo of punches, all of which were blocked. Lonis grabbed his arms, rotating them behind Grant's back and making him fall to his knees. He hissed in pain.

"Poor Sin," Lonis taunted, his voice tickling Grant's ear, "will you ever beat me?"

Grant growled and twisted his body, freeing himself from Lonis' grip. He turned, swiping out his leg and tripping Lonis, who fell back into the sand with an "oomph" and then laughed.

"You surprised me."

"You were getting on my nerves," Grant countered with a smirk. He held out a hand to help Lonis to his feet. "You have a bruise forming under your eye."

Lonis poked the swollen area where Grant had landed a punch earlier and then smiled. "I'm proud of you, Sin. You did well today."

A warmth passed through Grantham's body at Lonis' praise. He smiled. "Maybe one day I will be even better than you."

Lonis scoffed, clapping Grant on the back. "I don't believe that's true."

A trumpet sounded close by. He turned from Lonis to see the Trials Master coming from the direction of the village. He had nearly ten men with him, all dressed in black garments and holding trumpets with Opal Stone swords strapped to their sides.

Lonis whistled between his teeth. "The king has only been buried three days and they are already announcing the Trials."

The Master came closer. His broad shoulders stretched the fabric of his black tunic, his blond hair swept back from his face with too much oil, and curled over his pointed ears and collar. His beard was oiled as well and trimmed to perfection.

"Lord Grantham," the Trial's Master said in a booming voice as he held out a scroll tied with red ribbon and stamped with the Master's seal. "An invitation to the Trials."

Grantham bowed. "Thank you, Master Roxell."

The Master smiled and turned. More trumpeting sounded as he departed from the sand.

Lonis made a noise in his throat. "All that fanfare, and the whole affair was highly anticlimactic."

Grant shoved Lonis with his shoulder as he unrolled the scroll.

You have been cordially invited to participate in Elthare's 43rd King Trials!

Participating in the Trials is a great honor, and one that should not be taken lightly.
While it is not required for any member of any of the founding families to participate in the Trials, remember that it is a sacred duty that has been tradition for centuries.

In order to participate in the Trials, you must adhere to the following stipulations:
--You must be a member of the five founding families of Elthare
(Monneaire, Amadon, Pedgram, Sinero or Dominikov)

--You must be aged between twenty and twenty-five

--You must be of sound mind and body

The Trials will begin in a month's time. Please return a letter with your interest and be in Rivland by midday in thirty days. Failure to do so will be an automatic forfeit of your claim to the throne.

Your family will be invited to stay in the Champions' Manor during your time in the Trials, and you are allowed to bring one person outside your blood to be with you during this exciting time.

May the Gods bring you good fortune!
Roxell Vaslev, Master of the King Trials

Grant looked up from the Master's large scrolling signature at the end of the parchment and up at Lonis' eyes.

Lonis studied him, his brow furrowed. "Are you going to participate?"

Grant gripped the scroll, crinkling the parchment in his fist. He had no desire to be king, no desire to risk his life for the throne--

It's your duty, a voice that sounded eerily like his mother's entered his mind. She would have wanted him to enter.

Grant hesitated before giving his answer. "Yes. I am going to enter." His eyes met Lonis' again. "I want you to come with me."

Quickly, the realization of what he was signing up for settled in his gut, making him queasy.

Gods, what am I getting myself into? He shook his head.

Lonis remained quiet as he chewed on his bottom lip. He had an expression on his face that Grant had only seen once when Lonis' father had been severely injured in battle. "Sin--"

"Please." Grant stepped closer to his friend, gripping his arm, his eyes wide and begging. "I can't do this without you, Lonnie. Please, come with me."

Lonis nodded. Some deep emotion swirled in his eyes that Grant couldn't begin to decipher, the only thing he could make out in the honey-colored depths was fear. Lonis' hand rested on top of Grant's, warm and still a little sweaty from their sparring session. "I'll go with you, Sin. I'll be with you every step of the way."

Andalen strolled through the unusually quiet manor corridors. The servants were all gathered in their quarters celebrating Isa's nameday, so the halls felt colder, lonelier than usual. Her brother whipped around a corner, nearly smacking into her. She steadied them both with a hand on each of his elbows, noticing the piece of parchment in his hand.

"What's that?"

"A letter for father. It's a statement saying that I don't want to enter the Trials."

She blinked up at him, brown eyes meeting brown. "I was thinking..." she paused, unsure if this was a good idea or not, but she saw no other way. An Amadon had to enter the Trials, and she had always dreamed of being queen--she had to at least try. "I was thinking that I could take your place in the Trials."

Arlen raised an eyebrow at her, his mouth quirking into a confused smile. "What do you mean?"

"You can go to all the events like the parade and the dinners, and do the knowledge trial, and I'll do all the physical stuff." She took his hands in hers, pinning him with a stare. "I will become you."

Arlen chukled. "I hate to break this to you, Andi, but you're a girl. We're going to get caught."

"Please, If I chop my hair off and bind my chest, I'll look like you. We're the same height and from the back no one will be able to tell us apart" Now that the seed was planted, she wanted this more than anything. She wanted to be queen more than she needed air to breathe. "Please, Arlen. Let me do this."

"What if you actually win?"

"I haven't thought that far ahead, Ari. Please, I can't think of another way."

"This is a stupid fucking plan, Andi." He stared at her, mulling the idea over in his head. Finally, he sighed. "Fine, but if we get caught I'm blaming everything on you."

Andalen beamed. "Fair enough. Now let's go find some shears and Nix. She's not going to be pleased to hear this."

In unison they turned in the direction of her bedchambers. Andi looped her arm through Arlen's as he crumpled the letter to their father and threw it into one of the torches lining the corridor.

Chapter Seven

"Attention, Champions," a professional, clipped female voice sounded through the round, gold speaker on the wall of Khett's room. The voice belonged to Luane, the Champions' Manor keeper. She was a stern woman with severe features, and pin straight gray hair. "You will be leaving for the Champions Welcome Dinner. Please make your way to the foyer."

Khett straightened up from the open trunk with a tunic in his hand. He had only arrived an hour before and had hoped for some sort of reprieve before they jumped into the Champions' duties.

He had not seen the other Champions. Each of them had arrived at different times throughout the day, but he had heard Grantham Sinero's voice in the hall earlier, followed by that of Ikar Dominikov.

Footsteps on the floors above and below him sounded as the other Champions and their loved ones made their way down to the foyer.

"And so it begins," his mother said, fear laced her voice, mixing with pride. "Remember, my son, being king is in the Pedgram blood. What are the words on our family crest?"

"'Honor, truth and heart--long may they reign.'"

She gave a small, sad smile. "Your father would be so proud of you."

Khett dropped the tunic in his half-packed trunk and crossed the expanse of the room to sit with his mother on top of the red and black blankets of his new bed. He took her hand and gave her fingers a gentle squeeze. "I'm going to win, Mother. For him."

His mother sniffed, pushed her dark hair back from her face with her free hand, and then cupped his cheek; her fingers were cold against his warm skin. "I know you will, my son." She stood, pulling him up with her. "Now, let's go to the foyer."

Together, they exited the large, ornate room and descended the stairs down onto the first level of the Manor. He smiled charmingly at one of the pretty house servants as he passed, causing the woman to blush.

The walls and floors of the Champions' Manor were made from hard stone, marble and onyx, laced with gold. Murals of past Trials were painted on the walls and ceilings, and the colors, flowers and animals of the five founding families had been interwoven throughout the house. Khett wrinkled his nose at the purple and blue window drapings with small stags and crows stitched into the fabric.

Whose idea had it been to mix the Monneaire and Sinero colors?

Andalen and Arlen were hugging as he entered. Their parents stood close by, but distant from the words and affection exchanged between the twins. Phinn Monneaire stood with his younger brother and his seven-year-old sister at his hip, while his parents were huddled around them, sobbing onto each others' shoulder.

They fear for him, Khett realized, but it wasn't that same proud fear on his mother's face or in the Amadons, the Dominikovs, or in Lord Sinero's eyes. This was pure terror for their son's life. *And rightly so*, Khett's thoughts continued, looking at the young lord. Phinn, the youngest of the five champions, was built like a bird with a small frame and a face that made him look like a boy of fourteen rather than a man of twenty. The Trials weren't deadly, but they were brutal. They have left men permanently injured, and some had even been paralyzed after. From what Khett had heard, Phinn Monneaire was not a strong fighter.

A loud squeal came from where the Sineros stood, drawing Khett's attention. Grantham knelt in front of a young girl, holding out something in his hand. The girl laughed. "Thank you, Grant!" Then Grantham stood and looked at his companion, a tall figure with raven black hair and a sword at his belt. The man was built like a soldier with lean muscle and a rigid stance; the exchange between Grantham and his friend seemed tense and private, prompting Khett to turn away.

He turned to his mother. Tears streaked her face, and he chuckled at her foolishness. "I'm not going to die yet, Mother."

She gave him a watery smile, wiping at her eyes with the kerchief his father had given to her for her birthday, and pulled him into a hug. "Have fun, my son."

"Khett!" Nixema's voice drew his attention, and he pulled back from his mother to find the handmaiden in the small crowd. He hadn't seen her before when he surveyed the room, but she stood in a corner, draped in a simple but beautiful green dress. She waved him over.

He unwound his arms from his mother and picked his way through the families to stand next to Nixema. She smiled as he approached.

"Hello, Nix. What are you doing here?"

Khett followed her gaze to Andalen dressed in a jacket and trousers, her hair long and curly, but odd-looking. The color either too light or too dark, and the curls seemed different as well, looser, nothing like the tight spirals he was accustomed to seeing. Khett shook his head, thinking she was experimenting with a new style, before turning his attention back to Nix.

"Arlen brought me."

"He had no one else to bring?" Khett wondered, turning his gaze to the Amadons. Arlen looked ready to forfeit the throne before the Trials had even begun. Khett hated his friend being forced into something by his father that Arlen did not want to participate in. "No friends or a girl? It seems strange that he would bring his sister's handmaiden."

Nix made a face at him, something akin to her sucking on a lemon. "Arlen doesn't have friends besides you, and as for girls--"

"Hello."

Khett turned to see that Grantham and his companion had approached from their left. They were both wearing the Sinero colors, but Grantham's blue jacket was finer than his friend's and had small velvet crows sewn into the collar.

"Are we interrupting?" Grantham asked, bowing to Nix.

Nix smiled, showing the dip in her right cheek. "Not at all. I'm Nixema Maldreen, handmaiden to Lady Andalen."

Khett snorted, finding it strange to hear Nix call Andalen 'Lady'. Grantham looked at Khett with a curious expression. "Lord Khett, I didn't get a chance to tell you how sorry I was about your father's passing at the funeral. He was very kind to me when my father and I visited the castle last year."

Khett inclined his head at the Lord's words. "Thank you, Lord Grantham." He turned to the raven-haired man on his left with a nod. "I don't think I know who you are."

"You wouldn't," the man said with a smile, reaching out a hand towards Khett. "Lonis Hesito. I'm training to be a soldier in the Sinero Guard."

Grantham's arm went around the man's shoulders. "Lonis is my oldest friend, came to see me get maimed by you lot."

Lonis frowned, and his muscles tensed. "Not funny, Sin."

"Did you bring anyone?" Nixema asked Khett, pushing a blond tendril of hair off her shoulder.

"Just my mother." Khett had no one else he could bring, growing up in the castle had left him sheltered. His only friends had been Andalen and Arlen; any friends he made, when he had been allowed to venture outside the castle walls, were only kind to him in the hopes that they would one day be invited to the castle or to meet his father. Khett frowned. "I don't know who I would have brought."

Grantham clapped him on the back. "We can share Lonis," he said with a broad, teasing smile.

"I don't think your friend is too fond of that idea, Lord Grantham," Nixema commented with a giggle.

Petulance laced Lonis' voice when he replied, "I would've liked to have known that I was going to be passed around like a newborn babe."

Khett couldn't help but laugh, enjoying Lord Grantham's and Lonis' company. "Where are you from, Mr. Hesito?"

"You can call me Lonis; I'm not a fan of formalities. My parents are from the Republic of Kehan--from a small village in the Shuhai Valley."

Khett nodded. "I went with my father to the Republic two summers ago. It's a beautiful place."

"I wouldn't know," Lonis admitted. "I've never been."

A lovely woman with brown hair and dark eyes approached them from behind Grant. Khett smiled at her with a charm he reserved for the women he wished to bed. She returned his smile with a flirty one of her own. Grantham turned to find what had caught Khett's attention.

"Milden!" He hugged her and they both chuckled. "I miss seeing you around the village."

"I don't miss Oszerack, but I have missed you," she replied, pulling free from Grantham's arms.

"What brings you to the Manor?" Lonis asked after giving Milden a hug of his own.

"I'm the official seamstress for the Trials." She replied with pride. "Each of you are going to be fitted for a whole new wardrobe."

Khett pushed his way forward. "Hello," he said, extending his hand. His voice dripped with seduction. "I'm Khett Pedgram. I don't think I've had the pleasure of making your acquaintance."

She flashed him a disarming smile and curtsied. "Milden Oslan, assistant to Seamstress Ofra."

Khett whistled through his teeth. "You work for the royal seamstress? That's very impressive." He stepped even closer and lowered his voice. "When do I get the pleasure of you fitting me?"

"You'll be the first. You have my promise, Lord Khett." She whispered. She then stepped back and turned her smile on the rest of the group. "Excuse me. I need to discuss fabric choices with Lady Amadon."

Khett didn't take his eyes off the seamstress until Lord Monneaire blocked his view.

"She's Oszerackian?" he asked Grantham and Lonis.

"Yes," Grantham answered. "She was a ward at my aunt's orphanage."

Khett smoothed a hand over his styled hair. "I didn't know they made such beauty in Oszerack. I may have to visit your dirty village more often, Lord Grantham."

Grantham opened his mouth as if to argue, but Master Roxell clapped his hands twice to get everyone's attention.

"Champions, loved ones," Master Roxell called from where he stood between the foyer and the large hall that led to the dining area, "it is time the Champions take their leave. We have dinner waiting for the families in the dining room!"

Nixema disappeared to join the Amadons, and Grantham turned to Lonis, placing his hands on the other man's shoulders. "You're going to tell me everything that happens at dinner, and if there's anything chocolate for dessert steal some for me."

"Of course, Sin," Lonis replied with a crooked smile.

Khett turned away from Grantham and his friend to find his mother in the crowd, but she had already disappeared into the dining room with Lady Monneaire at her side. Khett felt a presence come up next to him, and turned to see Phinn at his side.

"Hello, Lord Khett."

"Lord Phinn."

"Your carriage awaits!" The Master said, ushering them forward.

Khett fell into step with Grantham and Phinn, but he could hear Ikar and Arlen behind them. They climbed into the black and silver carriage drawn by two black steeds, settling into the lush interior. Khett sat across from Arlen, smiling when his friend looked up at him.

"Here we are, old friend."

Arlen looked out the carriage window. "Here we are, indeed."

Khett's eyes cast downward. Arlen's hands were smudged with ink and charcoal. "You've been drawing."

Arlen looked down at his hands and then rubbed them on his gold trousers, smearing them with black. "This place begs to be drawn. Not that I have been successful at capturing its beauty." There was something flat about his voice. As if he had been deflated like an old balloon.

"You're an artist?" Phinn asked. "My brother paints."

"How old is your brother?" Arlen turned his attention from Khett to Phinn.

"Seventeen. He's really talented."

Khett kept his eyes on Arlen. When his friend smiled at Phinn it didn't quite meet his eyes. His brown skin looked pale and ashen. His eyes seemed lifeless--no, not lifeless--full of sorrow.

"I wished you hadn't gotten dragged into this, Arlen," Khett whispered. "You were supposed to go to school."

Arlen shrugged. "I don't want to talk about it, Khett."

Khett opened his mouth to argue, but thought better against it with the others in tow.

Next to him, Ikar shifted. Khett turned and looked at the Lord. His black hair tumbled around his pale forehead as he stared out the window at the passing landscape.

"That woman I saw you with earlier," Khett said to him. "The one with the red hair--"

"Be careful what you say, Lord Khett," Ikar said in a dry tone, turning to him with cold gray eyes, "that woman will be my wife one day."

Khett felt heat stain his cheeks. Ikar, two years younger than his twenty-four, had a way of making himself seem bigger than his skinny frame and older than the lot of them by ten years. "I was just going to say that I knew her brother, Briar Shaden."

"Also be careful what you say about Briar." His smile was as sharp and unforgiving as ice. "I would hate to have to kill you before the Trials even start."

"Aren't you a ray of sunshine?" Grantham commented. "Ignore him, Khett. The north winds have scrambled Dominikov's brains."

Ikar turned his sneer to Grantham. "And the southern sun has fried yours."

"There's no need to be rude to one another," Arlen mumbled.

Ikar and Grantham laughed. Ikar's sounded rusty like he didn't laugh often, while Grantham's was free like he had been laughing for as long as he had been alive. "Actually, Ikar and I have known each other for--what, ten years?"

"Eleven," Ikar corrected in his crisp tone. "The Sineros visit the north every year before heading out on a sea tour."

"We've arrived, young Lords," their driver said from his perch outside the carriage.

Outside the window, they had just passed through the castle gates. Khett swallowed, his throat suddenly dry. It had been weeks since he had lived in these walls--he and his mother had been forced to move into the Pedgram estate on the other side of

Rivland. He had expected things to be different when he returned. They weren't. Everything was still pristine and manicured, the same servants bustled busily through the grounds, and the same trees lined the cobbled road.

"Is it strange to be returning?" Arlen asked.

The carriage came to a stop right in front of the steps that led to the castle doors. The Trials Master stood at the top, hands braced behind his back. For a moment, Khett thought of his father standing on those same steps, hands braced behind his back, a smile gracing his face. He felt grief well up within him, pricking at his heart and the corners of his eyes. He choked back the sorrow and his tears, and turned towards Arlen.

"It's *very* strange." His voice sounded thick and foreign.

They all climbed out of the carriage and ascended the steps. The Master watched them with a small, self-important smile. "Welcome!"

Khett found it baffling to be welcomed to his own home by a man who had never lived there.

It's not your home anymore.

"Follow me, please."

They followed Master Roxell into the great hall, past the ballroom and the library until he came to a stop just outside the throne room. Khett swallowed. He hadn't been inside the room since the day his father died.

"Before we start dinner--"

The doors at the end of the hall banged open, and a figure strolled in from outside with an easy, unhurried gait; a tall and broad man with a shaved head, pale skin and a wicked smile that promised retribution if you crossed him.

"What the fuck?" Ikar whispered beside him.

"Sorry I'm late," the man said, coming to a stop before them and training his nearly black eyes on Ikar. "Hello, little brother."

"Lord Yvney!" The Master exclaimed. "We're so glad you could join us."

"I thought you said we had to be at the Manor by noon today in order to stay in the Trials?" Grantham asked, frowning at the newcomer. There was bad blood between the two men, Khett could see that in the way the two men stared each other down. They looked like two rabid dogs waiting to tear each other apart.

Yvney quirked a scarred eyebrow at Grant as he fell in line. "Hello to you too, Sinero."

Khett didn't personally know Lord Yvney, but he had heard stories, and he had heard enough to make sure he steered clear of the Lord.

"I did, but Lord Yvney had written a letter stating he wouldn't be able to make it by noon," the Master explained, "and in my humble generosity, I gave him a pass."

"I can't thank you again, Master Roxell." Yvney's smile was one Khett imagined a snake would wear--if a snake could smile--right before it attacked.

"You just wanted to make an entrance," Ikar accused.

Yvney shrugged at his brother with indifference before turning back to the Master. "Please, continue, Master Roxell. I didn't mean to interrupt," he said in a friendly voice that Khett believed didn't come naturally to him.

"As I was saying," Master Roxell continued. "Before dinner, I will tell you the expectations and rules of the Trials, and then you will meet with me one on one to tell me what ability has been passed down to you through your family name, but first, who wants to see the crown jewels?"

Murmuring followed the man's words. He shook his head at the lack of excitement among the young Lords and led them into the throne room.

The last time Khett had been in the room, his father had been reading a scroll that had came from the Dragon Queen. Now, the Pedgram throne had been removed, replaced by one made of gold with an ebony seat. At the bottom of the dais stood a table holding five purple pillows with five different crowns on top of each. Khett sought out the Pedgram crown with its rubies and onyx and found it at the end, the gold gleaming in the light from the torches above.

"There's rich history in these crowns," Master Roxell informed them, his voice echoing throughout the empty room. He went to the other side of the table and looked down at the five crowns with veneration, placing a hand over the Sinero crown, gold like all the others, but adorned with sapphires. "King Elric Sinero brought peace between the Lysins and the Eltharians."

He moved to the amethyst encrusted Monneaire crown. "After learning trolls were killing Eltharian children, King Hollis Monneaire had them banished from the mountains and removed from the kingdom."

"A Dominikov has yet to win a Trial," the Master said, placing a hand on the Dominikov crown, which had rubies like the Pedgram's, but lacked the onyx. He fixed his gaze on the Dominikov brothers with a smile. "Perhaps one of you will be the first."

He glanced at the Amadon crown, silver with emeralds and onyx. No one spoke of the Amadon's ruling in the past. Each had ended with death and destruction. Except One. "King Artus Amadon. He opened the castle doors to the common folk in the Harsh Winter and fed them from his own stores." Master Roxell sighed wistfully. "He sang hymns and told tales to keep up morale. I met my first wife during those hard months."

Khett wondered exactly how old Master Roxell was. The Harsh Winter was seventy years ago.

The Master didn't look older than forty, but there was a point to the tip of his ears that suggested elf blood ran through his veins. Elves aged at a slower rate compared to humans; they were almost immortal.

Master Roxell shook the memories free and moved to the Pedgram crown, looking at Khett as he spoke. "The Pedgrams have a long proud line of kings, but it was your father--King Jalinan--that brought real peace between the three kingdoms and the Republic of Kehan. It was your father who put an end to the War of Wars."

Tears pricked Khett's eyes, but he refused to let them fall in the company of others.

Master Roxell left the table and stood on the bottom step of the dais. "Sit," he commanded.

The wood creaked as they sat on the benches behind them.

"Each of these crowns has graced the heads of kings for many centuries. At the end of the Trials, one of you will be crowned, and you must uphold the same honor and authority as the kings before you."

"No pressure," Grantham whispered, his words carrying through the silent room.

Master Roxell smiled. "There, indeed, is great pressure, Lord Grantham." He was quiet for a few moments. "The Trials are not to be taken lightly, gentlemen. It is a great honor to serve in them, but they are dangerous. Only one man can be king."

Arlen stiffened next to him. Khett bumped his shoulder against his in reassurance. When Arlen looked at him, he gave him an encouraging smile, but it didn't seem to lessen his friend's nerves or end his sullen mood.

"The Trials will begin in three days time, starting with a test of your knowledge. Since you were babes you have been taught lessons in politics, arithmetic, philosophy, and many more subjects--all of that has been in preparation for the Trials. After, we will test your archery and hunting skills, and then will be the last but most important leg of the Trials: the battles." He paused, looking at them with excitement, but frowned when his enthusiasm was not matched. "The combined scores of your knowledge, archery and hunting tests will be used to determine who you will fight against in the battle rounds. Understood?"

"Understood," they said in unison.

"Excellent. Tomorrow will be the Announcement of the Champions. Tonight you are expected to get a good night's sleep and make sure you eat well."

They nodded. Khett shifted in his seat. Up until that moment the Trials had seemed more like a dream than a reality, but as he sat there listening to Master Roxell, the more the excitement and anxiety started to feel like a fist squeezing his stomach and heart. He felt sick and light-headed.

He looked at the Pedgram crown. *That's your crown, Khett. Win it for your father.*

"Now, Lord Ikar, stay with me," Master Roxell said, descending the dais to stand before them. "The rest of you can wait in the hall for your turn."

They stood while Ikar remained seated on the bench. As they departed, Khett overheard Master Roxell say, "Tell me, Lord Ikar, what is your ability?"

The door closed behind Khett before he could hear Ikar's answer. The other four were already sitting in the wooden chairs that had been brought into the hall, each of their faces drawn, except for Yvney, who smiled.

"I can't believe I agreed to enter the Trials," Phinn whispered, more to himself than to the others. "What was I thinking?"

"What *were* you thinking, time-thief?" Yvney barked with laughter. "Do you really think *you* could be king?"

The others gasped. The Monneaires were the poorest of the noble families, and they sometimes had borrowed money from Khett's mother and father to help pay for items they needed. There was a running joke between the other four families that the Monneaires used their ability to bend time to steal coin from people's pockets, but *no one* had ever called a Monneaire a time-thief to their face.

"Don't call him that!" Grantham seethed, his hands fisting, and his face contorted with rage.

"Why not?" Yvney asked, lounging in the wooden chair, leg slung over one of the arms. "Has his family paid back the coin they owe your family, Grantham?"

"That's not the point. You don't need to be a cock towards him."

Phinn's blush deepened. "I-I'm sorry. He's right, Grant. We owe so many people--"

Grantham patted his shoulder. "It's not your fault that your family fell on hard times, Phinn."

"No, it's your father's." Yvney laughed again. "He's the one who gambled away your family's savings and drank your coin. Do you blame your father for your family being poor, time-thief?"

The door to the throne room swung open. "Enough!" The Master's voice echoed through the hall. "Save that for the battles, Lord Yvney."

Ikar's eyes shot daggers at his brother, and he went to sit on Phinn's other side. Yvney shrugged and began picking under his fingernails with the edge of a blade.

"Lord Arlen?" Master Roxell said, his professional smile returning to his face.

One by one, the other lords entered the room with Master Roxell. The hall remained silent, even Yvney had stopped speaking. Finally, after

Grantham, Khett followed the Master into the throne room.

The crowns had been taken back to the vault, and Master Roxell settled onto one of the benches. He turned his smile to Khett as he sat opposite him.

"I knew your father," the Master said. "I was the Master when he won the Trials." Master Roxell's smile deepened, turning from professional to genuine. "Tell me your ability."

"I can manipulate the elements: fire, air, water, earth."

He nodded. "Yes, yes, but which one do you have true mastery over? Your father was a master of fire, which is yours?"

His father had hated his powers. *"We're the only people in all the world--besides the Lysins-- that think something as unholy as bending the elements to our will was something given to us by the Gods. We are not descended from the Gods, Khett. Witches are our ancestors, and the powers are a curse."*

Magic and the nobles' abilities were sacred in Eltharian religion. Witches and warlocks were servants of the Gods, ranked higher in society than merchants, but lower than nobles. To hear that his father had been pulling away from their Gods would have broken every Eltharians' heart. It would have broken Khett's mother's heart if she had known her husband had spoken such blasphemy.

He shook his father's words from his mind to think about the answer to Master Roxell's question.

He struggled to tame fire. Air and water came easier to him--he thought about how easily he could move boulders without touch, and how to make vines grow with just a simple thought. "Earth," he said. "Manipulating earth is the most effortless."

Master Roxell smiled. "The battles are going to be hard, Lord Khett, remember to use your powers wisely." He stood, putting an end to their conversation. "I'm famished."

He followed Master Roxell out to the hall where the others were waiting, fidgeting through their boredom, but still silent.

"Let the Dinner begin." Master Roxell clapped his hands and began another trek down the large halls.

"Finally," Grantham whispered under his breath as they followed. "I thought we were never going to eat."

Khett chuckled, despite the uneasy feeling in his stomach.

The Master led them to the dining hall where Khett's father had held holiday feasts and parties; the last feast held in the hall had been for his father's funeral. The room was as silent as it had been that day, and held wonderful but terrible memories of his father making speeches and kissing his mother while he ate chicken drenched in hearty gravy, and drank goblet after goblet of wine.

A large table had been set with seven chairs, and dishes covered every inch of the surface. Khett settled into a chair next to Arlen while a servant filled his chalice with wine. He piled his plate with meat, potatoes, bread and fruit; he felt like he hadn't eaten in days. Master Roxell sat at the head of the table, engaging Grantham in conversation. The low hum of voices filled the large room.

Ikar ate in silence. All around him the other competitors were talking about their families, their villages, or the recent festival in Palamar, but Ikar was all too aware of his brother sitting to his left, his presence a blight at Ikar's shoulder.

"You're awfully quiet, brother," Yvney whispered as he tore a chunk of meat off the bone. "Aren't you enjoying the dinner?"

Ikar whirled in his seat, pinning Yvney with a glare. "Why are you here? You had no interest in participating in the Trials when we got these invitations a month ago, so what changed?"

Yvney smiled in a way that always set Ikar's teeth on edge. It was the same smile he had when he won the title of Great Wolf Hunter of the North four years in a row, beating out Ikar by just a fraction of a point. The same smile he had worn when he let Ikar's rabbit escape when they were children and allowed his dogs to eat it as a treat, and when he had injured the boy who had bullied Ikar in their teens. Ikar had come to loathe and fear that smile. Even now, he shivered from the severity of it.

"It is a great honor to compete in the Trials, brother, don't you agree?"

Ikar didn't answer, and he knew Yvney didn't expect to get one.

"I realize that I have a duty to the Dominikov lineage, and why should you get all the glory?"

Ikar scoffed. "You're lying. The only reason you care about being a Dominikov is because of the wealth and status it brings you." His eyes went round. "I have been dreaming of the day I finally get out from under your shadow--our parents' shadow--for years. Can you not let me have this one thing to myself, Yvney?"

Yvney's grin sharpened. "Are you afraid of a little competition?" He sipped from his goblet and then turned toward Ikar, resting his arm against the back of his chair, and said, "Besides, brother, it is not like *you* are going to win the Trials. At least with me, our family has a fighting chance at the throne."

Ikar's blood went cold. He didn't respond, and pushed his plate away, unable to eat another bite. His brother's words brought his own doubts to the forefront of his mind. Perhaps Yvney was right: How could *he* possibly win the Trials?

Chapter Eight

Khett felt sick.

He made his way down to the dining room where voices drifted out into the rest of the Manor. He found the other Champions sitting at the large table, already dressed for the day. They were surrounded by their families and loved ones. Each of them looked as sick as he felt— all except Yvney, who smiled as he ate sausages and porridge as if it were another normal day in their kingdom.

Andalen stood from her seat and came to him, her face tight, but her smile in place, easing the vise on his stomach a fraction. She wrapped her arms around him, pulling him against her warm body. He held her to him as he inhaled her subtle lemon and vanilla scent.

"Are you nervous?" she asked into his shoulder.

"I'm fine," he replied into her hair, but noticed something odd about the texture, but he didn't question it. In that moment, as he held her, he was fine. He was more than fine. He pulled back and looked into her brown eyes. They were steady, which relaxed him even more. "It is nothing more than a test of my knowledge, and I have had the best tutors in the three kingdoms."

Her smile grew bigger. "I have no doubts that you will excel, Khett." She kissed his cheek and went back to her chair.

He maneuvered through the room until he found an empty chair between his mother and Phinn. He sat, pulling the plate of sausages towards him.

"How do you feel about today's Trial?" he asked Phinn as he piled food on his golden plate.

"Great, actually." The young Lord smiled at him, his eyes big and round, making him look boyish. "I have spent many hours in the library at our estate. I have studied nearly every subject there is. I've remembered every book I have ever read--word for word. Marklin, my brother, hates it. I am full of useless knowledge," he said with a laugh.

"You still have your library?" Khett asked, astonished. He had heard a rumor that the Monneaires had sold every last possession they had to pay off Lord Monneaire's gambling debt.

Phinn's cheeks reddened. "My books and Elodi's governess are the only things we have left, and I heard Mother and Father were going to fire her before I got invited to the Trials. Mother's books don't sell as well as they used to, and Father's debt keeps growing." He looked across the table at his family; his father was already glassy-eyed from wine. His mother frowned at her husband in disapproval. "Please, don't tell anyone what I told you. It is merely a rumor that we had to sell everything, but if it were known that it were true, I think that would embarrass my mother, and I don't want that." He looked close to tears. "I shouldn't have told you. I apologize. Mother says we should use discretion when talking about our struggles."

"I understand," Khett answered, uncomfortable at the shame in Phinn's blue eyes. "It must be hard on your family, and I do not wish to make it worse."

"Thank you. I appreciate that."

"Champions," Luane stood at the foot of the table, her hair as smooth and straight as it had been the last three days, her black dress pressed and wrinkle-free. Khett wondered if she owned other clothes. "Please, follow me to the carriages."

Khett stood with the others. He glanced down to see the three sausages still sitting on his plate. His empty stomach growled, but he had no time to eat, and he didn't think he could keep down food anyway.

Luane led them outside to where the Master's carriages waited, but Master Roxell was nowhere to be seen. Khett climbed into one carriage behind Phinn and Ikar, while Yvney, Arlen and Grant took the other.

"Where are we going?" Phinn asked as the carriage passed the gates of the castle and continued down the cobbled road into the city.

Khett looked out the window to see they had also passed the university. People milled around the grounds in groups, laughing and talking, and he wondered what it would have been like to be one of them, a commoner able to study whatever they desired. They had no ancient duty passed down to them through their family blood that obligated them to sacrifice their lives. What would it be like to be unencumbered?

But even as he wondered about a life he could not have, Khett loved the duty he had to his family. He had a purpose, and he found comfort in knowing he had something he was *supposed* to do with his life.

The carriages came to a stop just outside the Gods' Temple. The six of them climbed out, clustering on the white walkway leading to the marble building. Grantham looked ready to spit fire as he came to stand next to Ikar, while Yvney howled with laughter, and Arlen looked ready to cry.

"I forgot how much of a cock your brother can be," Grant seethed.

Ikar snorted. "And I keep forgetting to ask Mother if she's sure he's our blood. It can't possibly be true; my brother was raised by wolves."

Grantham laughed. "Unfortunately for you, I think he is, in fact, blood-related."

"The Gods cursed me with him," Ikar resigned. "Do you think I can trade him for another?"

"What happened?" Khett asked Arlen as he came to a stop at his side, ignoring the rest of Ikar and Grantham's banter.

Arlen ran a hand through his curls, his eyes brimming with unshed tears. "Please, Khett, I don't wish to discuss it."

Anger brewed in Khett's belly, and the ground shifted under their feet as if the earth were quaking. "Whatever he said, I will kill him."

"Leave it be, Khett." Arlen sniffed, and looked over at Yvney leaning against the statue of Nomir and chatting with a woman as she walked by. "I have never met anyone who got so much enjoyment out of causing other people pain."

The doors of the temple opened before he could ask Arlen what he meant, and Master Roxell strolled out, wearing his signature smile. He opened his arms wide; The silver of his buttons and jewelry glittered in the sun.

"Welcome, Champions!" He looked at each of them as if he was personally honored by their presence. "Today is the first Trial. You will be given four hours to complete the test. Top scores will be announced before the second Trial." He waited for them to acknowledge his words, and his smile grew, turning into a grin when they did. "Now, follow me."

He turned and led them through the empty temple, and back through to a hall that smelled strongly of incense. Golden doors lined the white walls, each closed and locked; only the priest's door stood open. He sat at his desk, reading a scroll. He smiled as they passed, wishing them luck.

They entered a large room, empty except for paintings of Kurem sitting on a throne of bones in the snow, and a painting of Nomir surrounded by flowers and holding a small babe. The symbol of the Gods was painted at the front of the room, an intricate twelve pointed star inside three circles with the words: *The Gods' favor is man's will.*

Six desks lined up in two rows of three with a larger desk sat before them. The tests were already on the surfaces with a pot of ink and a quill next to them. Khett chose the desk closest to the door, next to Arlen and behind Yvney. Master Roxell beamed and clapped his hands as if to get their attention, but they were silent and already turned towards the front of the room.

"Cheating will not be tolerated. You will be removed from the Trials if you are caught." His smile never fell from his face. Khett wondered if it hurt the man's cheeks to grin that much. "Remember, you have four hours. You may begin."

Khett looked down at the pile of parchment in front of him. He flipped to the back to see that the test was over three-hundred questions, and then read the first:

What brought the end of the Dragon War in the 1300's, and who was responsible for its end?

Around him, the scratching of quills had started, the only sound in the room besides the Champions' breathing. Khett dipped his quill in ink and answered the question.

Grant's hand was still cramped, even as he walked up the stairs of the Manor to his room. The test had been harder than he expected. He hadn't realized there were going to be so many questions, or that there would be some questions he had left blank because the answer escaped him.

Who the hell was Sedrik the Wise anyway?

He pushed the door open to find Lonis sitting on the floor in the middle of the room. His raven hair had fallen forward into his eyes as he thumbed Grant's blade. He didn't look up as Grant entered and settled on his knees in front of him.

"How was the first Trial?" Lonis' voice sounded more like gravel than its usual honeyed tone.

"Harder than I thought." Grant tried to catch his eye, but the other man kept his head down. "Who is Sedrik the Wise?"

"The first Trials Master," Lonis answered, finally looking up at Grant with sad, light brown eyes. "He helped write the laws of Elthare and the rules for the Trials."

"I should've had you take the test for me," Grant said, trying to lighten his friend's mood. He took the dagger from Lonis' hands and flipped it back and forth between his palms. "What is the matter?"

"Nothing," Lonis said, taking the dagger back and gripping it by its ivory handle. "Thinking."

"About?"

"I--" Lonis' eyes flipped up, and the emotion in the depths of his pupils choked Grant. He felt unable to breathe. The air hung heavy with so many unsaid words. "It's nothing, Sin."

Lonis crossed the room. He stood with his hand on the handle for a few moments with tense shoulders, and Grant wished he would say something, but he did not turn around. He did not say a word. Lonis opened the door and exited the room. Grant's breath left him in a small woosh, leaving him aching.

Ikar gazed at the animal-shaped hedges in the Manor's gardens. He stood in front of a large wolf, which reminded him of home. He missed the north, his manor, his bed. He missed the sad lute players who sat outside the shops and the smell of pine trees that came from the woods. He even missed the tavern and its drunken patrons.

"Here you are," Roslen's sweet voice came behind him, and he turned to see her picking her way over the white path, the skirt of her red dress gathered in her dainty hands. "I have been searching everywhere for you."

"And you've found me," Ikar said with a small smile. He went to her, pulling her to his chest and burying his face in her fiery hair. "What are you going to do with me now that you have me?"

"Wicked, wicked things, Lord Ikar," she whispered in his ear, tracing the shell with her lips.

She kissed him, engulfing him in heat and the smell of cinnamon. Her hands tangled in his hair, pale against the midnight strands. She rubbed against him, her small breasts soft against his lean chest. He brought his hand up, cupping one in his palm. She let out a soft moan, rubbing against his hardness, but he pulled back, breathless.

"Not here. The world can see us."

Her eyes blazed as blue and untamed as the ocean. "You know I've never cared about those sorts of things."

He chuckled, cupping her warm cheek with his long fingers. "My love, the exhibitionist." He kissed her again, light and chaste. "Come, let us make our way inside."

"We will," she said, pushing her body more into his as a slight breeze blew through the garden. He removed his black cloak and wrapped it around her shoulders. "But I have something to say first."

Ikar led her to a small bench further down the walkway and sank onto the iron frame, pulling Roslen to his side. Her ocean eyes were a calm before the storm. She pulled her bottom lip into her mouth, biting into the flesh with her top teeth.

"I've missed my bleeding for three months, Ikar."

Ikar's brows pulled down in confusion. "What do you mean? You are not ill, are you?"

Her eyebrow raised, and she smiled a little. "You really are very dense." She kissed him, softening the blow of her words. "I'm with child, my love. You're going to be a father."

Ikar's heart stopped in his chest. His lungs had stopped working for a moment. He stared at her, unseeing. His brain stuck on one word: father. *You're going to be a father.* Ikar stood as still as a statue. He feared if the breeze blew any harder, he would break into a million pieces like glass.

"Breathe, Ikar. " But when his chest still didn't rise and fall, she shook his shoulder and said with more urgency, "Breathe."

Even as he exhaled, her eyes were still worried, and she chewed on her lip. Her hands were cold in his. "Are-are you sure?"

"Quite. The doctor here in Rivland confirmed it this morning while you were at the Trial."

"Who took you?" he panicked. "You shouldn't have gone alone!"

"Briar was with me." She brought her hands to his face, cupping his cheeks, rubbing her thumbs along the sharpness of the bones. "Are you happy?"

A smile, big, broad and rusty from decades of rarely gracing his face, appeared. He gathered Roslen in his arms, pulling her into his lap. "More than I have ever been, Roz." He kissed her, losing himself in the taste of her sweetness. "Our parents are going to be angry."

"Why do you say that?" her voice light and giddy, even as her eyes dimmed at his words.

"We are having a child before we are married."

Roslen laughed. "They will be angrier if we do not have a boy."

"Right you are, my love." He kissed her again and again. "They will want an heir to carry the Dominikov name."

"I will be happy as long as our babe has your eyes," she said, resting her head against his shoulder.

"Oh, Gods, save our child from looking anything like me!" he joked, throwing his hands in the air. He looked up to the sky. "Kurem, make my child look like his mother."

Roslen giggled. "Or *her* mother."

Ikar smiled. "Or her mother." He looked down at Roslen, getting lost in her wide eyes. "I have never been happier than I am in this moment. Thank you, Roz."

"All I want is your happiness, Ikar. I need nothing more."

"You are the only person who brings me joy like this. You are the light that chases away the darkness."

He bent his head and kissed her for what felt like hours, placing his hand over her belly as if he could already feel his child moving.

Chapter Nine

"You're going to do well," Arlen assured Andalen four days after the first Trial.

She was dressed in his trousers and tunic, each made from a shiny, soft fabric dyed the colors of their family. He was adorned in the plain trousers and tunic she had worn to meet him, and her curly wig, with his face partially hidden behind the hood of her cloak.

"This is what you were born for."

Andalen itched at the uncomfortable bindings around her chest that made her small breasts virtually nonexistent. "Have you seen Nix? I wish to speak to her before I go out."

"I haven't," he said. "Do you want me to find her?"

"No. She's probably already in the crowd."

Outside the tent, the roar of the audience could be heard, chanting the names of their favored families. The Master was revealing the Champions' test scores, his voice carrying from the open field nearly fifty feet away. Arlen had done well on the knowledge test, tying with Khett for the highest score.

A small man, wearing a turban and a scarf over the lower half of his face, entered the tent, carrying a wooden box filled with brushes and paint. He looked around the clean tent with a bland expression, quirking an eyebrow at the trunk of clothes, a table of food and two chairs.

"Are you ready, Lord Arlen?" he asked, looking at Andalen.

Andalen's heart pounded. *Does he recognize that it's me?* But the man seemed too involved in his own work to care about her, and judging from his accent and his clothes, he came from Keresh. This man wouldn't have known what Arlen looked like.

Arlen turned away from the man, tucking his face deeper into the hood of Andi's cloak. His shoulders rolled forward as if someone were pushing on them.

She nodded. "Who are you?" She deepened her voice to resemble something close to a man's.

Behind her, Arlen snorted. The man looked at her like she had disrespected the Gods. "You do not *know* me? I am Hasa, artist from the fire lands."

"I'm sorry," Andalen muttered. "I didn't know."

"They say you are brilliant artist, and you don't know Hasa? What kind of artist doesn't know Hasa?"

She could feel Arlen's eyes on her, warning her not to mess up again.

The man came forward and painted her cheeks and forehead to resemble a fox, and then painted her lips black with a vertical gold line through the center. He stepped back, looking at his work. "You look like a warrior, Lord Arlen, a man made for battle."

Long ago, when the nobles fought in wars, they would paint their faces with the animal of their house. The common soldiers painted theirs in beautiful dots and lines; she much preferred the dots and lines to the face of an animal.

"Done. Now you know Hasa." He exited the tent, and Arlen turned, smiling slightly at Andalen.

"You really do look like a family soldier, sister."

She ran a hand over the very short curls atop her head. "I feel ridiculous. I didn't realize how much glamour and show went into participating in these Trials."

Arlen laughed. "It would not be very entertaining for the kingdom if there were no performance."

Another man came into the tent. "Lord Arlen? I'm to escort you to the field."

Andalen turned and hugged Arlen, wrapping her arms around his slender shoulders as nerves took over. "Show them what it means to be an Amadon," he whispered in her ear.

Andalen followed the man out of the tent and through the large field where the Champions were being held until the Trial began. There were several massive tents around her, the low buzz of chatter came from within some of them, but Andalen couldn't make out any words. The Trial Master's servants bustled through the field carrying trays of food, clothes, and bows and quivers.

They were stopped by a young man, no older than thirteen or fourteen if Andalen had to guess. He thrust a bow and quiver at her with no words. He kept his eyes down, showcasing a bruise on his cheek, yellow and purple as it healed.

Instead of taking the bow and quiver, she knelt in front of the child, and his eyes met hers, sad and blue. "Who did this to you?" she whispered in a deep voice.

He looked up at the servant escorting her, who was standing as stiff as a board beside her. "No one, Lord Arlen. Good luck." He threw the bow and quiver on the ground and scurried away.

Andalen frowned, watching the child disappear between Khett and Ikar's tents. She picked up the discarded items and then faced the other servant looking at her with a curious expression. "I do hope the Master is not abusing his servants."

The man met her look of apprehension with a smile. "Master Roxell treats us well...my brother is an easy target for the other servants because he is young."

"He's your brother?"

The servant nodded as he led her out of the field and down a tree-lined path. "Our parents died when I was young. I was the only one who could take care of Belmar."

"That is noble of you."

"It was my duty." The pride in the servant's voice made Andalen smile.

They came to another large field surrounded by spectators. They cheered as Andalen came into view. Banners of green and gold glittered in the sun.

"A-ma-don! A-ma-don!"

In front of her were six painted targets; circles of black, yellow and red on a white canvas. The

Dominikovs were already standing before their targets, bows at their sides and quivers at their back. They were dressed in red and silver garments with their faces painted to look like wolves snarling at their prey.

The Master stood on a dais off to the side, dressed in an elaborate silver and black cloak with his styled hair shining in the sun.

"Welcome, Lord Arlen!" he greeted, his voice carrying through the crowd. "Take a spot at a target of your choosing!"

The crowd cheered.

One by one, the other Champions were escorted onto the field, all of them painted to resemble their family's animal. Someone had put antlers on Phinn to make him look more like a stag. Khett stood on the other side of Lord Phinn, looking at Andalen with a mild, curious expression.

She turned away from him.

"Champions, welcome to the second Trial! For centuries it has been the great honor of the King to join his soldiers in battle! This Trial is to pay homage to all the kings who died protecting their kingdom!" The crowd's cheers rose, nearly drowning out the Master's next words. "The scores you receive today will be added to your test scores, and the two highest scores will receive an advantage at the next Trial!"

Andi's hands shook at her sides, her stomach lurched. *You are going to be queen. You are going to be queen,* she chanted to herself, but still, nerves wracked through her body. The sun was too hot, and the roar of the spectators too loud.

"Champions, nock your arrows!"

With a trembling hand, Andalen reached behind her and pulled one of the five arrows from the quiver, fitting it into the bow. She held the bow fast. The familiar feel of the firm wood steadied her nerves. She breathed in and out until the roar of the crowd fell away, and her breaths were all she could hear.

"Loose!" the Master called.

The arrow sailed from her bow, whizzing through the air until it slammed into the target with a loud *thwack*, hitting it dead in the center. Around her, arrows hit their targets, but none had hit the red as hers had.

"Nock!" the Master called again.

They repeated the action for the next four arrows. Hers hit the bullseye each time, a cluster of feathers and wood blocking out the red paint. As she lowered her bow she looked around at the other targets. Arrows stuck out from the canvas, most in the yellow painted on as the second inner ring. But there were two in the bullseye of Grantham's, and one in Khett's.

"The winner of today's Trial," the Master called, "is Lord Arlen!"

"A-ma-don! A-ma-don! A-ma-don!" the crowd cheered louder than before, and it rushed through her like a wave. She smiled with triumph, thrusting her bow into the air in time with their chanting.

Andalen sank into the chair inside the tent.

She had asked to be left alone. The rush of the Trial had left her feeling like a wind-up toy that had come to its end. She sighed, pulling the knee-high leather boots from her feet.

"I knew it was you out there," Khett's voice came from near the tent's entrance. She turned to see him standing just inside the flap with his arms clasped behind his back, his face still painted to resemble a hawk. "Where is Arlen?"

Andi sighed. She would never be able to lie to Khett. "How did you know it was me?" she asked as she untucked the tunic from the hem of her trousers.

"You stand differently than Arlen. You stand straighter, as if you're a tree in the forest," he answered, coming closer. He came to a stop at her left, close enough that she could smell the woodsy oil they had rubbed all over his body before the Trial. "And Arlen would not have been able to get all five arrows in the bullseye."

"You underestimate my brother, Khett?" She quirked an eyebrow at him, posed, waiting; a viper waiting to attack if he said one wrong word.

"Not at all, but he would not have been able to make those shots with his blindness."

Andalen could not argue with that, and she relaxed. "Are you going to tell the Master?"

Khett came to stand in front of her, smiling that smile that reminded her of mischievous children--the smile she had fallen in love with as a girl of sixteen. "No. I know how much you have always wanted to be queen. I will not tell the Master your secret, but you have to do something for me."

"What?" she asked, dubious of what this favor would be.

His cunning smile only grew bigger. "I will ask before the next Trial."

Khett came close, the smell of sweat and something strong and alluring emitted from his skin. He bent down to her. His brown eyes surveyed her face. It had been six years since she had ended their relationship, but she felt she would always be drawn to him, no matter where their lives would lead them in the future.

"Short hair looks good on you."

"Khett--"

Her words cut off when his mouth touched hers. She closed her eyes, giving in to the kiss only for a moment, finding it hard not to curl into the familiarity of his lips on hers.

Nixema.

She pushed at Khett's shoulder and wiped her mouth with the back of her palm. "What do you think you're doing?"

Khett looked away, ashamed. "I apologize. I think it's all the excitement."

He said nothing more and walked out of her tent.

Andalen cursed to the Gods.

Chapter Ten

After seven days of uneventful lounging around the Manor, they were taken to the woods again. *Why are all these damned Trials in the woods?* Ikar mentally grumbled as they trudged into a meadow in the middle of the Elthare forest. They lined up before Master Roxell in a large clearing with bows, quivers and swords strapped to them as if they were going into battle. The roar of the crowd from the perimeter where the grass bled into the treeline was deafening, but Ikar paid them no mind.

"Champions!" The Master announced, and the crowd fell into a hush. "Congratulations on making it to the third Trial! Today, you have been given weapons and a servant; they will accompany you into the woods to bring back the requested game!" Ikar's heart thumped in his chest, beating in time to the words Master Roxell spoke. "You are to hunt four ducks and a boar, and you will receive bonus points for any other kills you bring back!"

The crowd cheered.

The sun beat down on Ikar, stifling hot. He pulled the collar of his tunic away from his neck. *Gods, I hate summer.*

"You have until sunset. Failure to complete the Trial is an automatic forfeit."

Yvney leaned close to Ikar, and he could smell the wine on his brother's breath. "It's fortunate we are not hunting wolves, eh, brother?"

The ever lingering hatred for his brother burned Ikar's belly, sitting inside him like acid. He glared at Yvney, who only smirked at him. "You *stole* all of those kills from me, *brother.* I'm just as good of a hunter as you."

Yvney laughed, his eyes sparking with a challenge. "Alright, if you bring back a wolf I will give you my sword."

Ikar looked at the hilt of the sword strapped to Yvney's back. The weapon was long, sleek, and made from Opal Stone. The rubies in the hilt glittered in the sunlight. Ikar coveted that sword. He was supposed to get one of his own on his birthday, but since he failed to kill a wolf, he got nothing instead.

At least you weren't branded. The town had overlooked his failure when he announced his entry into the Trials. He had thanked Kurem that day; he had not wanted to mar the flesh of his back with a hideous mark.

"You have a deal, Yvney." Ikar smiled up at his brother.

Yvney returned the challenge with a scoff.

The Trial had already begun as they spoke. Arlen and Grant had been given rewards for having the highest scores during the Archery Trial. They were allowed to enter the woods an hour and a half hour, respectfully, before the others, but the Master announced that Arlen had given Khett the advantage earlier that morning. Ikar pulled away from his brother as Khett disappeared through the trees. He waited quietly with Grant, Arlen and Phinn until their turn. Yvney stood apart, waving at the women in the crowd.

The crowd chanted around them, filling the air with a mixture of their names and banners. Ikar saw one with a gray wolf's head and the words from the Dominikov family crest:

One of Many.

Bold silver letters on a blanket of red as dark as blood, and then he saw the person the banner belonged to. Roslen and Briar smiled at him from the crowd, their red hair nearly blinding in the sun. He watched Roslen's perfect lips form his name over and over again, and he smiled.

The Master signaled for them to enter the woods, after giving Grant his head start. Ikar looked at Roslen again, and she beamed, waving at him as he disappeared into the trees.

The woods grew quiet as he trudged through the overgrown brush and roots; he could no longer hear the crowd, but now heard only bird song and the soft rustle of leaves in the breeze. It took him several long moments to realize he was lost in the unfamiliar forest. Everything was too green and lush; he missed the knotted, black trees of the Althanen woods.

Ikar cursed and turned, choosing a different path than the one before.

He came to another clearing, where he found a servant in a simple red and silver tunic waiting with a cart and rope.

Only two carts remained, his and Phinn's. He frowned, realizing his brother had gotten there before him. The servant was a tiny thing with curly brown hair and an innocent face marred with blue and purple.

"Are you even strong enough to pull that cart?" Ikar asked.

One brown eye looked up at him as the other was swollen shut. As Ikar got closer, the extent of the boy's injuries became more evident. His lip was swollen, and his cheek was split and scabbed over with blood. Ikar knelt, taking the servant's small, dirty face in his hands. "Who did this to you?"

"Please, My Lord," his voice was small, terrified; a voice Ikar knew all too well.

Ikar had been younger than the boy when Yvney started beating him, and when the bullies in his village started picking on him for his pale skin and skinny frame.

"What is your name?"

"Bel-Belmar."

Ikar smiled at the boy and squeezed his shoulder gently. "If you won't tell me who did this to you, will you at least accept some coin for a job well done today?"

The boy's eyes widened, and a smile lifted, splitting the cut on his bottom lip. "Dolnik says I shouldn't take money from the nobles." His face fell, and he kicked at a pebble on the forest floor. "Thank you, My Lord."

"Who is Dolnik?"

"My brother."

You're wasting time, Ikar's brain warned him. "Is he the one that did this to you?"

Belmar shook his head. "No. Dolnik tried to get them off of me." He trembled, rolling the rope between his fingers. "Please, My Lord, we should begin the Trial. The others have already come and gone."

"Too right, Belmar."

Ikar stood to his full height. Unable to shake the look of fear, and bruising around the child's eye from his mind, he found a path and started along it with Belmar following behind. The trail twisted and turned, branching off into smaller, narrower paths that led deeper into the woods. Ikar frowned when he could no longer hear the rush of water, and the sun did not penetrate through the leaves as much. He looked up at the canopy of trees, and then back down the path they were following.

"I do believe we are lost, Belmar." His voice calm and light, but his heart hammered in his chest. Memories of getting lost in the Althanen woods when he was no older than Belmar pierced his mind.

For hours, he had walked around in the black woods, hungry and tired. Cold from the autumn winds. His Uncle Dietrick hadn't found him until the sun had nearly set.

Ikar shook his head, ridding himself of the memories, and turned to lead his small companion back the way they came. When they came to a fork in the path, he turned left instead of right, hoping to find something he could kill with the dull, steel sword rattling around in the cart Belmar pulled.

They walked for miles, following the twisting path until they came to the bank of the Roaming River.

"Ah, there we are," he said, clapping Belmar on the shoulder and smiling down at the boy. "I knew we would find it."

"Very good, Lord Ikar."

The tracks from the other Champions' carts were imprinted in the mud, but Phinn huddled on the river's edge, struggling to pull an arrow from the body of a duck. His servant looked on with pity. Ikar watched with mild amusement as Phinn struggled, holding back a chuckle when the naive Lord nearly fell into the water.

How did he get here before me?

Phinn was a kind man, but Ikar wondered if the young lord would be strong enough to continue in the Trials.

The servant took pity and plucked the duck from Phinn's hands and threw it into the cart.

"We'll deal with it later," she demanded, pulling the cart away from the bank.

Ikar turned his attention back to the task at hand when he could no longer hear the squeaking of Phinn's cart, and looked up and down the water as it flowed over rocks and made the lily pads dance on its surface.

There were no ducks in the area, all having flown away when the Lords had trampled onto the bank. Ikar silently walked along the river's edge after telling Belmar to stay with the cart. He had slung the bow over his shoulder, and it bumped against the leather quiver as he walked, a familiar weight upon his back.

Quacking came from a small break off the main river, and Ikar nearly cheered in triumph. He moved slow and quiet through the trees until they broke apart, giving him a clear view of five full-grown drakes.

He pulled out four arrows, hoping he would be able to nab these without having to give chase, and laid three in the grass next to him. He nocked the first arrow and let it loose, piercing two of the ducks in one shot. The others tried to take flight, but he already had the next arrow ready to go. It flew through the air, piercing another.

Fuck, he thought as the other two got away.

He looked down at the three dead birds in the water and went to them to pull the arrows free from their bodies. He held them by their feet as he trudged back through the woods where Belmar waited with the cart. The boy smiled when he came back.

"That was fast, Lord Ikar!" he exclaimed, tying the ducks together in the cart.

Ikar found himself smiling at the boy's enthusiasm. "Come, we must find another and a boar." He began walking and heard the squeak of the wheel as Belmar followed with the cart. "Oh, and a wolf."

"A wolf?"

"Yes, the biggest, ugliest wolf we can find."

The sun had nearly set, and Ikar's cart brimmed with four ducks and two boars. He had not meant to kill the second, but it had tried to attack him; he had no choice but to stab it through the neck with his sword. Belmar had nearly been sick when the boar's tusk had grazed Ikar's arm, and he had to prove to the boy that he had not truly been injured; the wound was nothing more than a small gash. Belmar had still vomited in the bushes.

Ikar walked through the woods, heading back to the clearing where the Master waited, with his shoulders rolled in and head bowed in disappointment.

"I'm sorry we didn't find a wolf, Lord Ikar."

He turned and smiled at the boy. "It is alright, Belmar. It was an idiotic bet I had with my brother."

"Well, you did capture two boars," Belmar offered.

"There is that, Bel. I hope they serve the one who nicked me for dinner."

"Me too!"

They broke through the trees, coming to the clearing where the Master waited; he looked mildly irritated about something, and Grant was nearly doubled over in the grass laughing.

Yvney stood off to the side, plucking under his nails with his knife, while Arlen and Khett were staring down at Grant as if he had gone mad. Phinn looked to be in a state of shock as he stood covered in blood over a pile of sick. His boar was still breathing, but not far from death. No one else had killed an extra animal, at least Ikar had that above the rest.

"All our Champions have returned!" The Master called. "In first place, we have Lord Arlen! In second, Lord Khett! Third, Lord Grantham! Fourth, Lord Yvney!" Each name was met with a roar of cheers. "Now, Lord Phinn did arrive before Lord Ikar. However, Lord Ikar brought back two boars, and Lord Phinn's boar is still breathing, so this will put Lord Ikar in fifth place!" More cheers mixed with some loud groans of discontent that came from where the Palmans stood. "And Lord Phinn is in sixth!"

Arlen, still dressed in a soft leather archery helmet, stalked towards Phinn's cart, driving a sword through the boar's heart. Ikar had not known the mild-mannered lord to be an expert at hunting and archery; it almost made Ikar like Arlen. Almost.

A hush fell over the crowd, and the Master cleared his throat. "Right.....well....." Ikar got a certain amount of satisfaction at seeing the pompous, well-polished man flustered. "That concludes the Hunting Trial."

Something caught Ikar's eye just beyond the trees--a flash of gray. He let out a laugh that sounded like cracking ice, drawing the attention of the other Champions and the Master.

"Something funny, Lord Ikar?" Master Roxell asked. The look of irritation he wore only moments before returned, twisting his brows and drawing his face downward.

Ikar ignored him. "It seems my luck has turned, Belmar," he whispered to the young servant as he drew the sword from the cart and left behind three gold coins that he hoped the boy would take.

"What do you mean, Lord Ikar?" Belmar turned, searching the woods for what Ikar had seen. "Is it a wolf?"

"It is indeed, my young friend." And with that, he took off at a sprint with Grant asking him where he was going, and the Master's voice carrying through the dusky twilight, both of which he pretended not to hear.

"Have you all gone insane!" The Master's voice followed him as he broke through the trees.

Perhaps, he thought to himself. He certainly thought he had a touch of lunacy since he was chasing a wolf through the forest with nothing more than a sword to arm himself. *You're not wearing protective gear, you twit.*

He stopped running, listening to the sounds of the forest, waiting to hear the wolf. Silence. Only the sounds of crickets and other insects that came out at night. He turned his head this way and that, trying to figure out which direction it had ran. And then he heard it, a twig snapping in the not-to-far distance.

He followed the sound, hoping to find his wolf, and he would. Tracking was in the Althanens' blood.

He walked for what felt like hours. The sun had fully set, and the moon had risen. Trees gave way to the rocky base of the mountains, and a wide, black mouth of a cave.

Gods, please do not let me get eaten by a bear.

Growling sounded behind him, and he whipped around, facing the wolf. Wild black eyes met his. Lips pulled back in a snarl, revealing yellow canines and dripping saliva. A smirk curved on Ikar's lips, pulling them back from his teeth until his snarl matched hers.

"Hello," he said. "Be nice, and I will kill you quickly."

The wolf let out another menacing growl before she pounced.

Chapter Eleven

Ikar dragged the wolf's body through the halls, leaving a large streak of blood on the marble floor as he limped through the Manor. The bite on his leg was wrapped with torn cloth from his tunic, but blood was already starting to seep through, dripping to the floor in small puddles. A servant asked if he needed aid, but Ikar refused the man with a curt shake of his head and pulled the wolf along until he reached the door of Yvney's room. He entered without bothering to knock.

Yvney sat in a chair by the fireplace, Milden's head was in his lap bobbing up and down. Yvney's eyes flew open at Ikar's intrusion, and he yelled. The seamstress scrambled to her feet, pink staining her cheeks. She adjusted her dress and patted her dark hair before skirting around Ikar and darting out the door.

"Be sure to return the favor, brother," Ikar said. "It probably wasn't easy for her to throw her pride out the window and service a cock like you."

"What do you want, Ikar?" Yvney snarled, tucking himself back into his pants and standing. He crossed the room, pouring wine into a goblet. "You irksome toad, Mother was going to send a search party for you. She thought her little babe got lost in the woods."

"I brought you a present."

Ikar dragged the wolf into the room, depositing it on the rug in the center. He took the chair Yvney vacated and warmed his chilled hands in the fire.

"Why did you bring this here?" Yvney asked, standing by the mantle, drinking his wine. His lip curled. "Our arrangement was that you find a wolf *during* the Trial, not after. You won't get my sword."

Ikar's eyes flicked to the sword hanging near the wardrobe. Its shiny handle absorbed the light from the fire in an almost hypnotizing way. Ikar shook his head and turned his glare back to Yvney. "I don't want your sword. I wanted to prove to you that I can kill a wolf. You're not the only wolf hunter in the Dominikov line."

Yvney laughed, and Ikar's hairs rose on the back of his neck. "You're a joke, Ikar. I still don't understand how you've remained in the tournament. You have no power, your intelligence is for shit, you may be good with a bow and arrow, but your sword work is lacking." He laughed again, and fire rose in Ikar's belly.

He jumped up, rushing his brother, pushing him back into the marble mantle. His forearm pushed against Yvney's throat, but his brother's dark eyes danced with glee, taunting him. The bite on his leg began to leak again, but he ignored it. "Why do you get so much pleasure from tormenting me?"

Yvney bared his teeth, reminding Ikar of the wolf right before she attacked. "You're weak, a stain on the Dominikov family tree." But there was something in Yvney's eyes that suggested he wasn't being completely honest. "Mother spoiled you rotten when she came home from the war, and it turned you soft."

Ikar's fist reared back and caught Yvney in the nose. His brother howled and fell against the wall. A well of satisfaction rushed through Ikar as he turned and headed for the door.

"Take your fucking wolf!" His brother yelled, his words muffled by the blood gushing from his nose. "It's bleeding all over the carpet!"

"As are you," Ikar returned with a smirk as he went to the door and turned back, looking at his brother. Yvney's face was covered in scarlet, his nose crooked from being broken by Ikar's fist, and his tunic wrinkled where Ikar had grabbed him. Ikar laughed. "I'm sure the servants know of some tricks to get blood out of the rug."

Andalen pulled her legs up under her on the garden bench as she ripped the bread in her hands to pieces, feeding it to the birds that surrounded her on the pathway. It was a chilly morning. Summer was slowly turning to autumn; Andalen's favorite season. Dew still clung to the petals of the flowers growing next to her, and when she breathed she could see it curl up before her like smoke from a chimney.

"You're going to make them fat," Arlen's voice came from behind her, where the path curved to go back to the Manor. He came around and sat beside her, taking the bread from her hands. "What are you doing?"

"Avoiding people," she replied with a laugh.

"Khett?" he asked, now tearing the bread and feeding the birds. His hands were covered with paint. He always delved more into his art when he was upset or stressed. "I heard about what happened."

Andi looked out at the gardens, lush and multicolored with marble statues scattered throughout the grass and golden fountains spitting water into ponds. "I'm sorry, Ari, I know how you feel--"

Arlen waved a hand. "You have nothing to apologize for, Andi. It is my cross to bear to be in love with someone who will never love me."

"All the same--"

"All the same, nothing. You're not at fault."

She smiled at him. "I wish you would stop interrupting me."

He pulled her against him, hugging her as he fed the birds. "I'm so proud of you, Andi. You're doing so well. First place across the board."

Andi sat up, pushing a short curl out of her eye. Their father and Master Roxell were coming down the stone path, the Champions not far behind. She squinted in the morning sun. Her father's face was red and angry.

"They've found out," she whispered, looking to her brother.

He swallowed. "Remember the plan, Andi. Keep a level head."

Together, they met the others on the pathway. Lord Amadon's eyes bulged from his head, his face was several shades of red and purple, and there was a vein on his forehead that looked near ready to burst.

"Explain yourselves!" he hissed, shaking with rage. He was still dressed in his sleep shirt, but a cloak was thrown over the fabric. "What is the meaning of *this*?"

"You still have not told us what *this* is," Ikar said, leaning against a tree, eating an apple. "You drag us all out here at sunrise, still dressed in our sleep shirts. I am freezing my balls off, and for what?"

Grantham laughed. "My sentiments exactly."

The master stood to his full height, combing a hand over his unoiled beard. It surprised Andalen how dull it looked without the pampering. "It has been brought to our attention that Lady Andalen has been participating in the Trials under the guise of being Lord Arlen."

"How-how did you find out?"

"Luane." The Master smiled in a way that wasn't pleasant. His lips pulled back to bare his perfectly straight teeth. "She's had her suspicions for weeks, and yesterday she saw Lord Arlen sneaking out of the stables after our return."

Grant laughed, several rocks hovering in mid-air before him. "I didn't even realize that was you at the hunt yesterday, Andalen!" His eyes swung from her to Arlen, and still, the rocks did not fall. "You both do look alike, but not enough that we should have been fooled. Well done!"

Lord Amadon breathed heavily and turned several shades of red again. "Lord Grantham, may I remind you that this is not a laughing matter."

Grantham's smile was big and bright. His levity was making Andalen's panic nothing more than a small seed in her mind. He lowered his hands, and the pebbles fell to the ground with a small clatter. "You may remind me, but I will think it no less funny. I think it's brave what Andalen is doing, and she should continue to do it." His green eyes met hers, and he smiled. "If that's what you wish."

"Thank you," her voice was small and breathless; a sound she had never heard come out from her own mouth before.

"She's a woman!" The Master raged. "Women are not allowed to participate in the Trials!"

"Correction," Arlen said, putting a hand on Andalen's shoulder. "There is no rule saying a woman cannot take part in the Trials. It's only stated that any eligible *member* of the five founding families aged between twenty and twenty-five can participate."

"For three centuries no woman has shown interest in taking part in the Trials."

"I'm sure that's not true," Andalen argued. "Maybe they were just too afraid. I'm not afraid to fight for what I want."

Master Roxell shook his head at her words and turned to the other Champions. "What do you make of this?"

"I say let her compete." Ikar flashed her a sympathetic look.

"And when it comes to the battles?" The Master argued. "You will have it on your conscience that you fought a woman?"

"Is it supposed to weigh differently on my conscience if she were a man?" he countered.

Andalen stepped forward, wiping her sweaty palms on her trousers. "All my life I have been training for this moment. I have been studying the politics and history of our great kingdom. I have been practicing with a sword and hand to hand combat. I'm not a dainty girl. I don't like knitting or learning the proper way to hold a teacup. I like hunting and fighting, and I'm good at it; I could kill a man while properly holding my teacup and reciting the Forty-Two Laws of Elthare.

"The Lysins have a queen who fights alongside them in battle, she rides dragons and beheads her enemies. I like to think I'm strong like her, and I want to compete in the Trials. It has been my dream to be the queen of Elthare. Please, don't take that away from me."

Halon's eyes searched hers. "Is this what you really want, Andalen?"

"It's all I have ever wanted, Father."

"Let's vote," Master Roxell interrupted. "All in favor of Lady Andalen continuing in the Trials."

Ikar and Grantham raised their hands. Khett looked sheepish, and near tears. Andalen went to him, pleading. "Please, Khett. You know this is all I've ever wanted." She lowered her voice. "You had no problem keeping my secret before, so what's changed?"

His brown eyes met hers, watery and distant. His hand cupped her cheek, and though she knew she shouldn't allow him the touch, she put her hand over his and held him there. She was aware of the closeness of Arlen, and the small shuffling he did behind her, but she didn't pull away. She allowed herself the small comfort of Khett's warm hand on her skin. "The thought of you competing in the battles--I can't bear it."

She turned away, and her eyes found Yvney. His hand was not raised either. He shrugged at her. "I don't care if you compete or not. I will defeat whoever stands in my way for the throne, whether they be man or woman."

"Pleasant as always, Yvney," Grant chided.

Master Roxell cleared his throat. "We still have to bring this issue to a council of the families. They will decide your fate, Lady Andalen." He turned to Arlen. "Yours as well, Lord Arlen."

Andalen had feared this. Whenever a large decision had to be made during the Trials or when no king sat on the throne, the five noble families formed a council to discuss matters and put them to a vote. The last time someone tried to cheat during a Trial, the council had voted to have him executed. Andalen opened her mouth to argue, but Khett's hand on her shoulder kept any words from leaving her mouth.

Arlen inclined his head, and his hands shook as he placed them behind his back. "I understand."

"They've been in there for days," Andalen complained, pacing the hall before the door that led into the council room. Her heart beat double time, and her stomach turned, nearly heaving everything she had consumed for lunch onto the marble floor.

"It has only been five hours, Andi." Arlen crossed one leg over the other, his hand holding open a book he had been reading. He seemed calm, but Andalen knew him better than anyone. She knew to look for the subtle changes in the tightness around his eyes, the slight tremor in his hands, and the way he kept clearing his throat. "Come, sit."

"I don't want to sit." Her boots continued to thud against the floor. "I want to know what they're talking about."

"We'll know in time."

She whirled on him and stuffed her hands into the pockets of her trousers. "Why aren't you more anxious?"

"One of us has to keep a level head."

"You don't think I'm level headed?"

"About as level headed as Isa during the Spring Luncheon." Arlen mimicked the panicked face Isa usually wore when preparing for the two day long event she had to cook for when winter ended and the flowers began to bloom.

That made her laugh, and she sat, pulling her knees up so she could rest her chin on them. Her hands were cold and frail. She was too hot and too cold all at once. "Do you think they'll arrest us?"

He closed his book, considering her words. "They might. We did deceive the crown."

She patted his hand where it rested on his knee. "I'm sorry for putting you through this."

His smile was tight and not quite forgiving. "Well, it's too late now. We've come too far."

The door opened, the sound loud in the otherwise quiet castle. Khett exited, and Andalen searched his features for some sign about their fate, but his face was unreadable. "They're waiting for you."

They stood and followed Khett into the room. The other Champions, and the Lords--and Lady Monneaire--of each house sat around a large wooden table atop the dais. Two chairs stood before the steps leading up to the table; they were wooden and rickety, and creaked as Arlen and Andalen lowered themselves into them. Even though her father was on her side, she couldn't meet his gaze.

The faces around them remained unreadable, even as Master Roxell stood, and Khett took his seat. He rounded the table, hands behind his back, his hair and beard gleaming in the light of the lamps as he looked down on Arlen and Andalen. "The council and your fellow competitors have come to an agreement."

Andalen shifted in her seat. *Oh, Gods.*

"It has been decided that Lady Andalen may continue in the Trials, but must take the Knowledge Trial for herself. Lord Arlen's scores will be erased and replaced with her own." He cleared his throat before continuing, "As a punishment for deceiving the crown, Lady Andalen will pay the royal bank five-hundred gold coin and begin the battles with a penalty."

She could live with their decision. She wasn't worried about what was going to happen to her. "What about Arlen?" She looked at their father.

Lord Amadon looked ill, and she saw it then, how much it pained him to make this decision. The others sat still beside him, eyes averted, faces drawn.

Master Roxell answered, "Lord Arlen will be stripped of his family's title and branded a deserter."

"No!" Tears blurred her vision, and she jumped up. Her stomach felt hollow. A hand came down on her shoulder, pushing her back into her seat, and she looked up into the stern eyes of the Master's guard she had not noticed before. She turned back to Master Roxell and the council. Her father. "No, please. It wasn't his idea!"

"There's no other way, Lady Andalen." His eyes darted away from hers as she met his. "We'll allow Lord Arlen to remain with you during the Trials, but as soon as they are over he will be branded and exiled."

Sorrow and guilt clawed at her from the inside, tearing her apart, stripping her, leaving her bare and empty. "Please," she begged. Arlen would be a pariah, a wanted man if he ever stepped foot on Eltharian soil again. He would have to take the last name of an Odenmal orphan if he did not choose a name for himself. "There has to be another way. Father?"

Halon wouldn't meet her eyes.

"Andi." Her brother's soft voice came from beside her, and she turned her head, meeting watery brown eyes. His face was calm. A small smile graced it. He had accepted his fate. She wished he had fought, kicked and screamed along with her. How could he just accept that this was happening? "We knew it would come to this."

"I did not! I didn't know you would be banished from Elthare!" She was crying freely, tears streaming down her face like waterfalls. She had expected to be jailed together, possibly beheaded, but not this. She hadn't expected to be separated from him. "Ari, this is the end."

He took her hand, turning towards her. "This isn't the end. You will fight, and you will win. You will be the best queen Elthare has ever witnessed."

"Do you accept these conditions?" The Master asked.

Arlen turned his head. "We do," he said before Andalen had time to argue.

Chapter Twelve

The Rivland tavern was not like the taverns in the other villages. Like everything else in the city, it was marble and gold, and the smell of body odor and stale alcohol was absent. The patrons were quiet, talking in their small groups over their drinks, whispering in corners about their classes at the university or talking about their different trades in tones so low, Grant could hear his own breathing.

A lute player sat on a stage, dressed in common, but still fine fabric. He was a handsome fellow with blond curls and a square face. The barmaid brought him a drink, which he accepted with a smile as he continued to play. She made her way back to Grant's table, his pint of ale in her hand and a smile on her pretty face.

"Here you are, love." She set the ale on the tabletop and leaned over, offering him a peek down her shirt. "I have a room above if you are interested."

Grant leaned back and folded his arms, appreciating the way the light hit the barmaid's face. "Oh?" He picked up his ale and took a long drink as the lute player watched him, a smile curving on his square face. Since entering the Trials the prospect of bedding random men and women had raised significantly, which amused Grant.

"I'm rooting for you in the Trials," the barmaid said, coming around the table to sit in the seat that had his boots on it a moment ago; she didn't bother brushing off the dirt. "I grew up in Oszerack. In the orphanage."

Grant snorted. "Another Oslan in my life," he scoffed. Oslan being the surname given to the orphans of Oszerack. "Milden was enough, thank you."

Their relationship had ended in a fiasco. He had proposed on the eve of his twentieth birthday, and she flat out said no, offering no further explanation before she fled the village to live in the northwest. It was only last year that Grant had gotten the reason for her answer. He should have known that he would never have been able to tie Milden down. She was independent and free-spirited. Being the wife of a Lord would never have made her happy.

The barmaid's eyes brightened. "I know Milden. She was with me at the orphanage. We're very good friends."

"As were we." He leaned forward, placing his elbows on the table, running his fingers along the rim of the glass. "What's your name?"

"Pialma."

"Pialma." He was tempted by her offer; she smelled a little like roses and wine. "I thank you for the offer, but maybe another time."

Her face fell. "I didn't mean to overstep."

Grant smiled and stood, bumping the table, which made the three empty glasses clatter and the half-empty one sway slightly. "You didn't overstep.

Your invitation was lovely, and any other time I would gladly accept, but it would be unfair to accept your invitation when my heart belongs to someone." He dug some coins from his purse, placed the amount to pay for his drinks on the table, and handed her the rest. "Give these to the lute player. He plays well." He looked over at the man, returning his smile with a wink.

Grant turned and exited the tavern. The night was chilled, promising the arrival of autumn. He pulled his cloak around him, hating the cold north-west breeze that came off the ocean.

"You need thicker clothes," Milden's voice came from his left.

He turned, spotting her standing in the doorway to the dress shop. Her dark hair hung loose around her shoulders, and a pencil stuck behind her ear.

"Perhaps you can make me some," he replied, crossing the white cobbled street to her, dodging Rivs as they made their way to their destinations, all dressed smartly in their fine attire.

"Perhaps," she echoed with a smile, leading him into the shop.

The shop was warm and smelled like some sort of spice. The Seamstress, Madame Ofra, was behind the counter showing a woman a pair of boots that would go well with the trousers and coat she had picked out for her husband.

"Is it true you bedded Yvney Dominikov? That man is a massive ass."

She smirked at him over her shoulder. "It's true. He may be an ass, but he's handsome, and he was nice to me."

Grant grumbled. He couldn't argue with that. Yvney was handsome, but he doubted the man could be nice.

"He tried to blackmail me, Milden."

"Yes, I know." She let out a little chuckle. "But he's tried to blackmail everyone."

"You sound as if you like him."

Milden shrugged. "Maybe I do."

Grant opened his mouth to ask how she could possibly like someone like Yvney Dominikov, but she cut him off before he could get anything out.

"You smell like a pub floor," Milden said, wrinkling her nose.

"Thank you!" He beamed. He wanted to know more about what she found so attractive about Yvney, but found this to be a much better topic of conversation. "I just came from the pub, where sadly I was not on the floor, but on a chair. I did make friends with the barmaid. She knows you."

"Pialma," Milden said with a smile, going around the counter next to the seamstress and pulling a measuring tape from underneath. "She's a nice girl. Too forward."

Grant laughed as Milden began measuring his shoulders. "Hypocrite. If I remember correctly, I believe it was you who kissed me first behind the orphanage. And you like sex just as much as any man I have come across."

Milden's eyes were distant and fond, lost in the memory of their past relationship. "Did she make a pass at you?"

"She did," Grant replied with a smile. "The lute player was rather handsome as well," he whispered.

"Zasha. Do you want me to set something up with him? He's a man with your preferences."

"Shh," he hissed, eyeing the other women, but they were still engrossed in their discussion. "Are you trying to get me arrested? I would not fair well in a cell."

She just shrugged. "I'll add a cloak to the list of items I will be making for you."

"How much for the cloak?"

Milden turned with a mischievous grin. "The Master is paying for the Champions clothes for the Trials. He can pay for your new cloak as well."

"I do like the sound of that." He pulled her into a hug, her body familiar and warm against his. "Thank you."

Shortly after, he left the shop and continued on his path to the Manor, which was dark when he arrived. A servant opened the door for him, and he asked where everyone had gone off to.

"There is a theatre troupe in the square, and they have gone to watch. However, Lord Arlen and Mister Lonis are in the drawing room."

He thanked the servant and strolled through the Manor's marbled halls, his boots thudding against the floor, and his hands stuffed in the pockets of his trousers. The drawing room was quiet and empty, but evidence that someone had been there was still scattered throughout. There were cards on the table as if they had gotten up halfway through the game. Half drank goblets of wine still sat on the surface, and the decanter was nearby, almost empty. The room smelled of spicy, sweet tobacco; the same type Lonis had smoked when they were teens.

He continued through the house, heading up the stairs to his room. He passed Lonis' door when he heard passionate grunting. His heart seized, and he felt like he couldn't breathe as he pushed the door open.

Quick, hot, nasty betrayal rushed through him.

Lonis' back, bare and muscled, dripped with sweat, and long dark legs wrapped around his waist as he pumped forward and back. Arlen's face was contorted in ecstasy. Lonis' head was thrown back, and Grant hated that even now he thought Lonis looked beautiful as jealousy and anger ripped through him.

Bile burned his stomach. *Run*, his mind yelled, but he couldn't. He was glued to the spot, hand on the door, eyes wide, watching the horrific scene before him.

Lonis' eyes opened, and his head turned. Honey eyes met Grant's. The pleasure in his irises gave way to guilt and regret. "Sin."

His hips stilled, and Arlen looked at him and then at Grant. The bliss on his face was erased, replaced with embarrassment, and his eyes went wide. Pink tinted his cheeks. "Grant--"

The words shattered him, breaking the spell that had held his body frozen, and he ran. He ran as fast as he could down the hall to his room where he threw up in the wastebasket before sinking to the floor, feeling numb and hollow. His skin itched like there were insects crawling all over him, and his eyes burned with tears.

Knocking sounded at his door. "Sin, please, talk to me."

He didn't get up. He curled himself into a ball on the sapphire rug in his room, staring at the shadows that the moon painted on the wall.

"Sin. Please."

He woke to see Ralsair sitting on his bed. She was dressed in her favorite pale pink dress, and her hair was braided with ribbons tied around the ends. "Why are you on the floor?"

"I heard it was better for your back." He stood, stretching. He sat on the mattress next to her and tugged on her braid. "Did Mikhial do these?"

She nodded.

"He's getting better." He crossed the room to the basin. "Why are you not down at breakfast?"

Grant leaned forward, splashing water on his face, hoping to wash away the memory of the night before. Gods, he could still see it. *It* was already burned into his brain: Lonis' hand on Arlen's thigh, the look of bliss on their faces. It churned in his gut, and he wished he could hate Lonis, or at least forget the way it hurt to see him fucking someone else, but he couldn't. For as long as he lived, he could never hate Lonis.

"I want to go riding. There's a horse in the stables named Sunshine, and Luane says I can ride her." She jumped up and ran to the window. "Look! You can see her!"

Grant rubbed the water from his face with a large cloth, and then went to the window, where he could see the stable boy leading a beautiful white mare by the reins around a paddock. Ralsair's face was split with a wide childish grin.

He envied her joy in that moment.

"You know I hate riding, Ral. Why don't you ask Mikhial?"

"He took the train to Oszerack to see the Vintner's daughter, and Lonis said he has sparring with Lady Andalen. And Pa is in the city."

Grant tensed at the mention of his friend. "Was he at breakfast?"

"Pa?"

"Lonis."

"No. He and Lady Andalen went straight to the combat house after he woke up."

The combat house was a small building on the other side of the Manor's property where the Champions could go to practice their hand-to-hand, archery and swordsmanship. Grant and Lonis had spent many afternoons in the house sparring and cracking jokes. He shook his head and turned away from the window.

"Let me get dressed, Ral, and I'll meet you at the stables in twenty."

But before Ralsair could leave, Luane's voice filled the space. "Champions and loved ones, please meet in the drawing room."

Ralsair frowned at the circle on the wall Luane's voice projected from. "We're not going to go riding, are we?"

Grant knelt in front of her, taking her shoulders in his hands. "We will, Ral. I'm sure whatever Luane has to say will only take a few minutes. Go wait in the hall while I get dressed, and we will walk down together."

He stripped out of his grimy, day-old tunic after the door shut behind Ralsair, and replaced it with one that was the color of beach sand, and then pulled a vest over that. It had been two months since he had dressed in the Oszerackian fashions, and he missed the simplicity of the tunic and vest. He ran his fingers through his still damp hair and then met his sister in the hall so they could walk down together.

Ikar smirked at him as he came into the drawing room, his cool gray eyes on the tan shirt and pants Grant wore. "Feeling nostalgic, Sinero?"

"I'm not the only one," he commented, looking at Ikar's boots. "I don't think you have a need for fur; it's not that cold yet."

Ikar crossed his arms over his skinny frame. "Come, sit. Be my companion as Luane bores us with more news."

He sat as Lonis and Andalen entered the room. Lonis' eyes met his, and he moved to take the chair on Grant's other side, but Lord Monneaire--who smelled of alcohol despite the early hour-- got to it before him, and Grant let out a relieved breath. Lonis frowned and made his way to another chair on the other side of the room.

Luane and Master Roxell entered, both dressed in their usual attire: a stiff black dress for Luane, and a fine black and silver coat for the Master. Both looked out at them, smiling.

"Ah, she finally brings us good news," Ikar whispered.

"Welcome to the beginning of the Battle rounds," Luane exclaimed with a broad smile. "Each one of you has shown tremendous skill thus far in the Trials--"

Grant tuned her out and turned to Ikar. "Should we be offended that she finds such joy in the prospect of us injuring each other?"

He chuckled. "Probably."

"The battles will start in one week," The Master continued where Luane left off. "The first battle will be between the Champions with the top two scores!" His smile faltered when no one's enthusiasm matched his. "We have decided we will throw a ball in the Champions honor tomorrow night at the castle before the battles begin!"

That did pique the interest of the noble families. Chatter buzzed through the room like a swarm of bees, and the air shifted into a jovial light.

"Roz will be pleased," Ikar said, looking at the woman with bright red hair. "She's been wanting to go to a ball since we were children." Her eyes met his, and her smile was like the sun. Grant understood why Ikar was so taken with the young woman.

"How are your parents receiving the news that you and Roz are with child?"

"They keep calling it 'the Bastard,' but I think Mother is happy. Her parents are overjoyed. I'm just worried about how the kingdom will receive the babe once it's born."

"Nobles have been having bastards since the creation of Elthare, Dominikov. You're just carrying on the tradition."

Ikar hit Grant's shoulder. "Roz and I will be married."

"Before or after the babe is born?"

"Fuck off. And what about you? When are you going to settle down and start having bastards of your own?"

"Maybe never." Grant searched for Lonis in the crowd and found him near the doors, engaged in a conversation with Arlen. His light mood darkened, and he turned back to Master Roxell. "Maybe I'm destined to be alone forever."

"And they call me dreary," Ikar joked, crossing one leg over the other so his boot rested on his knee.

"Who are Champions in first battle?" Lady Dominikov asked in her heavy Lysin accent.

The Master smiled and ran a hand over his beard. "Lady Andalen and Lord Khett."

The room fell silent.

Chapter Thirteen

The string quartet played a slow waltz, and the room was lit with bright laughter and conversation. Everyone from Oszerack to Alithane had been invited to the Champions' Ball, and they had turned up in their finest dresses and coats. Women's faces were painted with rouge and kohl, enhancing their delicate features. Couples danced to the music, and servants wound through them, carrying trays of food and wine.

Grant, dressed in a sapphire velvet coat with silver buttons and black pants with new leather boots, twirled his sister around the floor; their laughter bounced off the walls as they spun. Mikhial danced with the Vintner's daughter, Hanali Nihat. And their father had found the company of a Palman school teacher, an elegant woman with graying brown hair.

Grant had not seen Lonis since the previous day. He had been avoiding his old friend, which had not been difficult given the Manor was rather large, but Lonis was somewhere in the ballroom. Grant could feel his friend was close. Lonis' presence was like his heart beating in his chest, pumping in the rhythm in which he breathed. Lonis would always be an extension of his heart, no matter how much that pained him.

The quartet changed songs, easily bleeding from one to the next, and Milden appeared next to him, dressed in a gown that seemed to reflect the lights from the candelabras. She smiled, her brown eyes sparkling with joy. "May I cut in?"

Grant set Ralsair on her feet and held his hand out to Milden. He smiled down at his sister. "Save me a dance for later, Ral."

She laughed, yelling, "I will!" as she scampered off towards Kal, who was stuffing his face full of bread and grapes. He blushed as Ral came close and pulled him to the dance floor.

Grant turned, sweeping Milden into his arms, and twirled her into the middle of the floor. She giggled, throwing her head back as her small chuckle turned into a laugh, reminding him of their time together: the many afternoons they spent by the river, the kisses they stole behind buildings in the town square, and the first time they had made love. The memories washed over him in a wave, overshadowing the heartbreak when she had refused his hand and left Oszerack and him behind.

They swayed in time to the music, her head coming to rest on the lapel of his coat. "Did you not have a date?" he asked. "I'm sure you would have had many men asking you to the ball."

"And you would be correct," she replied. "None that I enjoyed the company of beyond their skills in bed."

"Not even Yvney?"

"Yvney asked Sherideen Closs."

"He's a fool." He chuckled. "Someday one will capture your heart. I just hope it's not Yvney."

"And they'll want to cage me," she said, her tone put out.

He thought of the words she had spoken years ago: *I am a dove, Grant. I long to be free, to feel the wind upon my wings. I can't be a dove if I am married; wedding bonds are a cage I will never be captured in.*

He tucked his fingers under her chin, making her eyes meet his. "If they love you, they will not dare cage you." He smirked. "And just to be clear, I still mean someone who isn't that insufferable oaf."

She smiled. "You were the only man who has ever truly loved me, Grant."

He let her put her head back against his chest. His heart ached with the sadness in her voice. "I don't think that's true. What about Phinn Monneaire? I've seen him staring at you from afar. Your presence makes him blush."

"Phinn Monneaire!" Her voice was incredulous. "He's nothing more than a babe!" She hit him in the chest, which made him laugh. "Now, stop saying such ridiculous things, and let me enjoy our waltz."

They danced in silence, enjoying the familiarity of each other's company. When the song ended, Milden stepped out of his arms with misty eyes. "Thank you, Grant," she said with a sad smile.

"Millie?" He took a step forward, his hand outstretched. His heart broke for her, but he did not know how to help. "What happened? Did I do something wrong?"

She shook her head. "You did everything right. You're perfect." Her hands clamped over her mouth, trying to hold in a sob, and she scurried away from him, pushing through the throng of bodies until she disappeared behind the heavy dark wooden doors.

Grant's heart felt heavy as it pounded against his ribs with sorrow and pain and the love he had felt for Milden all those years ago.

He searched for his sister and found her still dancing with Kal, which made him smile, and he decided to let her enjoy her friend's company for a while longer before he stole her away again. He wove his way through bodies, clapping Ikar on the shoulder as he danced with Roslen, and rolling his eyes at Master Roxell, who was dancing with a woman who looked to have just stepped foot into her womanhood.

"Come to my estate. I have a collection of pottery from the Republic of Kehan. Given to me by the president himself," he heard Master Roxell say to the woman as he passed.

Yvney sat in the corner, drinking by himself, watching the festivities with a dark expression. The girl he brought with him was dancing with another gentleman not too far away.

"Have you seen Milden?" Yvney called.

"No," Grant replied and headed to the gardens. They were lit with torches lining the stone paths, fountains spewing water to the sky, and the smell of flowers perfumed the air. Couples meandered through the gardens, canoodling under the light of the rising moon.

"You've been avoiding me, Sin."

Grant closed his eyes at the sound of Lonis' voice. Pain--white, hot and sharp--shot through his heart. But he had missed Lonis over the last day. He missed the familiar presence at his side, and the way he could count on Lonis to laugh at his jokes when no one else would. "You're correct."

Grant lowered himself to the stone edge of a fountain. The golden cherub's horn spouted water into the large pool at his back. He looked up at Lonis and wished he hadn't. Lonis was wearing a coat and pants colored blue and silver, his raven hair was oiled and slicked back from his face, making his high cheekbones seem sharper.

Gods. He swallowed. Looking at Lonis was like looking at the snow-covered trees in the winter. All at once: it calmed him, filled him with serenity and took his breath away.

"We should talk, Sin."

He turned his gaze out to the gardens where two lovers were kissing near the apple trees. "I don't wish to speak of that night. It's still burned into my mind, playing on loop. It fucking taunts me."

Lonis sat on the lip of the fountain next to Grant and plucked at a loose string on his pants, but said nothing.

"I apologize if I ruined that night for you, Lonnie."

Lonis' smile was lopsided, not quite full, but present. "You didn't. I'm happy you walked in when you did."

Anger burned through him, and his eyes burned like the Infernal Flames as he glared at Lonis. "You wanted me to see that?"

"Of course not." Lonis took a coin out of his pocket and flipped it into the fountain. "Your intrusion cut things short."

Grant stood and closed his eyes, pinching the bridge of his nose. "I *apologize* that you did not get to finish, Lonis!" He rounded on his friend, his hands shaking, his blood boiling. "Please, go find Arlen and continue! I'll keep guard! We wouldn't want anyone else interrupting, would we?"

A pain developed just behind Grant's eyebrow. He could see Lonis' sweaty back. His hips thrusting. Grant wanted to scream.

Lonis jumped up from the fountain, his hands up in surrender. "Don't twist my words, Sin. That's not what I was inferring. I don't wish to continue what I started with Arlen. Tell me why it bothers you." Lonis came closer, grabbing the lapels of his jacket, pulling Grant against him. His breath fanned Grant's face, smelling of wine. "Tell me, Sin. Tell me what *exactly* you want from me."

It would be so easy to press even closer and--.

Grant huffed and pulled away from Lonis. "I don't want anything, Lonnie. I hope you and Arlen are *very happy* together."

Grant threw up his hands and stalked away.

Arlen drank another goblet of wine. All around him people danced and gossiped, enjoying themselves, but their laughter was like an annoying pest buzzing in his ear that he wished to squash under his boot.

Lady Andalen and Lord Khett. The Master's voice had been ringing in his head since the previous morning, mocking him.

The two people he cared most about in the world were going to fight like animals vying for territory. Punching, kicking, mangling. The only rule: *Do not kill your opponent.* He could not bear to see either of their pain.
The Gods were cruel and merciless.

He reached for another goblet.

"I think you've had enough," Khett said from the seat beside him. The table was empty, the others were on the dance floor, and Grant was standing in the doorway leading out to the garden, looking more agitated then he had at the beginning of the night.

Arlen turned to Khett. There was a woman sitting on his friend's lap. He frowned at the girl; he didn't remember seeing her there a moment ago.

"You have to forfeit," Arlen pleaded.

Khett smirked and laughed, but the smile didn't reach his eyes, they were full of fear. Khett squeezed the girl's middle, drawing her closer and kissing her cheek. "Do you have faith in me, unlike my friend, here?"

She nodded. "Of course I do, Lord Khett."

Khett kissed the girl, their sloppy sounds irritating Arlen even more.

"Be serious, Khett." He gulped down half the goblet before continuing. "You know how skilled Andi is in combat. You will not win."

Khett frowned and then whispered in the girl's ear. She nodded and stood, smoothing out the skirt of her maroon dress. Khett fixed his charcoal coat and picked up a goblet, smoothing his hair out in the reflection of the gold. "I have a duty to my father to win this tournament," he explained, leaning forward on his elbows. "The Pedgrams have been kings more than any other noble family. It is in my *blood* to rule this kingdom, and I will not give that up without a fight."

Arlen reared back as if Khett's words had injured him. He blinked at his friend, the drink making his thoughts foggy and slow. "But...you love her."

He nodded. "She is the only woman I have ever really loved, and she would think me a coward if I didn't compete."

Arlen's insides twisted in knots. The alcohol sat sour in his stomach, and he feared he was going to be sick. Was he being overdramatic? The fights weren't to the death--but an image of their Uncle Velros popped in his head. After the 42nd King Trials he was broken so bad he was in a coma for a full year.

"Do you truly think you can bring yourself to fight her?"

Khett was silent for several long moments. "I will have to." He stood and walked away.

Arlen sat with his sullen thoughts. Another goblet had found its way into his hands, and he saw Andalen dancing with the old baker from Odenmal. He downed the contents of the goblet and pushed through the people, tripping over his own feet and landing sprawled on the dance floor. The music continued, though the dancing around them had stopped.

"Arlen!" Andalen squealed, helping him back onto his feet. "Apologies, Mister Ewin."

"None needed." The baker smiled and bowed. "My hip is creaking; these old joints aren't what they used to be. Thank you, Lady Andalen. For indulging this old man with a dance." He exited the dance floor.

"Dance with me, Arlen." Andalen gave him no choice, she placed her hand in his and stepped in time to the music. Once they started spinning in time to the music, the other couples followed suit, some whispering about the scene Arlen had made. Andi's green dress whipped around them as they spun. "How much have you had to drink?"

He ignored her. "Please, Andi. You must not go to the Trial. I can't--I can't bear it if you or Khett are permanently injured. Remember Caldon Monneiare?"

Caldon had died three weeks after his Trials, succumbing to the injuries he had sustained in the Coliseum. Arlen had nightmares of Andalen's death. He didn't think he could bear it if she died as a result of the Trials.

She shook her head, her mouth pulling to a frown. "I didn't come this far to be branded a deserter."

He stopped dancing, but they kept the pose, looking at each other, each begging for the other to understand. "But it's okay for me to be branded and kicked out of Elthare because of your wishes and dreams? I gave up everything for you to compete in the tournament, and you can't give me this?" He felt as if an invisible hand was squeezing his heart. "Please, Andi. *Please.*"

"I'm sorry, Ari." She resumed dancing, but her steps were stiff and rigid. "And I already gave Khett up for you." She paused, and the quartet slipped into another song. "You may think me selfish, but it's my dream--my duty to be the first woman to complete the Trials."

"What about your duty to me?"

"I'm sorry, Ari. I wish there was another way."

Tears gathered in his eyes, and Andalen pulled him into a hug. "I can't bear it."

"You will have to," she whispered, her tone soothing, although her words were not. "We both have to."

Andalen sat on the marble steps of the castle, watching the carriages whisk the citizens of Elthare back to their homes. The moon hung full in the sky, and the stars shimmered against velvet black, though storm clouds were rolling in from the ocean.

"Did Arlen ask you to forfeit?" Someone said from behind her. Andalen turned her head, finding Khett leaning against a marble pillar. There was lip pigment on his collar, and his coat was unbuttoned, revealing the white tunic underneath. He came forward and settled on the step next to her. "He asked me when we were sitting at the table."

"When that servant was on your lap. I saw."

He smiled and tilted his head. "Fresia."

"You never remember their names," Andalen sounded astonished.

He leaned over, whispering, "I remember yours. And hers."

She pushed him away with a laugh. "Yes, he asked me to forfeit."

"You won't."

She smiled. He had always known her so well. "No. I *can't*." She needed to continue the Trials. She had given up so much to be where she stood now.

She leaned into him, and he wrapped an arm around her shoulders. They sat like that for several long moments before Khett spoke again. "I really am sorry, Andi, for kissing you that day in the tent. I never wanted to come between you and Nix."

Andalen had come clean to Nixema about the kiss; her handmaiden hadn't spoken more than three words to her in nearly a month. "I appreciate that." It still pained her, the ending of their relationship. She wondered what would have happened had they married as planned before she ended things to preserve her relationship with Arlen. "Nix is still mad at me. She refused to come out of her room tonight."

"I should make my apologies to her as well."

"You should." Andalen pulled back and looked into his oak eyes. "She considers you a friend."

"I consider her one as well."

Andalen settled back against him, tucking her chin into his chest, drawing comfort from the presence of her childhood friend and first love. Being in his presence was like coming home after a long journey overseas. It was the same feeling she had when she was wrapped in Nixema's arms.

"Are you scared?" she asked. "About the Trial."

He reached a hand out toward the bed of flowers a few feet away, and Andalen watched, mesmerized, as a single daisy was plucked from the bunch by an invisible force and floated to his hand. He smiled at her as he tucked the stem behind her ear and then wrapped an arm around her, but she still felt the chill of the night air.

Khett gave her his signature smirk, but his eyes looked dull. "Terrified."

Andalen nodded in understanding, she was also rather frightened of their upcoming battle. "How are you...with your father...?" She had never had to talk about death so seriously. She wasn't sure what to say to Khett regarding the former king.

"Fine." Khett looked away from her. "Dandy."

"No, you're not. You haven't been the same."

Khett regarded her with a frown. "I haven't?"

"No. It's as if you have given up. You seem..." She searched her mind for the right word, "...apathetic."

"I'm not apathetic."

"You can talk to me, Khett."

Khett looked away from her again, then stood. "I don't have an answer for you, Andi," he said in a flat, robotic tone. "I'm fine."

He walked away before she could say anything else.

Chapter Fourteen

"You will win this," Khett's mother said. Her voice held no room for argument.

She sat on the lounge in his room, her black and red skirts falling over her ankles, covering her feet. Her dark hair was done up in an elaborate bun, rouge stained her cheeks, and kohl lined her eyes. If Khett hadn't seen her crying the night before, he would have believed that the Trials had not phased her. Being the former queen, his mother was used to putting on a brave face.

"You don't know that, Mother."

He stood, grabbing a pastry from the tray that had been brought up to his room. It was customary that the Champions spent time with their families in the days leading up to the battle. They were allowed private meals away from the other nobles, and activities had been planned for the families to enjoy together. The day before, he and his mother had ridden horses out to the beach and had a picnic in the sand. They had spent the day visiting his father's grave, and he had gone to the Temple for service as a favor to his mother.

His mother's eyes narrowed, holding back tears. "Maybe not, but I have to believe it."

He sat, tearing the pastry to pieces. He was too nervous to eat, and he feared if he ate anything it would come back up.

The door to his chambers opened, and a maid entered. Her russet-brown hair was loose, flowing down her back in a pin-straight waterfall. She wore a plain silver dress with a black pin holding the fabric in place at her shoulder. Khett sat straighter as Fresia came closer, smelling of fruit and flowers. He had the distinct pleasure of knowing that she tasted like honey between her legs.

"It's time to get ready, Lord Khett," she said, bowing at the waist.

"Thank you, Fresia."

She bowed again and exited the room. Khett stood and turned to his mother. Her lips pursed and tears gathered in her eyes again, spilling down over her cheeks. He went to her, kneeling in front of her. Her hands came up, cupping his face.

"I've prayed to the Gods, Khett. They'll watch over you."

He no longer believed in the Gods. How could he after They took his father, and he was stripped of his title as prince and forced to leave the castle, the only home he had known for twenty-four years?

They're testing you, a voice sounding an awful lot like his mother whispered in his mind.

I have no time for tests.

Khett kissed his mother's cheek and stood to exit the room, finding Fresia standing just outside the door. Dallin stood with her, hands fisted at his side and even he looked close to tears when Khett came into view.

Khett chuckled, clapping his steward on the shoulder. "Go be with my mother. Maybe you two can cheer each other."

"Are you sure, My Lord?" Dallin's voice was shaky. "I can accompany you."

"Please, Dallin, watch over my mother." Khett cursed the way his voice cracked on the last word. He had tried not to let the fear get to him, but he could not deny he was terrified.

"Yes, My Lord." Dallin bowed and disappeared into the room.

He turned to find Fresia looking at him, her brown eyes sad, her pretty face drawn.

"Not you too," he complained, reaching out to tuck a strand of hair behind her ear and cup her cheek. He didn't know what was so special about the servant, but after that first night he had taken her to bed, he had been unable to think of anyone else. They had spent the last three weeks lost in a small bubble of their own making. Only when she was called away for her duties, did Khett finally get out of bed and join the others for sparring lessons or activities around the Manor.

She cleared her throat. "Come, Lord Khett."

She turned and led him through the halls of the Manor to the baths. The room was expansive and decorated in gold and onyx. Three large pools were set into the marble floor, filled with water as clear as the blue sky. The air was thick with humidity and the smell of flowers. The only sounds in the room came from the city outside the open balcony doors.

Fresia led him to the bath closest to the balcony that overlooked Rivland; the white marble of the buildings blared in the sunlight. Fresia made quick work of removing his clothes and settling him into the bath. The hot water soothed his disquieted soul, unbinding his tight muscles. Soft hands rubbed his arms and chest, smoothing sudsy goat milk soap over his skin.

"Remove your dress," he said in a lazy voice. "Join me."

Fresia giggled. He looked behind him in time to see her unclip the band on her shoulder, and her dress fall away, revealing milky skin. His eyes raked over her appreciatively.

She entered the bath, straddling his hips as he wrapped an arm around her, pulling her body more flush to his so they were skin to skin, her breasts soft against his hard chest. Her arms went around his neck as her sad brown eyes searched his.

"I'm scared for you," she whispered. "I've heard tales of the permanent damage sustained at other Trials--"

He placed two fingers under her chin, bringing her attention back to him. "Let's not speak of this," he said, and then he kissed her. His free hand cupped her backside, kneading the flesh.

Fresia giggled as Khett pulled her to him, her hands splayed over his naked chest, hair oil still on her fingers. She was dressed now, her cheeks still red from the pleasure he had given her. He stood in the middle of his room, wearing trousers, and nothing else, with his hair dripping down his face and back.

He kissed her again, tangling his hands in her still wet hair. She pulled back with a laugh. "I'm never going to get you dressed if you don't stop."

He chuckled. "I would rather just stay here with you." He released her so she could resume her duties. "Do I get armor? A weapon?"

She nodded, her voice was tiny when she answered, "You'll be granted these things after you arrive at the Coliseum."

She finished rubbing the perfumed oil through his hair before reaching for his tunic, an elaborate burgundy and charcoal coat, and then helped him into them. When he was dressed, she paused with a small smile on her face.

"You look so handsome."

He looked in the mirror hanging next to the fireplace. "Are my looks the only reason you went to bed with me?"

She laughed, the first genuine laugh she had all morning. "Maybe at first, but they're not the reason I kept returning."

He turned to her, one of his hands cupping her hip. Fresia was a beauty and a delight to be around. The idea of properly courting her teased his mind. Andalen had moved on, and it was time he did too.

Mother wouldn't be pleased; she's a maid. The thought made him smirk.

"I'm cheering for you, Lord Khett," she said, bringing her lips to his. "Come. The carriage is waiting."

The Manor was quiet, the other Champions and their families had already been escorted to the King's Coliseum. He wished he could have spoken to Andalen or Arlen before the Trial, but he would not see them until he was out on the field.

Fresia accompanied him to the carriage where the driver and Dallin were waiting. He climbed in, winking at Fresia as the carriage pulled away.

They rode in silence. Dallin plucked at a string on the carriage seat with worry, and Khett was afraid if he opened his mouth nothing but vomit would come out. When they arrived at the Coliseum, the roar of cheering assaulted Khett's ears, amplifying his nerves. His hands shook as the door opened, and he exited.

A servant escorted him and Dallin through a small wooden door into the underbelly of the Coliseum. The winding halls smelled damp like mold, but were quiet, the cheers muffled by many layers of stone and dirt. The halls were dim, lit only with a few low burning torches, but clean, and free of the rats he had expected to see.

"Here we are, Lord Khett," the servant stopped in front of another wooden door. He bowed and scurried off down the corridor.

Khett entered the room to find it full of tables holding weapons of every kind and more armor than he had ever seen in his life. Another servant, a woman with graying hair, stood at the front, polishing the jeweled hilt of a sword.

"Lord Khett," she said with a smile. "Right on time. My name is Raina. I'll get you outfitted with armor. During the Trials we allow daggers, clubs, hammers, and bows and arrows. You may choose from any of those." She gestured to a table holding all the weapons she listed. Their white blades glittered in the light.

Raina fastened his arms and legs with shiny gauntlets, and a shield on his left arm. He did not receive a helmet or a breastplate to guard his heart.

"Pick a weapon," Raina commanded as she tied up the leather on his side, joining the chest and back plates. "All our weapons are made from Opal Stone and forged by the royal blacksmith," she said with pride. "The finest weaponry man can find."

Khett walked around the room, noticing that several spots stood empty; Andalen had already been there and chosen her weapons. He knew she would have picked the bow and arrow, but several daggers were missing as well. He picked up a few daggers, their white blades sparkling in the light, and strapped them to his waist and thigh. He picked up a lightweight spear with a deadly Opal Stone head. Raina assured him he could use it during the Trial as well.

"I'm ready." His voice shook with fear.

Raina smiled at him. "Good luck, Lord Khett. May the Gods grant you good Fortune."

Another servant led Khett and Dallin through another door, deeper into the bowels of the Coliseum. They walked down many dimly lit corridors, heading straight for the center of the structure. As they walked, the roar of the crowd became louder and louder. He could hear the Master, his amplified voice shook the stones.

"Ladies and gentlemen, welcome to the King Trial Battles!"

"Wait here," the servant said, pointing to another wooden door. "When Master Roxell calls your name, enter the field." The servant bowed and then he was gone.

Khett entered the room, blinking at the sudden onslaught of bright afternoon sun. The room was small with only a wooden bench, which Dallin sank onto, twisting his hands in the fabric of his trousers. There were three stone walls, the fourth was made of iron bars. Through the bars Khett could see the stadium. He was underground; a set of three steps was just beyond the bars, leading up to the field. He could see part of the audience, their cheers drowning out the Master's words. "Our Champions have Three minutes inside the arena, each strike equals one point. The round ends when I ring the bell, or one of the Champions can no longer stand on their feet."

Bile rose in Khett's throat.

The Master stood at one end of the Coliseum, on a platform built into the raised walls where the audience sat. The other Champions sat behind him, dressed in elaborate coats.

Below Master Roxell were two banners nailed to the stone wall; one was the Amadon colors with their family motto: *The people are our strength.* The Pedgram banner had the words, *Honor, truth and heart--long may they reign.*

"Today, we have the great honor to witness history, a woman will be fighting in the first battle of the forty-third King Trials!" the Master exclaimed.

His words were followed by the buzz of whispering at this news and cheers. "Lady Andalen entered the Trials under false pretenses, but out of the goodness of my heart, I have allowed her to continue in the tournament."

Khett scoffed, anger burned in him along with the fear. They should have known the Master was going to take the credit for Andalen continuing in the Trials. He could see the other Champions frowning at Master Roxell as he continued speaking.

"With top scores across the board, please welcome, Lady Andalen!"

The iron bars on the other side of the field lifted, and Andalen entered the arena, her face calm, unworried. Her hair was styled so each ringlet fell around her head like a perfect spring. She was dressed in gold trousers and a green tunic, armor gleaming in the sun. Her quiver was strapped to her back, and her bow was gripped in her hand. Several daggers were strapped to her waist and thighs. Cheers thundered, and all around her green banners waved in the air. She stood in the center of the arena, looking around the audience with feigned confidence, but even from where Khett stood he could see the bow shaking in her hand.

"Next, please welcome Elthare's favorite son, Lord Khett!"

The bars in front of Khett lifted. He turned to Dallin to see tears streaming down the man's face. "Your father would be proud, Lord Khett." He cleared his throat. "May the Gods bring you favor."

Khett nodded and ascended the stone stairs onto the dusty field. Cheers erupted all around him, and the women called his name. He saw Fresia in the crowd wearing a red rose, the Pedgram flower.

'Good luck,' she mouthed to him.

He turned his head towards Andalen. Her brown skin seemed to shimmer in the sun, and the kohl around her eyes made them darker. A golden lily, the Amadon flower, was painted on the part of her chest that was exposed, a symbol of luck and strength.

"Let the battle begin!"

The stadium filled with cheers, but neither of them made a move. They circled each other, and Khett's hold on his spear became sweaty. For several long moments, neither of them spoke as they created a round path in the sand.

"Fight. Fight. Fight." The chant of the crowd started out as a whisper, but then erupted like a tidal wave. "Fight! Fight! Fight!"

His sweaty grip slackened, but he adjusted his hand, holding the spear tighter. His legs shook as he continued wearing down the sand. "I don't wish to fight you, Andi."

There was a hesitation in her stance, a flicker in her dark eyes as they shuttered, and then she flew at him. One second she was across from him, and the next her fist was connecting with his jaw. He stumbled back, and in his shock, he let go of his shield. He worked his free hand over his jaw, popping the bone.

He looked at her stunned. "Andi--"

An arrow flew at him. It was as if someone had flipped a switch in her brain, and she attacked him as if he were nothing more than a common enemy.

He saw her hesitation, but he also saw the warrior within her that would stop at nothing to bring down her opponent.

With his hand shaking, he hovered it over the earth. His powers made the rocks and sand at his feet fly through the air. A boulder slammed into Andalen's chest, knocking her back into the stone wall.

He gave her no time to react. He threw his spear, catching her in the shoulder. She screamed out in pain. He backed up to the other side of the arena as she pulled herself from the ground, blood dripping from her wounds. She turned, slamming the spear against the corner of the wall where she had exited from. He winced as the spear crunched against the stone, and the end of it broke off, leaving a jagged two-inch wood stake in her shoulder.

She turned, blood coating her skin and tunic; her eyes teary and narrowed with determination.

"Andi!" He yelled over the cheering.

An arrow slammed into his leg, just above his knee. He howled and fell to the floor, crying out as pain wracked through his body, so intense it nearly blinded him.

"Get up!" He heard a voice from the crowd, louder than the rest, and found his mother leaning over the wall, horror clouding her face. Tears streaked her pale cheeks black with kohl. "Get up, my son. Fight!"

He gripped the end of the arrow, snapping it off. He stood, struggling to his feet, and putting all his weight on his good leg.

Andalen rushed at him, two daggers in hand. Her bow lay a few feet behind her, forgotten. She threw one dagger at him, but he dodged. He swung at her, but she ducked.

He called on the wind, and it blew her back several feet. She tumbled through the air, slamming into the stone wall again. She crumbled at the base, groaning. She didn't get up. Blood poured from her nose and the cuts on her arms and face. But she was still breathing, the unsteady rise and fall of her chest was proof she still lived.

The crowd cheered.

He felt numb.

He fell to his knees in the dirt. Pain, a different kind than his injuries, bubbled up in him and spilled from his eyes. He sobbed as the crowd cheered around him. His heart, broken and mangled, hammered in his chest.

"The winner of the first--"

The Master's words were cut off by the sudden movement under the rubble, as several rocks tumbled from the heap.

"Andi!" Khett breathed, but was too shocked to move. "Andi!"

She struggled to her feet, her face covered in bruises and cuts. Her left ankle was odd, broken from her toss through the air. She hobbled toward him, dragging her left leg behind her, a dagger in her hand.

Still, Khett did not move.

He saw her as a child, picking daisies in the gardens while their parents discussed the kingdom's politics over goblets of wine. When she was fourteen and could brandish a sword better than many of the soldiers in his father's guard. At sixteen, when her curls tumbled over her face and dripped into her eyes after she had jumped into the river with all her clothes still on. It was then that he had realized he loved her. At seventeen, when she kissed him for the first time, and her lips were soft against his, her body warm as she pressed against him under the apple tree. Then, three weeks later, after they had lost their virginity to each other. At eighteen, when she said no to marrying him, and yet he had still loved her. At twenty-one, when she entrusted him with the secret that she was bedding her handmaiden. And at twenty-four when he saw her on the platform at the train station in her green dress and hat, the pure joy in her eyes when she looked at him. And even though he regretted it, he thought of the day he kissed her in the tent after the second Trial, how familiar she had felt against him after so many years.

How was he supposed to defeat someone he had loved before he even knew what love meant?

She was only a few steps from him now, and yet, he still didn't move.

"Khett," she whispered, her bottom lip was split, trickling blood. "Khett."

"It's okay," he responded. He laid his sword next to him, surrendering himself to her. "Let loose, Andi."

She paused. Her hand holding the dagger shook. "What?"

"Punch me. Kick me. I refuse to be branded a deserter, but I surrender to you."

"Khett, don't say such things."

He shook his head. The crowd had fallen silent, straining to hear their conversation. He could hear his mother sobbing, but he couldn't bring himself to look at her.

"Khett, I don't think I can."

"You can." He reached up, taking her free hand. He kissed the knuckles. "You must. Please."

"Why are you doing this?"

"I will always love you," he whispered, bringing her knuckles to his cheek and leaning into the touch.

He took her other hand, the one that held the dagger, and stabbed it into his own shoulder.

Master Roxell rang the bell.

"The winner of the first battle is Lady Andalen!"

Andalen gathered Khett in her arms, her dagger still protruding from his shoulder. He had passed out from the pain, and she was glad for it.

Several servants swarmed the field, pulling Khett from her grasp. Two of them helped her to her feet, ushering her back inside the Coliseum.

The crowd cheered her name, but she barely heard them.

"Will Khett be alright?" she asked one of the servants.

"The doctors and a warlock will have a look at him," the servant assured her. "Let's get you in a bath."

A witch waited in the Bathing area with a doctor. They both assessed her and deemed she had sustained no real damage from the fight.

"You were so brave, cousin," the witch, Tulis, exclaimed. She was several years younger than Andalen, but had risen quickly in social status to become an official sacred being. She was blessed with the Gods' protection and honored at many religious celebrations.

"Thank you, Lis." Her voice held no inflection. She wanted nothing more than to sleep and see Khett.

Tulis healed Andalen's wounds, all the while talking a mile a minute about the battle, her mother and brother, and the journey she planned to take when she turned eighteen.

Andalen barely heard a word her cousin spoke.

After Tulis left, Andalen was led to the baths. Servants washed her, cleaning the dried blood and grime from her skin.

Halfway through, the door opened, and Nixema burst in, her chest rising and falling rapidly. Andalen's tears watered at the sight of her handmaiden.

"Leave us," she commanded the other servants.

Quickly, the three women left, leaving Andalen alone with Nixema.

"You fought bravely," Nix breathed out.

Andalen broke down. Large, fat tears rolled down her cheeks. Her sobs echoed off the walls.

But Nix was there to hold her. She climbed into the bath, skirts and all, and pulled Andalen into her plump frame.

"It's alright, love," she soothed. "It's alright."

She pulled back, tangling her hands in Nix's hair. "I'm sorry about the kiss with Khett, Nix. It meant nothing. I promise you, it meant nothing."

Nixema studied her for a moment as if trying to see if Andalen spoke the truth, and then she kissed her.

And for that moment, everything else paled in comparison to the feel of Nix's lips on hers.

Chapter Fifteen

Mealtimes were quiet and strange without Khett. Ikar kept looking at the chair he usually sat in on the other side of the table; it stood empty now. Since he lost the Trial, he and Lady Pedgram had already been escorted back to their estate on the south-western side of the city, near the ocean. They had left with a tearful goodbye.

"Is it true you bought servants from Master Roxell?" Grant whispered over their dinner. "Why?"

Ikar had no explanation for the madness that drove him to Master Roxell's ridiculous manor, which was decorated with ugly chotskies from around the world, in order to purchase Belmar and Dolnick for the price of ninety gold pieces. Each.

Perhaps the brothers were the physical embodiment he wished he had with his own brother. More likely, Ikar had gone mad.

"I needed more servants and felt like spending some coin," Ikar answered. "Why else?"

He looked around the table as he picked at his stew and bread. The others talked amongst themselves, their whispering a slight buzz in the quiet dining room, like a small infestation of gnats around the dinner table. Ikar frowned when he realized his brother was missing.

Where has he gone to now? He wondered, frowning at Yvney's empty seat.

"Good evening," Master Roxell entered the room with his signature smile in place. Luane stood at his side, hair in a sleek bun, but she was frowning. At least she could read the room better than the Master. "It has been a week since Lord Khett left, which means it is time to announce the second battle."

No one spoke, and Master Roxell frowned at their lack of excitement. What was there to be excited about? A friend was gone, not dead, but scarred. And more were going to follow suit, maybe even end up worse off. Ikar wondered if it had been this hard for previous Champions during their Trials. The noble families had always been close; it could not have been easy for any of them to combat their friends either.

Master Roxell's boots scuffed against the floor as he came further into the room. His hair was tied back with a strip of leather, showing the tips of his pointed ears. He came to a stop in front of the table, between Ikar's mother and Lord Sinero. He smiled again.

Ikar set his spoon down and took Roslen's hand in his. He felt unsteady ever since Khett and Andalen's battle. He had known he would possibly lose a limb, or end up brain-damaged like his cousin during this tournament, but he hadn't thought of the gravity of the situation until he had seen a battle first hand. He placed a hand over her stomach, which had grown in the past months, swelling with his unborn child.

I have something to live for now. He thought it better if he bowed out of the tournament, get branded a deserter, which would mean he would be kicked out of Elthare. But he could go to Lysic or Soldare, or one of the far, *far* away lands overseas with Roslen. He had heard Keresh was lovely this time of year.

Roslen leaned forward, her fiery hair brushed over his bare, pale arm. "You will not quit," she whispered into his ear. "You will finish these Trials. You will fight."

He pulled back and smiled at her. It still amazed him how well she could read his moods. "Yes, my love."

Despite his agreement, he still wondered if forfeit would be a better option.

She kissed his cheek, leaving a trail of fire on his skin. The squeeze he gave her hand was gentle, and then he brought it up to his lips, kissing the knuckles.

Master Roxell cleared his throat, and Ikar realized he was not the only one who was having a side conversation. Grant and Lonis were whispering on the other side of the table, and Andalen was speaking to Lady Monneaire in a low voice. He looked over at the Master, catching the man's frown as he ran a hand over his beard in irritation.

"As I was saying," he said, piercing them all with a frustrated look. "The second battle rounds will begin in three days. The competitors in this round have the lowest scores of the competition."

Everyone looked at Phinn, they all knew he had done well in the knowledge round, getting the second highest score out of the six of them, but his archery and hunting skills were severely lacking. It was rumored that it was his servant girl who had brought down the boar during the hunting Trial, and he had only killed one of his ducks. Even Ikar, one to never believe rumors, could see the truth in that. Phinn had admitted that he didn't have the privilege of learning combat and hunting as the others had in their youth. He was sure the young lord didn't even know how to hold a sword properly.

Phinn blushed, burying his head in the large porcelain bowl of stew.

"The next battle will be between Lord Phinn and Lord Yvney," Master Roxell said.

Ikar felt a small smile creep onto his mouth. His brother had one of the lowest scores in the competition.

Hooray for small victories.

Ikar's boots clicked against the floor as he searched through the Manor's halls for Yvney. He wanted to be the one to deliver the news that his brother had one of the lowest scores and would be fighting next. He felt sorry for Phinn, of course. There was no way the skinny man was going to best his brother.

Having searched the entire house, he headed outside. It was colder now as the summer began to move into autumn. The trees were starting to change color, and the autumn winds were picking up, biting into his skin. But still, it was nothing compared to the winds in Alithane.

He searched the grounds, the gardens and the stables. As he came to the combat house, he heard voices drifting out from inside. The door was ajar, showing a large room with weapons adorning the walls and a tan padded floor. Yvney's back was to the door. Ikar made to turn, thinking his brother was with Milden again. He didn't wish to witness whatever they got up to in the shadows.

Yvney was a vile creature, but then Ikar had seen that the person his brother was around the seamstress was not the same person that tortured Ikar. Yvney treated Milden with respect and gentleness. The dichotomy confused Ikar, and he admitted made him angry. Why couldn't Yvney have shown that same compassion to his own brother?

The person in the combat house was not Milden, but rather a man with graying brown hair.

The man was older, maybe in his fifties--it was hard to tell in the yellow light coming from the single lamp in the room--with a long beard. The man stood with a regal air, tall and confident. Imposing.

"You owe me money," Yvney snarled at the man. "15,000 gold pieces. I have not received any of the things you've promised me."

The man smirked. "You will have your money shortly, Lord Yvney. I promise you."

"I'm starting to think that your promises mean horse shit," Yvney huffed. "And your daughter? Does she know you've promised her to me? Do I get to see her?"

"She knows," the man said, circling around Yvney as a shark does it prey, "and though she's not happy about the deal, she has agreed to marry you, should you win the Trials."

I knew it. Ikar had known that the shit Yvney had fed him about competing in the Trials for their family name and honor was all a lie. His brother had always been driven by two things: money and women.

"You make sure I get my coin, King Pytir." Yvney turned then, and Ikar could see the cold hatred in his brother's eyes. The look a snake gets right before it strikes, but the king looked unmoved by his brother's poisonous gaze. "If I don't have my coin before sunrise tomorrow, I will kill you."

Why does the King of Soldare care about our Trials? But then Ikar answered his own question. The King wanted access to the Opal Stone mines.

Ikar felt like such a fool.

"Don't make idle threats, boy. You wouldn't want to make an enemy out of me." With that, the king strolled towards the door. Ikar had no time to get away. He stood frozen in spot as King Pytir opened the door and exited. His brown eyes fixed on Ikar, and he smirked. "Are you going to tell someone what you heard?"

"I..." Who would believe him? Elthare had an allegiance with the Soldaren King. Soldare was indebted to them; if he soiled the king's name, it could start a war between the two kingdoms. Wars had been started for less. "I didn't hear anything."

The king's smile grew. "Good answer, boy."

Ikar watched as King Pytir disappeared from view through the trees that surrounded the Manor's lands. Once he could no longer see the Soldaren king, Ikar entered the combat house, finding Yvney leaning against the large post in the center of the room as if all the wind had been knocked out of him. He looked up as Ikar entered.

"What do you want?" He demanded, standing straight and curling his upper lip.

"Of course you lied to me. I can't remember the last time you told me something true," Ikar accused, coming closer. His hands shook at his sides. "I should turn you in to Master Roxell."

"Here is some truth for you." Yvney stalked toward Ikar, his hand on the hilt of a dagger tucked into his belt. "If you turn me in to the Master, you little bug, I will squash you. I will drive this blade deep into your chest and watch the life leave your eyes."

A sarcastic quip died on Ikar's tongue. He shook with fear now, the rage dissipating, dropping from him like water washing away dirt. "You would kill me?"

Several emotions played on Yvney's face: hatred, guilt, regret, contempt. He settled on a sneer. "You're lucky I haven't killed you yet, *little brother*."

Despite the many years of knowing how much his brother hated him, the knowledge that his brother would kill him brought a pain to his chest like nothing he had ever felt before. He shook his head, trying hard to get rid of the feeling. "I'm not going to tell anyone." His voice was small, distant. He didn't recognize it as his own.

"Why are you here?" Yvney leaned back against the pole, scrubbing a hand over his face. "Did mother send you?"

"No. She doesn't know you're out here." Something flashed in Yvney's eyes at those simple words, a look of deep hurt and longing. "The second battle's been announced."

"Oh? Who's fighting?"

"Phinn Monneaire--"

"Filthy time-thief," Yvney spat.

"--and you." Ikar had expected to feel the satisfaction of telling his brother this, but he felt nothing. His mind was still locked on the conversation he had witnessed between his brother and the King of Soldare.

He thought about how Yvney would kill him with little to no remorse. *I am nothing to him.* That feeling weighed heavy in his chest, making it hard for him to breathe.

Chapter Sixteen

The tavern was near empty. The barkeep was wiping down glasses with a cloth, and the lute player was packing his instrument in its case. There were only three patrons huddled over pints of ale in the far corner, with books scattered around the table between them. Ikar's gaze landed on the bar, where he found Phinn sitting on a stool and sipping on his apple wine. Ikar winced at the look of dejection on the man's face. He had hoped to drink alone, but found himself strolling to the bar where Phinn sat.

"You look like shit," he said, sliding onto the stool next to Phinn. "Are you thinking about the battle?"

Phinn snorted. His blond hair had fallen in his blue eyes, making him look younger. "I wasn't even thinking about that."

"What can I get you?" the barkeep asked.

Ikar waved the old man away and turned back to Phinn. "What has you so down then? Has your apple wine gone sour? Who drinks apple wine anymore?"

"Milden Oslen."

"She drinks apple wine?" Phinn shot him a look. *Right. Now is not the time for wit.* "Did you fuck her too?"

Phinn's face puckered, and Ikar snorted that Phinn took offense to his blunt words. "I did, but not in the way that you are thinking."

Ikar's laugh was as sharp as a blade. "Is there another way to fuck someone? I thought it was fairly straight forward."

"It was nothing more than a transaction. Not the carefree tumble you believe occurred." Phinn looked at him with the pathetic expression of an animal that had just been kicked. "After my parents lost everything, I took a job to help bring in some income." Red splashed across his round cheeks, and he looked out across the bar at the other patrons who were pouring over the stack of books in front of them. They looked to be legal counsel or at least studying law at the university. "I'm not proud of the job, but I was good at it. Made a lot of coin."

Ikar leaned forward on his elbows, studying the young lord. He already knew where this was headed, but he wanted to hear the full story from his companion's mouth. "Now, I am intrigued. What was this job?"

"Have you ever heard of the Masked Man?"

Ikar leaned back. He had not been expecting *that*. "Yes. He's a male whore from Palamar, and his sexual prowess is known throughout Elthare, blah, blah, blah." He waved a hand through the air. "A woman in Alithane raved about him. The man sounds like a myth to me."

Phinn swallowed, his cheeks becoming even redder. "That man is me."

Ikar was stunned into silence. He couldn't take his eyes off the young Palman lord, and then he laughed, a short guffaw that was cut short at the end. "You're not as innocent as I would have guessed!" He clapped Phinn on his shoulder. "This is very intriguing, indeed! Do the others know?"

"Only Grant." There was a story there, but Phinn's shoulders curled in as if he were ashamed, so Ikar held his tongue. "It's not funny."

"On the contrary, it's hilarious." Ikar sobered under the angry gaze of his companion. "Alright. What does this have to do with the dressmaker?"

Phinn scrubbed a hand over his hair and leaned back on his stool. "She was one of my customers. We met twice a month." He paused to stare in misery at his apple wine. "I've fallen in love with her."

"What do you mean?" Ikar asked, flagging down the barkeep. It looked like he would need a drink after all. He had not expected the young lord to start spilling his guts all over the bartop.

"She's just so...beautiful. Perfect. And she tastes of strawberries."

Ikar shook his head. "What is so enchanting about this woman? First Grant, then my brother, and now you. Is her cunt made of magic?"

Phinn made another face. "Must you be so crude?"

Ikar just shrugged, signaling for Phinn to continue.

"I told her tonight, after dinner, how I felt about her." He paused to order another drink. "I told her everything about me, about being the Masked Man."

"She laughed?" Ikar guessed from the tears that had formed in Phinn's eyes.

He nodded. "She told me she was in love with someone else, and even if that weren't the case, I was too young for her. I'm only two years her junior!."

"I don't think she means in age, Phinn. We have these homeless dogs in Alithane that follow you around the village, waiting for you to show some affection or to drop scraps of food. You remind me of those dogs."

Phinn opened his mouth, then snapped it closed. His eyes burned like blue fire. "I'm not a dog!"

Ikar just shrugged again.

They sat in silence for a few moments, and then Phinn said, "I'm afraid, Ikar. I'm going to lose tomorrow."

"You don't know that, Phinn. You could beat my brother--" he trailed off. Both of them knew that wasn't true. Phinn's defeat was as sure as the sun rising in the morning. "You could always forfeit."

Phinn shook his head rapidly, again reminding Ikar of a dog. "I can't. My father has already disappointed my mother so much. I can't be another disappointment to her. She was so proud when I entered. She thought if I could win, we could use the crown to restore our family name."

He clapped Phinn on his shoulder. "I understand, Phinn." He drank the rest of his drink and slammed the cup on the counter before he stood. "Come. Let me show you some fighting stances. If you can't beat my brother, let's at least make it so that you can hold him off for a while."

Phinn grinned and stood from the stool. "Everyone says you are as cold as ice because you never smile, but I don't think that is true. I think you hide behind your flippant comments and scowl."

"Aren't you the observant one?" Ikar gave him a wry chuckle, his mouth never turning into a smile. He said nothing more as they made their way out of the tavern and into the night.

Grant flipped his dagger in the air, catching it by the handle.

"What are you doing?" Lonis' voice came from behind him.

He turned to see his friend standing by the stairs, dressed in leather gear with a wooden sparring sword slung over his shoulder. Lonis had been helping everyone in the Manor hone their fighting skills. Grant was proud of how he had became friends with the other noble families.

"Studying physics." In truth, he was questioning why he had entered the Trials in the first place. He had no desire to be king.

Lonis came forward, moving as silent as a breeze through blades of grass. When he was close, Grant could feel the warmth of him, smell the sweat he had worked up in the combat house, and the scent of the oats and honey soap from the baths.

"I'm so tired of this, Sin."

And he looked tired. There were giant circles under his eyes, and he had lost a lot of his tawny color since they left the south. Grant felt guilty. It was his fault Lonis was so thin, so worn. His friend spent so many hours worrying about him.

"Tired of what?"

"This silent treatment," Lonis whispered back. "It's been *weeks* since you said more than a handful of words to me."

He wanted to go back to the way things were, but how could they? He was a noble, a *man*. Being with Lonis in the same way he had been with Milden would get both of them arrested. He had bedded men and women and people who didn't identify as neither man nor woman in the past, but never had he wanted to be in a relationship after Milden shattered his heart. Not until now. And now, it felt impossible. What would people say if they got a cottage together? Grew old together and never took wives? It was Grant's dream, but it seemed like a dream that wouldn't come true.

Grant swallowed at the knowing look Lonis gave him as he pushed closer to Grant. Nothing separated them now. He could feel Lonis' chest rising and falling, his gaze intense.

Does he know my fears? Does he know my desires?

Of course he did. Lonis always knew what Grant was feeling.

But the way Lonis' lithe body pressed him against the wall showed that he was everything but afraid. Lonis was ready, so why wasn't Grant?

"I-I'm sorry I've been shutting you out." Grant felt too hot, too exposed. He pushed against Lonis, and they parted, standing feet from each other. "But that night still haunts me." It was partially true, he could still see thrusting hips in his mind, but more than that, he was afraid. He was more afraid to commit to Lonis than he was to compete in the Trials. He had no idea what he was meant to do.

Lonis scoffed, and his eyes narrowed again, this time in anger. "Let it go, Sin. I have, Arlen has. If you keep wallowing in it, there will be no beginning for *us*."

The breath whooshed out of Grant's body. He wished he could take Lonis into his room and forget about everything, conquer his fear, but he stood his ground, tightening the grip on his dagger. "Maybe that's how it's supposed to be, Lonnie."

Lonis was silent, and his eyes widened at Grant's rejection. He stumbled back a few steps as if he had been slapped. "That's bullshit, and you know it."

Grant was silent, and took a whetstone from his pocket. Lonis held his hand out for the stone and dagger. He hated the technique Grant used to sharpen his blades.

Grant took a step forward, settling the dagger and stone into Lonis' palm, but he didn't let go immediately. "Maybe it would be easier if you forgot about whatever we could have, and find it with someone else." His voice was only a notch above a whisper. "Like Arlen perhaps. I can't deny that he is a good man."

"I don't want Arlen."

Grant felt tears burning his eyes, but he refused to let them fall. Instead, he walked away, leaving Lonis and his dagger behind.

Chapter Seventeen

Grant's boisterous laughter bounced off the walls of the dining room. His sister was in a fit of giggles by his side, and they were both covered in dirt and grass, having been thrown from their horses earlier that morning.

Arlen sat at the other end of the breakfast table, wedged between Lord Sinero and Grant's older brother, Mikhial. He picked at his porridge, eating small rabbit bites every few minutes. Andalen frowned at the bags under her twin's eyes.

"Champions," Luane came into the dining room with a jingle of the keys at her waist. "It's time. Please, head to your rooms. Servants are waiting to get you ready for the second battle."

Andalen and the other Champions stood, saying goodbye to loved ones. She turned, catching sight of Phinn talking to his brother and sister outside in the gardens. She had grown fond of the young lord over the last few months. His innocence reminded her so much of Arlen when he was younger.

She followed Grant and Ikar, who had not joined his mother and father in wishing Yvney good fortune. The three of them were quiet as they made their way up the stairs.

When they parted, Andalen entered her room to find a servant girl laying out her finest dress. She looked up when Andalen entered. There was a red rose pinned to her simple black dress.

"I'm Fresia. I've been tasked with getting you ready for the day."

"You have a rose attached to your lapel. Is that in support of Khett?"

The woman looked away, soothing out non-existent wrinkles on Andalen's dress. "The Lord and I are...close." The servant blinked as if she had not meant to say the words aloud.

"Ah." She felt sorry for the poor girl. Another one of Khett's conquests that thought what she had with former prince was special. "Well..." She was at a loss for words. "Shall we get me dressed?"

Fresia flashed her a grateful smile and then set to getting Andalen ready for the day. She didn't protest the dress the servant had laid out for her. In fact, it was one she didn't hate as much as the others. Milden had created it to mirror the fashions of Lysic. The fabric was loose, comfortable, and easy to move in. The dress was green with beautiful golden lilies threaded throughout, and the hem hit just above her ankles. The belt was braided and gold as well, the ends draping down her slender hips.

"You're a vision," Fresia breathed.

Andalen smiled at the servant. "Thank you."

Fresia styled her hair, curling the springs around a slim modern rod that heat up in the flames from the fire, so they were perfectly formed. She fit a golden headband over Andalen's hair and then lined her eyes in kohl.

Once dressed, Andalen hurried down the stairs to meet the others at the carriage. Grant and Ikar were already standing on the outside steps, both handsome in their coats. Grant's was blue with silver buttons. His brown-black waves fell over his eyes. Ikar was dressed in a red coat with gold buttons. His inky hair was slicked back from his face, making his cool gray eyes stand out against the morning sun.

The carriage came around the bend of the tree-lined road leading up to the house, oil-slick black against the green foliage.

They climbed into the carriage with the help of a footman. Andalen arranged her dress, so it covered her legs, as Grant settled in beside her. Ikar stretched out on the other side of the carriage with a raised eyebrow.

"Do I smell?" he asked. "No one wants to sit near me?"

"Yes, the north stench clings to you, Dominikov." Grant laughed.

Ikar rolled his eyes. "And the south clings to you, Sinero."

Andalen shook her head at their antics, used to the banter between the two Lords. "And what do I smell of?" she asked.

Grant smiled. "Wheat and the sea."

His answer made Andalen laugh. "At least you're honest, Grant. Most men would try to flatter me by saying I smelled of some flower or fruit."

"Yes, well," he flipped his hair from his eyes. "I'm not trying to bed you."

That only made her laugh more. She was pleased that they treated her as they would each other. She wasn't just a lady to them; she was a friend. Or at least she hoped they were friends.

They spent the ride observing the landscape and arguing about which was better: the north, the south or the east.

When they pulled up to the King's Coliseum, they were ushered through the winding halls by a surly, elderly woman with a hunch in her back. The halls were lit with torches, the smell of dirt and sweat hung heavy in the air, and the crowd could be heard, loud and unbridled. The cheers were a mix of all their names; the Elthare people didn't know who would be fighting until seconds before the battle began. Andalen smiled as she heard her name in the crowd. Pride welled in her chest.

They were brought to a narrow hall with an opening at the end that led to the Master's balcony.

"Wait here," the servant barked and shuffled away.

"She was pleasant," Grant commented, leaning against the wall with one leg folded over the other.

Ikar stood next to him, arms folded, face apathetic. "She reminded me of my grandmother."

"Ladies and gentlemen!" The Master's voice echoed throughout the arena. Andalen could see his back through the opening at the end of the hall. His blond hair was loose, the black fabric of his coat pulled over his broad back. "Welcome to the second battle! Today's competitors have great skills in one or more areas, and have been paired together based on their scores so far in the Trial--"

"He conveniently left out that they were the lowest scores," Ikar mumbled.

"Shh," Andalen scolded, elbowing him in the ribs.

"First, let's introduce the champions that will not be participating in today's battle!" The crowd cheered. "Our charismatic lord from the south--Lord Grantham!"

The cheers grew to a deafening roar. It was no secret that Grant was favored to win the throne. He was handsome and charming, and the love he showed his sister had won over many of the Eltharians.

Grant winked and pushed off the wall. "See you out there."

He walked to the end of the hall, raising his arms as he reached the end and exited onto the Master's balcony. The roar of the crowd grew even louder. A chorus of "Si-ner-o! Si-ner-o! Si-ner-o!" followed behind the cheers.

"Next up," Master Roxell called, "One of our lords from the chilly north--Lord Ikar!"

Ikar rolled his eyes as he uncrossed his arms, his face never morphing into anything more than a small quirk at the corner of his lips. He strolled to the end of the hall, eyes fixed straight ahead. The cheers were less than what Grant had received, but still loud. He gave no show that he was affected by the praise as he took his seat behind Master Roxell, next to Grant.

"And last, the greatest surprise we have seen during these Trials, a history in the making--Lady Andalen!"

Andalen stepped forward, her heels clicking against the gray stone floor. She blinked in the brightness of the sun, waving to the crowd.

"Am-a-don! Am-a-don!"

All around her was a sea of people in different colored clothes. Fashions from every part of Elthare could be seen: the simple vests from Oszerack; the harem pants of Palamar; the conservative coats of Rivland; the durable leather jackets of Odenmal; and the fur-lined cloaks of Alithane. All colored and dyed to represent the Champion they supported.

The majority of the clothes and banners were blue, but it made her happy to see more green than red and purple. The green of her family was worn mostly by women. However, some men sported emerald and gold, as well. A group of women on the other side of the arena held a sign with gold lettering and an amateur drawing of a lily.

ANDALEN IS OUR QUEEN!

Andi smiled, raising a hand in their direction before taking a seat.

Grant leaned over Ikar, smiling at her. "Looks like you've become a favorite."

"Give one more cheer for these three Champions!"

The crowd erupted like a volcano spitting lava, singing a chorus of their names. The entire arena shook with the stomping of feet.

The Master waited for the cheering to die down before continuing. "Now, help me welcome our first Competitor. Our Palman Champion--Lord Phinn!"

The cheers for Phinn were small compared to those for Ikar, Grant and Andalen. The Eltharians wearing purple were few and far between in the ocean of blue, green and red.

The stones under their feet rumbled as the iron gates beneath them opened. Phinn entered the arena looking confused and dwarfed in his armor. His grip on the handle of his spear was unsure and loose.

"Gods," Grant breathed, "this is going to be painful to watch."

"Let's hope he remembers what I taught him last night," Ikar mumbled.

"There's nothing we can do now," Grant replied. "I only hope he armed himself with daggers like I told him."

Andalen leaned forward in her chair, feeling sorry for their young friend. She said a prayer for him, begging for the Gods to guide him through the battle.

"Next The Great Wolf Hunter of the North--"

Ikar made a sound in his throat, something akin to a growl and a whine.

"--Lord Yvney."

The iron gate on the other side of the arena opened, and Yvney strolled out with a cool confidence. His chest was bare, showing dark hair and the bulge of his muscles. He wore his armor well. Each plate was molded to his skin as if he had been born to wear it. The grip on the handle of his war hammer was sure, and the smile on his face conveyed how much he lived for combat.

The cheers erupted, and the Althanen section jumped to their feet. "Yv-ney!Yv-ney!"

Yvney's smile grew, making him look cruel and feral. He raised his hammer in the air and let out a guttural roar.

The crowd ate it up. Even people not wearing the Dominikov red cheered for him.

"Begin!"

Yvney didn't hesitate. He charged at Phinn, raising his weapon over his head, and swung his hammer. Phinn ducked, rolling into the dirt, but lost his spear along the way. He jumped up, his hair and clothes covered in dust. His hand went to his belt, removing a dagger. He threw it, but his aim was off. It flew over Yvney's shoulder, bouncing off the stone wall behind his opponent.

Part of the crowd groaned, and the other half cheered.

"Come on, Phinn," Grant urged. His body tensed, and he balanced on the edge of his seat. "Come on."

Ikar looked just as tense. The expression on his face wasn't as easy to read, except for the tightening at the corner of his eyes, and the way he held his body bound and straight.

Master Roxell smiled, enjoying every minute of the competition.

On the field, Yvney attacked again, but Phinn dodged. One moment he was standing in front of Yvney, and the next, he was behind the larger man.

He removed another dagger from his belt, plunging it into Yvney's shoulder.

The crowd cheered, some chanting, "Mo-nneaire! Mo-nneaire!"

Yvney only jerked at the injury and turned, swinging back with an open hand, knocking Phinn down into the dirt. Phinn bled from his nose and lip as he clamored to his feet, and Yvney laughed, the sound carrying throughout the arena on a wave. He said something to Phinn that had the young lord shaking, but Andalen couldn't make out the words from where she sat.

Yvney struck again, and Phinn dodged once more. This time, Phinn stood at the other side of the arena, nearly twenty feet from where he had been only moments before. Andalen noticed that the sun had moved across the sky; it seemed like an hour or two had passed in only a few moments.

Yvney howled, more out of frustration than pain. Daggers that had not been there only moments ago were protruding from his chest, shoulder, legs. Blood dripped down each injury, smearing red against his skin, matting into his chest hair.

"STOP THAT!" he yelled, pulling the daggers free from his flesh. "FIGHT LIKE A MAN!"

It seemed to happen in one fleeting moment. Yvney charged forward, his steps wide and heavy as he pulled a dagger from his belt, plunging it into Phinn's neck. Phinn's body sputtered, flickering at the edges as he tried to use his powers. Blood spurted, drenching Yvney and the sand in red. Phinn fell to his knees.

A scream erupted from the stands. Marklin jumped up, racing to the edge of the wall that separated the stands from the field. "Phinn!"

Yvney raised his hammer and swung. Phinn's head flattened into the dirt. His body went still.

Yvney stumbled back, dropping the hammer.

Thick and heavy silence fell over the crowd, and then as if a giant storm erupted, the spectators yelled their outrage.

"Murderer!" they hollered.

"Fiend!"

"Cheater!"

Yvney stood in the middle of the field, blinking down at Phinn's corpse as if he was not sure what had happened. Master Roxell stood and signaled guards on the periphery of the Coliseum. They swarmed the field, grabbing Yvney by the wrists and hauling him away.

"Where are you taking him?" Ikar demanded from beside Andalen.

"He will be locked in a cell in the Round Tower." Master Roxell shuddered as he looked down at Phinn's body. "Murder inside the Arena is a punishable offense, Lord Ikar."

Andalen shut out Ikar arguing with Master Roxell, and the jeering from the crowd as Yvney was dragged away. She looked down at Phinn and whispered, "May Kurem lead you to the Gates."

Chapter Eighteen

It was too quiet.

Kelmen Stocke hauled in the nets he and his partner, Benox, had cast into the ocean for fish. An odd feeling sat in his gut, a clenching of the muscles that made him queasy.

"Somethin's not right," he said to Ben. He paused, looking around him, but it was only three in the morning. No one was out yet. No other fishermen would be on the shore until five--he liked getting to the beach early, so he caught the best fish.

"Yer so paranoid." Ben began plucking fish from the nets, throwing them into the buckets sitting at their feet. "Remember when ya had that bad feeling two weeks ago, and ya just had ta shit?"

Kel shook his head. "T'is different, Ben. Somethin's wrong."

"Do ya have these feelings cause yer Ma's a witch?"

Kelmen ignored his friend's taunting and looked out at the black water. Something was on the horizon; a massive black shadow moved slowly across the water. Kel squinted. "I tink there's ships--"

Ben's head shot up, and his gaze caught on the large black shapes cutting through the ocean. "Kel?"

Something whizzed through the air, slamming into Benox. Kel froze. A large ball, much like one for a cannon, but made of wood with iron spikes protruding from it, pierced through Ben's skull. Blood pooled in the sand around his body.

Run!

Kelmen sprinted across the beach, heels kicking up sand behind him. He had no idea what direction he was heading. He just had to get away. The spiked cannonballs flew over his head, slamming into the dock and buildings near the shoreline. People scurried from the falling structures, screaming.

"Help!" Someone yelled, but Kel kept running.

He soon found himself at the mouth of a cave at the base of the cliffs, and he paused, panting.

"Gods, what do I do?"

"You talking to yourself, lad?" A man came out from the shadows, dressed in the tanned hides of the Mezeran people. He was older than Kelmen by many decades, but there was a wild look in his eyes. "You ran right into the jaws of death, didn't you, lad?"

Kel's whole body shook with fear, but he had to keep going. He had to warn the village.

The man stalked closer. His heavy boots dug into the sand, his furs dripping with water from the sea and the light rain that had begun to fall. He grinned, brown teeth flashed in the light of his torch. A heavy axe swung with each step.

Kelmen looked around for something to use as a weapon, but saw nothing.

He turned and ran.

Kel ran in the direction of the shouting in the village; there was no other way to go.

Mezeran soldiers ran toward Odenmal from every inch of the beach. *How did they get to shore so quickly?* But Kel could not ponder the question. He had to keep moving.

A discarded axe lay in the sand, and he picked it up, astonished by the weight of the handle and blade.

A man nearby stalked toward a woman, a sinister grin spread across his face, barely hidden behind his beard, as he began to untie his trousers. The woman fell back, tripping over her own feet. She scooted back from the Mezeran, tearing her dress.

"Help!" She called.

No one helped her. Odemalians scampered for safety. Another woman eyed the fallen female, and Kel could almost see her thinking: *Better you than me.*

The Mezeran raised his long, crude blade.

"No!" Kel shouted. He found himself in front of the woman, raising the axe. The sound of the blade hitting the head of the axe he held pierced over the sounds of shouting and crying. The impact shook his whole arm.

There was a sudden whoosh as the shop next to them went up in flames.

Kelmen pulled back and swung the blade, hacking into the man's neck. He didn't remove the man's head cleanly, but rather left a bit of muscle that made it seem as if the Mezeran's head swung on a hinge as he fell back onto the road. His blood ran with the rain through the cracks in the cobblestones.

Kel turned to the woman. Her large green eyes were full of tears. There was a cut on her face, and blood trickled down into the neck of her dress.

"Can ya walk?"

The woman nodded and took Kel's hand.

Together, they ran through the village. He stopped when he saw two Mezeran women advancing on a girl about thirteen. She was dressed in the Lysin fashions--she must have been visiting from the other kingdom for the Trials--and her brown hair was plaited. She cowered against a wall, whimpering as the women advanced on her.

"Marta!" A man screamed.

He ran toward the women, and Kel began to raise his axe, but it was too late.

The smallest of the women stabbed the small girl through the heart.

The man stopped, falling to his knees on the cobblestones. "Marta!"

The women descended on the man, but he didn't try to run. He looked up at them with tears streaming down his face. Kelmen quickened his pace to protect the Lysin man, but the tallest woman slammed the butt of her sword into his head, knocking him out cold.

As one, the three turned, spying Kelmen.

"Shit." He turned and hightailed back to the woman he had saved. "Run! Head fer the station!"

All around them chaos had erupted. People were pulled from their homes and murdered in the streets. The Mezerans looked like an infestation of bugs. There were so many. Everywhere he looked, they seemed to multiply.

"Keep goin'."

The woman kept pace with him, and they finally made it to the train station. The only part of Odenmal that had yet to be overtaken by Mezerans. Other Odemalians were taking refuge in the station.

"We have ta get out of 'ere," Kel warned them. "They'll be comin' soon."

"Where do we go?" Someone asked.

"We go through tha woods. Ever'one's in Rivland fer tha Trials. We have ta get there and warn tha Nobles."

Kelmen expected them to argue, but no one did. They all clambered to their feet, some clinging to the person nearest to them out of fear. The woman he had helped earlier grabbed his arm. Her nails dug into his flesh, but Kel ignored the pain as he led thirty-five people to safety.

Chapter Nineteen

Master Roxell's words echoed through his head. *The next to fight are Lord Grantham and Lord Ikar.* His chest tightened as he tried to eat his eggs and potatoes.

Lonis had shoved back from the table following the Master's words, stomping up the stairs to the Sinero floor.

After breakfast, Grant went to Lonis' room and pushed open the door. The room was smaller than Grant's, but still lavish in style and colored with blue and silver. The rising sun bathed the room in golden light. Lonis sat on the floor by his bed, his dark head bowed over Grant's dagger in his lap. When he looked up, his tawny face was tracked with tears. He sniffed.

"I haven't seen you cry since you broke your arm when we were children," Grant said, trying to lighten the mood but failing.

"Sin--" Lonis' voice shattered like fragile china.

Grant crossed the room, sinking to the floor at Lonis' side. He wrapped an arm around his shoulders, drawing Lonis' warm body against him. Lonis sniffed again, burying his face into Grant's neck.

"Tell me why you're so upset, Lonnie. It's not like I am going to die."

"Poor choice of words after what happened to Phinn." Lonis sniffed again. "I'm afraid of what is going to happen. You remember your Uncle Rhys? He was never the same after the Trials."

"I suppose no one will ever be the same after getting hit in the head with an iron hammer."

"Be serious, Sin." Lonis reached for Grant's hand, and long, golden fingers wrapped around his. His touch sent Grant's heart fluttering, and his entire body was on fire.

Gods. What you do to me.

"You won't lose me, Lonnie." Their bodies crashed together as Grant wrapped his arms around Lonis' shoulders. "I promise not to get hit by any hammers."

Lonis chuckled slightly. "Why can't you ever be serious? Promise me you'll be alright tomorrow."

He couldn't promise him that. He swallowed. "I'll try. For you, I will try."

They hadn't walked far. The tracks seemed to extend forever. Kelmen, who could only tell time by the position of the sun in the sky and not by the clocks a smarter man had invented only forty years prior, looked up to the sky. According to the sun, they had been walking for hours, and they were no one near Rivland.

Kelmen heard movement behind them.

"Tighten up," he hissed to the others. "Keep movin'."

They moved as quickly and as quiet as they could, but a knot formed in Kel's stomach with every step. The Mezerans had found them.

An arrow whizzed out from somewhere between the trees. The point slammed into the chest of the man directly behind Kelmen. He fell, his head splitting on the iron tie.

"Run!" Kelmen screamed.

The people scurried down the tracks as the Mezerans broke through the trees, giving chase, picking people off one by one.

Arrows and axes flew, few missing their marks, but many finding homes in heads and backs. Kelmen grabbed the hand of the person nearest him, dragging her along.

"Keep up."

She kept pace as Kelmen veered from the rails into the woods, hoping to lose the Mezerans in the trees.

"Where do we go?" the woman asked. It was not the same woman he had saved earlier, but a Kereshi woman with leaves stuck in her wild, windblown hair. "Where is safe?"

Kelmen stopped, hiding both he and the woman behind a large tree root. "We're not going to make it to Rivland in time," he told the woman. "There's a witch that lives not far from here. She can get a message to the right people in Rivland with magic."

The woman nodded, cursed in Kerish, and the pair ventured out into the open again, weaving and ducking through branches until a cottage came into view with smoke curling up from the chimney.

"That's the house." Kel felt a smile form on his face.

"Thank--"

The woman's words were cut short, and her body jerked next to Kelmen's. Her eyes flew wide. Over her shoulder, two Mezerans were approaching, one with an axe. The other's axe was sticking out from the Kereshi woman's back.

Kelmen ran towards the cottage, his body tingling slightly when he breached the magical wards the witch had surrounding the small structure. He swung the door open and slammed it shut, leaning against it to catch his breath.

The witch, who had been sitting on her rocky floor communing with the spirit world, opened her eyes and greeted Kel with a familiar smile.

"My dear son, what trouble have you gotten into now?"

The sound of screaming came from outside as the Mezerans tried and failed to step through his mother's wards.

Chapter Twenty

The iron bars of the small stone room were still down with sunlight and wind coming in through the slats. Grant held two *padarés*, a traditional Eltharian weapon that looked like a small bow made from wood with a leather handle, but the curved end was bladed with a short, thin Opal Stone dagger sticking from the middle of it.

Holding the *padarés* brought back memories: practicing them with Lonis' father when he was a boy and still learning how to hold a sword. He had adored the weapons since he had seen them hanging from Mister Hesito's belt, the razor ends glittering in the sun when he walked.

For his sixteenth birthday Lonis had bought him this pair with coin he had saved up over the years. The wood was nicked, and the leather worn with years of use.

Grant was shirtless, and silver paint decorated his tanned skin. Strapped to his belt was his grandfather's dagger. He wasn't armed with any blades from the Arena's armory. He wanted to be holding the weapons that meant the most to him during his battle against Ikar.

"You will do well--"

His father's words were cut off by the door Grant had just come through opening again. A different servant entered. His eyes were drawn, and his mouth pinched. "Lord Sinero, Lord Grantham, follow me."

"What about my battle?"

"I'm sorry, sir. The Trials have been postponed until further notice."

"Why?"

"Please," the servant wrung his hands in his faded white tunic, "Master Roxell will explain everything."

"Attention!" he heard Master Roxell's voice beyond the bars. "I regret to inform you that The King Trials have been postponed due to a rising issue." Outrage followed his words, but he projected his voice over the noise. "Please remain calm and seated until a servant can escort you."

Curious and alarmed, Grant followed the servant and his father out of the tiny cell and down the round hall of the Coliseum.

In nearly five hundred years, a Trial has never been postponed.

Something was very wrong. Dread filled Grant's stomach like lead.

The servant was quiet as he led Grant and Lord Sinero deeper into the Coliseum. There was a chill this far down, and the walls were darker, stained with soot from the fire fifteen years before.

The servant opened a door and ushered them into a semi-round room where Ikar, Andalen, Arlen and Khett had gathered. Their parents were hovering around them, the buzz of conversation dying when the door closed behind Grant.

Grant went to stand with the others. Ikar was dressed for battle in the same leathers and metals that adorned his body.

"What happened?" he asked.

Andalen and Arlen's faces were grave; Arlen looked as if he had been crying.

"Odenmal," Ikar answered. "It's been attacked. Only a handful made it out alive and sought refuge in Alithane."

"What?" Grant blinked slowly, trying to comprehend what he was hearing. "By who?"

"Lords, Ladies," Master Roxell entered the room. His face was drawn and slightly gray. "Please, have a seat."

There was a great amount of shuffling before everyone was either sitting in a chair around the large wooden table or--in Ikar's case--leaning against a wall. Master Roxell remained standing, running a hand over his beard as he paced the small area between the door and the table.

"I had just received word from Elbatha, the Wood Witch, that Odenmal has fallen into the hands of the Mezerans."

"The Mezerans?" Lady Dominikov questioned. "The small kingdom in East?"

"Not so small anymore," Lord Sinero said. "They have taken over Oïosa and Rahji."

"Yes, but those are tiny islands," Lady Amadon chimed in, laying a hand on her husband's arm. "We are a kingdom."

"That doesn't matter." Ikar pushed off from the wall and tucked a strand of his hair back into place. "It seems the Mezerans will keep moving west until they control every piece of land in Wehlmir."

"And we will make sure Elthare does not become a part of Mezerah." Master Roxell finally stopped pacing and stood at the head of the table. "The Wood Witch believes they will split and move up to Alithane and down to Oszerack. We'll send troops out to stop the Mezerans from advancing deeper into our kingdom."

"We need help," Andalen said. "The Mezeran army is bigger since they acquired Rahji and Oïosa. They outnumber us." She stood, and Grant could see her calculating something in her mind. "Even if every man of age fought alongside the Royal Guard, we would still be outnumbered."

"How do you know that?" Grant questioned.

Andalen cut him a look. "I do my studying, Grantham. Military strategy interests me."

Grant was impressed, though he would not admit it to Andalen. "Touché, Andi." He turned from her to address the room. "What do we do? How do we stop the Mezerans from taking our kingdom?"

"We'll ask King Pytir and Queen Selia. The Dragon Queen has helped us before, and Soldare owes us for bartering peace with Lysic," Lord Amadon interjected.

For the next hour, the families strategized. They planned to send out a draft to every able-bodied man over the age of sixteen and would send a large group of soldiers to Alithane and Oszerack to defend the cities. Arlen and Andalen volunteered to go to Soldare while Grant and his father went to Lysic.

Once the meeting was over, Grant hurried through the Coliseum to find Lonis. All the Noble children and the others had been taken to a room further down the hall. He pushed the door open to find Lonis sitting in a chair, puffing on a pipe full of sweet-smelling tobacco. Ralsair was in the corner playing dolls with Phinn's younger sister, while Marklin and Mikhial played cards. Nixema was alone, knitting a string of patterns into what looked like a giant purple snake.

"I thought you stopped smoking," Grant commented, crossing the room to Lonis.

"Only because you don't like the smell," Lonis gave him a small smile, "but days like this call for a vice of some sort."

Grant sat opposite of Lonis, their knees brushing as he got into position. "You could always find other ways to relieve stress. I keep offering to call one of the Night Houses."

Lonis made a face. "No."

Grant chuckled, but sobered quickly. "You heard about Odenmal?"

Lonis nodded. "The servants are talking about it." He paused and sucked on his pipe. "I'm guessing there is going to be a draft?"

"There is. Promise me you won't die."

"Can't promise that, Sin. It is war after all."

"At least promise to think of me as you die."

Lonis' eyes flicked to his, raking over his face as if taking in his features and committing them to memory. "You will be the only thing I think of."

"Lonnie…" the words he longed to say to his oldest friend were on the tip of his tongue, but instead he said, "I'm leaving for Lysic."

"When?"

The door opened, and his father beckoned him over. Grant sighed, standing. "Now."

Lonis stood too, and Grant reached out for him. The world narrowed, fading to black at the edges of his vision until all he saw was Lonis' face. He pulled Lonis to him. Their bodies molded together, hip to hip, chest to chest.

"May Nomir grant you fortune," he whispered.

"And you, Sin. We will see each other soon." Lonis pulled back, digging into the pocket of his tunic. "I bought this for you. I was gonna give it to you after your battle."

Grant took the bar of his favorite chocolate; a note was attached to it. He began to open it, but Lonis stilled his fingers.

"Read it on your travels."

"What does it say?"

Lonis' smile was crooked. "You'll find out when you read it."

Chapter Twenty-One

The Round Tower was a hidden fortress deep in the woods between Alithane and Rivland. The progression of ten-thousand soldiers heading to Alithane trotted past it without so much as a glance, but Ikar pulled on his horse's reins and looked up at the stark gray building with its razor wire wrapping the roof and the field of thorns below. He could feel the dull buzz of magic in the air; wards put in place by witches and warlocks to keep the prisoners from escaping. There was only one way in or out of The Round Tower, a small door at the base that was guarded by a brute of a warlock named Obe.

"We have to keep moving," a man behind him hissed. "We have to make it to Alithane before the enemy."

Ikar glanced at the man dressed in the white and gold of the Royal Guard. If there were a king, the man would be wearing a pin with the family animal and one of the five noble colors.

Ikar briefly wondered what it would be like to see a wolf head pinned to the man's chest and a cape of silver and red on his back.

"If I am going to die defending my city, I would like to say good-bye to my brother first."

The man's lip curled. "Your brother is a murderer."

"Nobody's family is perfect."

Ikar broke off from the progression, his horse huffing at the sudden change in direction.

"We won't wait for you!" the Guard hollered.

"I didn't ask you to!"

Ikar dismounted his horse and tied the reins to a tree. "You stay here," he told the creature. "Neigh if anyone comes."

He walked up the thin path to the door where Obe waited.

"What do you want, Dominikov?" Obe grunted, hand twitching above his sword. "No visitors."

"Come on, Obe. I just want to see my brother."

"Master Roxell said no visitors."

Ikar smiled. "Remember when we were kids, and you fell into the river and nearly drowned because you didn't know how to swim?"

Obe rolled his eyes. "Why are you bringing that shit up?"

Ikar pulled out his coin purse, tossing it in his palm. "I went in after you and saved you." He opened it and began counting out gold pieces. Obe's eyes watched him hungrily. Ikar was one of the few that knew the warlock loved nothing more than money. Obe had a gambling problem, and Ikar was not above exploiting that. "Then I spent a whole summer teaching you how to swim, and you said you owe me. You remember that, Obe?"

"Yes, yes, I remember." Obe was practically drooling at the gold in Ikar's hand.

"Well, I'm cashing in that favor." He closed his palm over the coins and shoved his purse back into his pocket. "And I'll throw in fifteen gold pieces if you let me in to see Yvney."

Obe made a weird rumbling noise in his throat. "Fine."

The warlock unlocked the Tower door and led Ikar through. The interior was dull, lit only by single candelabras every ten to twenty feet. And it smelled of blood, piss and body odor.

Yvney doesn't belong here. Sure, his brother was the world's biggest pain in the ass, but he didn't belong in the same place they held Elthare's worst criminals.

"How has he been doing?" Ikar asked Obe, sidestepping a man reaching through the cell bars for him, calling out to him, humping the bar door in Ikar's direction. Ikar kept his face neutral; he wouldn't show how much these people terrified him.

"You'll see."

The Tower had a staircase that spiraled through the center of it, leading off to hallways of cells. There were a dozen cells on each floor and a total of five floors. Each cell was filled with four or five men and women.

Guards ignored Ikar--at least he thought they were guards. They looked just as rough as the prisoners.

Obe stopped in front of a cell on the fourth floor. There were only three men in the cell: two skinny men who looked to be part Kereshi, and Yvney, huddled in the corner.

"Brother."

Yvney looked up, and the look on his broad face would forever haunt Ikar's dreams. He looked worn, his eyes faded and dull. His skin was yellowish-gray, and he was dressed in an oversized tunic and trousers with a number over the left side of his chest, 0493553556. His head was still shaved, but there was a large scab covering the left side of his skull, and blood that had trickled from the wound had dried down his face.

"Ikar," he rasped. "Why are you here?"

"We're at war, Yv. The Mezerans have invaded Odenmal. I wanted to see you." He held his breath as Yvney moved, gingerly getting to his feet. He put all his weight on his left side, and his right ankle looked swollen. "You don't belong here."

"I do. I killed Phinn." His lip trembled slightly at the mention of Phinn's name. He closed his eyes and shuddered. "I've never killed anyone before." He opened his eyes again, training them on Ikar. "I deserve this punishment."

Ikar ignored the audience they had and focused on Yvney. "Don't say that. It was an accident."

"There's something wrong with my powers. They consumed me. I felt trapped inside a cage of anger and hate." Yvney paused, his eyes tearing. "Leave, Ikar."

Yvney turned his back to the cell bars and sank to his knees, facing the wall. With nothing left to say, Ikar turned to follow Obe back down to the entrance.

"Brother?" Yvney's voice stopped him, but he didn't turn around. He couldn't look at Yvney and see the haunted expression, the guilt. "I never truly hated you."

Ikar didn't know what to say. He didn't know if Yvney was looking, but he nodded and followed Obe down the stairs.

This is my kingdom.

Khett looked around the countryside as he followed the progression to Oszerack. The sky was a beautiful powder blue, cloudless, and birds chirped up in the trees.

As the former Prince, Khett's duty to protect Elthare was greater than those around him. This was the land his forefathers built. The Eltharians were *his* people.

He would fight to his very last breath to make sure Elthare didn't fall into enemy hands.

"You're quiet," Lonis commented.

He put his hand over the necklace tied through a buttonhole on his coat. Fresia had given it to him just before they departed and made him promise he would return. He had been courting her since he returned to his estate in Rivland and found that he was beginning to grow quite fond of her.

"Thinking."

"Aren't we all."

They were silent for the rest of the ride; the only sound was the clip-clop of the horses' hooves.

They made it to Ozerack just before the sun set, but the village was quiet. The gates were open when last Khett heard they had been closed.

"Draw your swords, men," Lieutenant General Morin commanded. "Proceed with caution."

Khett drew the sword his father had gifted him on his deathbed. Rubies encrusted the hilt, and the Opal Stone shimmered in the sun. Out of the corner of his eye, blue sapphires caught his gaze. He turned to see Lonis brandishing the sword he had at his hip, but Khett hadn't noticed the blue jewels or the S engraved on the handle until that moment.

"Is that Grant's?" Khett asked, recognizing the steel. "He showed it to me not too long ago."

Lonis smiled at the blade tenderly. "Dumbass gave it to me before he left."

Khett wanted to ask what weapons Grant had taken instead, but the soldiers were moving again.

As they entered the village gates, the smell of death hung heavy in the air. Bodies littered the roads, flies buzzed.

"We're too late," Lonis whispered. His face was pale with shock. "Mallery." His gaze was held on the body of a plump woman, her red ringlets dyed with mud and blood. Her blue eyes stared open and unseeing. "She's the baker's wife."

"Eyes peeled, lads," one of the Royal soldiers warned them.

"Father?" Lonis called out to a Keynan man dressed in Sinero blue. "Where's mother?"

Mr. Hesito's skin paled, and he led his horse to Lt. General Morin.

"Sir? My wife."

Lt. General Morin nodded gravely. "Where would she be?"

"At the Sinero Estate."

"Take some men with you, Nei-yu."

Mr. Hesito gathered twenty men, including Khett and Lonis, and they rode to the other side of the village.

"No one's left alive," Lonis whispered.

The Sinero estate was still standing, the iron gates closed and locked. The buzz of wards enveloped it. Khett sighed in relief. There was hope blooming in his chest.

"Meena!" Mr. Hesito yelled, climbing down from his horse. "Meena!"

The door to the manor opened, and a slender woman with the same tawny skin and blue-black hair as Lonis stepped out, followed by a handful of men, women and children, most of the Sinero servants, and a few villagers as well.

"Nei-yu!" She ran to the edge of the garden, just before the line where the wards began. Tears streaked her face. "Lonis, my son!"

"Mother." Lonis clambered down from his horse and raced to just before the fence. "Are you alright?"

"The Mezerans--"

"We saw," Mr. Hesito interrupted. "Are you the only ones left?"

"I think so. We tried to take in as many as we could, but the Mezerans were vicious."

"Can you lower the wards?"

Mrs. Hesito turned to tell someone to remove the wards, but the sound of maniacal laughter stopped her. Out from the alleyway stepped ten Mezerans, hair wild and skin scarred in elaborate designs. No two looked the same, one man was pale with red hair, Khett guessed he was from Oïosa, one was a woman with red-brown skin and thick black hair, and yet another was the color of the Pepperwood trees with hair the color of blanched sand.

"Elthare's elite guard," the red-haired man teased. "Only twenty of you? I'm insulted."

"There are more in the village," one of the soldiers dressed in Amadon green said.

"Oh, we heard you coming. The thousands of your finest soldiers will be no match for Mezerah's Mighty Hand. More of us will come, and we will come in droves."

"And we will kill every last one of you." Khett held his sword fast.

The man laughed. "Young Prince Pedgram. Although, you're not a prince anymore, are you? Your kingdom has some odd traditions, prince."

"Enough talk," another soldier dressed in Royal white and gold barked. He charged at the Mezerans, swinging his sword.

The Mezerans dodged, and the woman swung her axe, slicing a long, deep gash through the soldier's horse. The horse whinnied in pain, falling to the ground. The soldier rolled away to avoid being crushed, but more Mezerans appeared from the shadows and descended on the soldier. His screams cut through Khett's eardrums.

The Mezerans started forward, and the Elthrians met them mid blow. The sound of swords clanging against sword and axes filled the air. Grunts and screams followed.

Khett stabbed his blade through the neck of a Mezeran, only to be pushed away by another. He fell to the cobbled street, cracking his head against the stone. Blood flowed from the wound into his eyes, but he climbed to his feet, rolling out of the way of the sharp axe that would have met his sternum.

He kicked up, connecting his boot with a Mezeran's face. She fell back, and he fell upon her, slamming the hilt of his sword into her nose. His powers flowed through him, and the street lurched like a wave, cracking down several hundred feet. The Mezeran fell into the chasm, screaming.

Behind him, he heard the sounds of grunting and steel against steel. He turned to see Lonis engaged in battle with two Mezerans. Khett climbed to his feet, driving his blade into the back of one man and using his free hand to push the other man into the dark hole he had made.

Lonis toppled over with the other on top of him. Two daggers swung violently; one cut Lonis' arm, and the other stabbed into his shoulder.

"Lonis!" Khett yelled, lunging forward and driving his axe through the Mezeran's skull.

The man fell forward onto Lonis, but Khett didn't pause to see if Lonis was okay. He turned to kill more Mezerans, driving his blade into their bodies and using his powers to rain rock and rubble down on their heads.

Then something flashed silver in his eyes, and he fell to his knees.

Blood poured from the gash on his neck and down the front of his tunic. The last thing he saw were wild Mezeran eyes and a wicked smile.

Then everything went black.

Chapter Twenty-Two

They had been at sea for three days, and it would take another two to reach Soldare, and another to reach Lysic. Grant was already ready to die of boredom. And worry.

Was Lonis safe? Had the Mezerans attacked the other villages? Were they going to survive this godsdamned war?

He paced the large wooden deck of the Royal ship, nibbling on the last bit of chocolate Lonis had gifted him.

"You didn't even share," his father joked.

Grant huffed. "This was my gift. If you want chocolate, then find someone who will buy you some."

Lord Sinero laughed.

Andalen and Arlen looked ready to be sick. They were clinging to the rails of the ship for dear life, and their dark skin had been tinged green since they left the docks in Rivland. Arlen had already lost his breakfast and lunch that day.

"Come sit with me, my son."

Grant rolled his eyes, but obliged the old man, settling onto the deck as his father tied knots into a piece of rope. Grant looked up at Captain Wilnen, who looked more like a pirate than the Captain of the Royal Naval Guard.

"Have you read Lonis' note?"

"No." The paper, though thin, had felt heavy in Grant's breast pocket since he placed it there. He was afraid to read the words. What if it was a letter to tell him goodbye? That he had moved on? Grant closed his eyes, and pain began throbbing at his temples. What if it was a letter declaring his love for Arlen?

"When you told me you cared more about who a person is than what's between their legs, what did I tell you?"

"You said you were proud of me for trusting you enough to tell you and to be careful, so I didn't get arrested." Grant was still surprised at his father's acceptance. Often he wondered how his mother would have reacted to the news. Would she have been as loving as his father? "Why are you bringing this up?"

"What else did I tell you?"

"You want me to be happy." Grant shifted awkwardly. He so did *not* want to have this conversation on the deck of a ship with a crew of fifty and Andalen and Arlen only feet away. Even if his father was speaking low, and no one was paying attention to them, Grant still felt exposed.

"Exactly. And do you know when I see you at your happiest? When you're with Lonis. You and he have been close over the years, but something changed three years ago. You seek him out. You look at him the way I looked at your mother. You're like magnets, positive and negative. You're the sun and the moon. Opposites, but one cannot exist with the other. You love him?"

"Really, Father. Can you not do this now?"

Lord Sinero smiled. "Take it from someone who lost the love of his life. You should tell him how you feel, son. We only have a limited time in this world."

Grant scrambled to his feet. "Thank you for making things awkward. Excuse me while I jump into the shark-infested waters."

Instead, Grant disappeared into the galley. He made sure he was alone before pulling Lonis' letter from his pocket.

Sin,

5,528 days.

That's how many days it has been since you said hello to me when my family moved into the Sinero Estate.

I am not a man who writes flowery prose or dramatic declarations of love. I deal with facts and logic. I am rational, calculating, reasonable. You are the opposite, in case you were wondering.

Here are the facts:

One: I love you. I have loved you every day for 5,528 days.

Two: That night with Arlen was a mistake. It was the one time in my life that I did not act rationally, and it almost cost me you. I have never been so scared in my life until the moment I saw you standing in that doorway. I hope you will forgive me.

Three: We are at war. Either one of us could die tomorrow, and I don't want to leave this world without telling you how I feel.

Four: You are everything to me, Sin. There has never been anyone else. You are it for me, and you always will be.

Return to me, Sin. I'll be waiting.
Love, Lonnie.

Tears hit the parchment, smudging the ink. Emotion swelled Grant's chest, his heart filling until it was nearly painful. He knew what he needed to do. He had spent too long denying the obvious.

Grant folded the letter and put it back into his pocket, holding his hand over his heart.

He placed his head against the wall and closed his eyes, conjuring Lonis' face in his mind.

I'll return, Lonnie. I promise.
Gods, this war needs to end soon.

Tall tan buildings could be seen in the distance. Andalen had never been so thankful to see land as she was in that moment. She contemplated kissing the dock once she stepped off the ship.

She toyed with the necklace Nixema had given her for her birthday. She never left home without it, and over the last few months it had become a lucky charm of sorts.

"I've never been to Soldare," Arlen said, leaning against the ship's rail. "Is it true they mark magical beings and imprison them?"

"It is," a sailor replied. He lifted his sleeve. On his bicep was a large red circle with a curved diagonal line running through it. "My Father is an ogre. I was born in Soldare, and when King Pytir's soldiers found my home, they killed my mother and father and branded me. I was still young, so they wanted me to work in the mines. I escaped after three weeks. Captain Wilnan found me on the beach. He made me part of his crew. Soldare is a dangerous place for magic folk."

"That's awful!" Andalen exclaimed.

"That's the law." The sailor shrugged. "We should dock in a little over an hour."

Once they were docked, Andalen, Arlen and a handful of their family's Guard were met by King Pytir's advisors and Prince Hektor. Hektor sneered at Andalen.

"We meet again, Lady Andalen."

"Charmed," she spat out.

"Your hair is shorter." The Prince tipped his head to the side, considering her appearance. "You look very much like a male."

Andalen refrained from rolling her eyes. "That's the point, Prince Hektor. Please, lead us to your father."

Prince Hektor turned and led the consort down the sandy beaches to the heart of Solterra.

Solterra reminded Andalen of Odenmal. Everything from the buildings to the roads to the dirt was brown. The fashions of Soldare were simple, plain dresses and tunics dyed the natural colors of the earth.

Prince Hektor rambled about the mines and how the kingdom was producing more gold than ever. His words reminded her of what the half-ogre said on the ship, and she wanted to ask the Prince if he got satisfaction from treating magic folk like slaves, but she kept her mouth shut.

The castle stood proud in the center of the city with stained glass windows portraying the God and saints of Soldare's main religion. Hektor led them into the great hall, footsteps echoed off the gold-threaded onyx floors.

King Pytir sat on his throne, and it too was made from onyx and gold. He merely nodded in greeting as Andalen and Arlen approached, each bowing to show respect.

It was well known that the Soldaren King suffered from gout, but his illness was never mentioned, and he acted as if he were still as virile as he was at the age of thirty. Although, he remained sitting even as a handful of servants brought forth wine and cheese.

"Lord Arlen, Lady Andalen, what brings you to my kingdom?"

The King's attention was turned toward her brother, but Arlen remained silent. He had always been shy. Andalen was used to taking the reins in social situations. She stepped forward.

"Your Highness, Elthare is under attack. The Mezerans outnumber us greatly..." Andalen paused. She was not a woman who usually begged, but to save Elthare, she would grovel. She would kiss the King's feet if she had to. "Please, King Pytir, we desperately need your help."

Her words were met with silence. The King sipped from his gold goblet, eyes never leaving Andalen's face.

"And why should I risk the lives of my soldiers for you? Was it not the Eltharians who turned their backs when we needed aid against Lysic only twelve years ago?"

Arlen stepped up to Andalen's side. "You owe us. You attacked Lysic without provocation, and in the end, it was Elthare that brought peace. If it were not for our late King, the dragons would have burned your kingdom to the ground."

Andalen groaned. Arlen may have been shy, but when he spoke, he didn't filter his words. She had always been much more diplomatic.

Prince Hektor laughed. "So, you do have claws after all, Lord Arlen. I always thought you to be a timid mouse."

Arlen ignored the prince. "Without help from your army, Elthare will not survive this invasion."

The King leaned forward slightly, shifting his weight off his left leg. His sneer sent goosebumps down Andalen's arms. "My answer remains unchanged." He stood, and a servant appeared at his side to escort him from the room. "Soldare will not come to save you. Hektor will escort you back to the docks. Hopefully, your boat has not left yet."

He hobbled from the room. Andalen, stunned for words, wracked her mind for something to make the King provide them with some sort of help, but she could think of nothing.

"Elthare will remember this!" Arlen shouted.

Hektor laughed. "If your kingdom lives to see tomorrow."

The boat was just about to set sail to Lysic when Andalen and Arlen approached. Grant met the siblings on the deck, cutting a look to Prince Hektor on the slated dock. "Vile creature," he muttered. "What happened?"

"Soldarens are assholes," Andalen replied. "Hopefully, we'll have better luck in Lysic."

Arlen huffed and plopped down onto a barrel of gunpowder.

"Ari?" Andalen questioned with worry.

"I'm not a timid mouse!" he hollered.

Grant chuckled. "Who said that?"

"Hektor," Andalen clarified as the boat pulled from the dock, heading north. "Ari, you are kind of...introverted. Everyone knows it."

"Doesn't mean I'm timid."

Andalen sighed. She didn't want to have an argument with her twin. Besides, she was already beginning to feel sick as the ship began to push through the water. She ran to the rail and lost the remaining contents of her stomach to the sea.

Chapter Twenty-Three

They were evacuating Alithane. All ten-thousand soldiers marched Althanens from their shops and homes, and into the forest. At the town's edge, many of the soldiers remained behind while the rest--a thousand or so--saw that the people made it to Rivland safely.

It had been a week since Ikar and the others arrived in his town, but there had been no attacks from the Mezerans. From the fire message they had received from the warlock and witch accompanying the troops in Palamar and Rivland, things have been quiet there as well. Hours later, the heads of the noble houses decided to evacuate Alithane citizens to Rivland, and the remaining Oszerakians to Palamar.

If the Mezerans came for the northern city, there would be nothing left but empty homes and nine-thousand soldiers to greet them.

The only thing that matters is that they don't get Rivland. Halon Amadon's voice in his head was not something Ikar welcomed. He would rather hear an ear-splitting scream.

But Lord Amadon was right; if the Mezerans took the castle, Elthare would truly be gone.

Ikar ushered a woman and her child with a missing leg onto a cart being pulled by her feeble, old donkey.

"It would be easier for you to travel on one of the soldier's horses," he told her.

"I won't leave Barley behind."

Briefly, he wondered if that was the donkey's name or the boy's.

A cold wind blew in off the ocean.

"Ikar!"

A small, teenage girl named Winny ran from the inn, holding a large basket of bread and fruit. She was a cousin to Roslen and Briar, but lacked their fiery red hair. Hers was a mousy brown that matched her eyes.

"Win, didn't I tell you to leave already?"

"When have I ever listened to you?" she countered with a smile. "I'm leaving now, but Lady Dominikov is looking for you."

"My mother? Why?"

"How should I know?" She ran past Ikar, and one of the soldiers helped her onto the back of his horse.

The town was near empty now. All that remained were a few stragglers and those that refused to leave. The baker was still inside his shop, but the shutters had been drawn and locked. Ikar had begged him to go, but Mr. Pilsen had always been a stubborn fool.

Ikar found his mother in the empty tavern. She was behind the bar, pouring dark whiskey from a bottle into a large gold cup. Outside, the soldiers could be heard shouting orders to the Althanens.

"*Mën Syebek,*" She slurped at the drink, "you have done well."

"Thank you, *Mater.*"

She circled the counter, coming to stand in front of Ikar. She placed a rough hand on his cheek. The scar on her chin pulled as she smiled. "I'm very proud of you, but it's time to go now."

"Go?"

"To Rivland with others. The *verend* are coming. You must go."

"I can fight." Ikar couldn't just *leave* her behind. "This is my city!"

Lady Dominikov smiled again. "And you have done it proud, but we must protect castle."

"You're not coming."

"No. I stay here, help beat *verend.*" She kissed Ikar's forehead, then each cheek. The Lysin way of saying good-bye. "Remember, *mën Syebek, serdhe ivë drahker layüt.*"

Ikar swallowed. *The heart of the dragon beats within you.* Another Lysin custom. One that fellow soldiers told each other before battle.

Ikar pierced his mother with cool gray eyes. "We will survive this."

"I pray to Gods that we do, Ikar."

Despite his unease at leaving his mother behind, Ikar nodded, kissing her on the cheek. He exited the tavern and found his horse where he had left it. A soldier was just exiting the town, and Ikar galloped on the white steed to catch up with him.

"You know, I was raised in Alithane," the man said, turning his head to look at the empty town. "My father worked in the coal mines."

Ikar was not one to make small talk, but things change during war, so he supposed he could at least make a friend while they traveled back to Rivland; he needed the distraction from the sick feeling in his stomach. "I hear the mines are haunted."

The man laughed. "They very well could be."

"You smell like animals." These were the first words Roslen uttered when Ikar found her in the castle gardens. She giggled. "But I will hug you all the same."

"I'm honored," he said, deadpan, wrapping her in his arms. "How is our child?" Ikar kneeled to kiss her swelling belly.

"She can probably smell you in there."

"How do you know it's a girl? It could be a boy."

"Or it could have horns," Brair's voice came from the other side of the wall. He laughed. "But Uncle Briar will still love him, her, it."

"Hush, Bri," Roslen tutted at her brother.

Briar came around the wall. His eyes looked glassy as if he had been crying. "I'm glad you're back, Ikar."

"You mean you're glad I didn't die."

Briar smiled slightly. "They closed the gates to the city. No one is coming in or going out."

"What about Grant and the others?"

"They're en route to Palamar," Ikar answered. He had just come from a strategy meeting with the General of the Royal Troops, Master Roxell, and the heads of the noble families who had stayed in the castle. "The Palman docks remain open, but only until sunrise. If they don't make it back in time--"

"They will be lucky," Roslen interjected. "They won't have to fight."

Ikar laughed. "You didn't hear Andalen before they left. She is ready. She wants all the Mezerans on the end of her arrows."

"They're not bringing the Palmans here?" Briar questioned, plucking a rose from the soil.

"Don't let the servants see you," Ikar warned, chuckling. "They'll have your head for ruining the royal flowers." He wrapped an arm around Roslen and kissed her temple. "No. There are too many people in Elthare to fit in Rivland. The only thing we can do is fortify both cities and hope for the best."

"You were never one for optimism," Roslen said. "What do you think is going to happen?"

Ikar mulled it over. The realist in him believed they were doomed; the Eltharians were outnumbered, and the Mezerans have already taken over two cities. They continued to move west, and for every Mezeran the Eltharian soldiers killed, two more popped up in its place. So, yes, Ikar believed they were doomed. But he wanted to believe they were going to come out of this with their kingdom still intact. He wanted to believe that he was going to be able to see his child grow, and also marry the one person he loved more than life itself.

"I don't have an answer for that, my love, but I am praying to the Gods that we win, and to send every last Mezeran to the fucking Infernal Flames."

The city was quiet when they pulled into the dock. Above, Grant could make out the large outline of twenty dragons and their riders.

Queen Selia hadn't provided them with her entire army, but she was willing to lend twenty of her dragon riders, and 50,000 troops. The sea behind them was littered with Lysin ships.

Lord Monneaire and Lady Pedgram met them on the shoreline. Lord Monneiare appeared to be sober for the moment, but Lady Pedgram's eyes were swollen and red.

"You did well," she praised Andalen, Arlen and Grant. Her eyes slid over them to Lord Sinero. "The Soldarens refused?"

Lord Sinero shrugged. "Did we expect anything else?"

"I suppose not."

Behind them, the Lysin soldiers rowed small dinghies to the shore. The twenty dragons landed on the beach, kicking up white sand in every direction. The leader dismounted her dragon and met them on the wooden docks.

"I am Geta." Her Lysin accent was very heavy, and there was a roughness about Geta that Grant hadn't experienced before. "It is honor to come to your aid."

"We appreciate it," Lord Monneaire extended his hand toward the dragon rider. "Come. We have set up camp in the Atrium."

The tense quiet in Palamar made Grant uneasy. He was used to music and dancing, the smell of cooking meat filling the air. The multicolored lights that usually lit the streets at night were dowsed, bathing the different colored buildings in shadows.

Grant followed behind Geta and the others, hanging back with Andalen and Arlen. "Something's wrong. Did you see Lady Pedgram's eyes?"

"She had been crying," Andalen agreed, fiddling with her necklace. "You don't think Khett--?"

Arlen stiffened and quickened his pace to catch up with the former queen. They stopped to speak while the others continued down the cobbled streets to the Square.

Behind them, Arlen let out a loud, gut-wrenching wail.

"Oh, Gods," Andalen whispered and doubled back to her brother.

Grant kept pace with Lord Monneaire and the others.

"How did it happen?" Grant asked. "With Khett?"

"Oszerack was ambushed. He's not dead. The Warlocks have been working to heal him."

Grant let out a sigh of relief before he thought: *Lonnie.*

Grant's eyes met his father's, but he couldn't ask. He couldn't bear to bring the words to leave his lips.

"The Hesitos?" Lord Sinero asked.

"Alive."

Grant released a breath and quickened his footsteps. He needed to see Lonis, make sure he was still whole. Still alive.

The Atrium sat middle of Palamar; it was a large multicolored building with no roof, adorned with gold filigree and marble pillars. For hundreds of years, festivals and live performances had been held in the vast structure. Several tents, ranging from being able to hold twenty people, to only being able to hold one, stood erect in the open space. There was hardly enough room between each one to walk.

Which one is Lonis in?

Grant scanned the canvas as if the blank, beige cloths could give him the answer. He broke off from the group and began winding his way through the ropes and stakes.

Voices murmured low in each tent, but none of them were Lonis. He heard Milden in one, talking to Ralsair. And next to that, he finally heard the warm, familiar tones he was searching for.

He pushed up the flap to find Lonis and Nixema chatting in the semi-dark. A glowing stone sat between them, casting eerie shadows across their faces. Nixema hurried to her feet.

"You're back. Andalen, is she--"

"She's fine," Grant assured her. "But they just found out about Khett."

"Gods." Nixema scurried from the tent.

Lonis rose to his feet. He was so tall that his head brushed the canvas above.

"Did you bring help?" Lonis asked, inching closer to Grant. He looked unsure of himself. Grant could almost see him thinking: *Did you read my letter?*

"I brought dragons." Because he loved nothing more than to irritate Lonis, he then launched into his adventures on the sea. He told Lonis about Andalen and Arlen throwing up into the water, stargazing with his father and learning the life stories of the crew. As he spoke, he could see Lonis' impatience growing, and Grant couldn't help but smile. "Rookery really is an awful cook."

"Grantham."

Grant blinked. "I hate when you use my whole name." He stepped forward and kept walking until he and Lonis were chest to chest. "I read your letter."

"And?"

"And I am not prone to flowery prose and dramatic declarations of love!"

Lonis laughed. "You are the most dramatic person I know, Sin. Remember when we were sixteen, and you wrote that poem for Milden? She threw it in the river." Lonis laughed again. "Or when we were ten, and your Pa banned you from going to the bakery after lessons, and you thought you would literally die if you didn't have a roll every day. You claimed you *needed* them to survive through your lessons."

Grant clamped a hand over Lonis' mouth. "Stop talking and kiss me."

Lonis' eyes twinkled as he leaned forward and pressed his lips to Grant's. His arms slid around Lonis' neck, fingers tangling in the black hair at the base of his neck.

Everything around them: Every sound, every second, the entire world seemed to fade. It was only them, and this moment.

The moment their entire lives had been leading to since Lonis came to live at the Sinero Estate.

Once their hands began to roam, and the kiss became more passionate, Grant wondered how he had gone so many years without this. Without Lonis. How had he not combusted with sheer want? How did he survive being around Lonis day after day and not felt his hands on him, or his mouth on his.

Lonnie is right. You are dramatic.

Grant told his brain to fuck off and enjoy the moment.

"Say the words," he demanded, working his lips to Lonis' jaw. "I want to hear them out loud."

Lonis placed his fingers under Grant's chin and met his eyes. "I love you, Sin." He kissed Grant again. "It has always, *always* been you."

Grant beamed. "Now say them again."

Lonis chuckled. "Why do I feel like this is going to become a thing?"

"Because you're a smart man, and it is." Grant pulled back, toying with Lonis' hair. "I can't pinpoint the exact moment I started loving you as more than a friend, but I do love you. So much." Grant hit his shoulder. "See? That was not at all dramatic."

Lonis chuckled and rolled his eyes. "I take back everything I said about you, Sin. Please, tell me more, in your undramatic way, how much you love me."

Grant silenced Lonis by kissing him again.

Andalen stepped into the small tent they kept Khett in. The small area smelled of herbs and smoke, and too many bodies pressed into one space. Lady Pedgram hovered by her son's head, smoothing his chestnut hair back from his pale, clammy face. Fresia sat at his side, his limp hand gathered in her lap. Petau bent over Khett, brushing a sickening green salve over the wound at Khett's throat. He muttered an incantation under his breath.

No one spoke for several moments, watching the warlock work. When he paused in his spell, he looked over at Andalen and Arlen, giving them a small, uncomfortable smile.

"Cousins. I am glad to find you well."

"Petau." Andalen took a step forward. "How is he?"

Andalen couldn't take her eyes off Khett's body. He hardly looked as if he were breathing. His skin was nearly gray. Blood had dried on his uniform, staining the red fabric a deeper color around the collar.

"He isn't healing." Petau ground some sort of purple herb with a pestle. "I'm afraid Kurem will come for him before the week is out."

"There is nothing you can do?"

Fresia tensed at Andalen's question.

Petau looked grave. "Even magic has its limits."

Andalen looked behind her to her brother. Arlen's face was smooth in shock. His hands gripped the fabric of his shirt. Tears slid down his umber face.

"Ari."

Andalen gathered her brother in her arms, holding him tight, allowing her brother the moment of sorrow when she herself wanted nothing more than to sob for the man before them.

The flap of the tent opened, and a man no older than seventeen strolled in. He looked very much like Khett, but he was more slender, and his eyes were green, and with darker hair. He held himself with the same Pedgram confidence as Khett and the King before the Illness took him.

Behind him, an elderly woman peered into the tent with a click of her tongue.

"It smells like death in here."

"Who are you?" Fresia asked, clinging even more to Khett. "Only Khett's friends and family are allowed in here."

"Lucky for you, love," the man said. "I am the latter. Aunt Lily, please clear the room so Bethanie can work. She will heal Khett."

"Chris--" but something in her nephew's gaze stopped her, and she nodded. "Everyone, please, leave."

Despite the unease in Andalen's gut, she followed the others outside. Something unsettled her gut, but she was so desperate for Khett to live that she ignored it.

Chapter Twenty-Four

The tent they had another strategy meeting in was large enough to fit a full-sized table and eight chairs. Grant stood at the front of the tent, near the entrance, and away from General Anrick Sinero. His uncle had always believed Grant to be spoiled and soft. Anrick had wanted Grant to train in the Royal Guard like his cousins, Johan and Vilhem III. Instead, Lord Sinero had raised Grant to be educated not only in combat, but in arithmetic, the arts and literature.

The plan was changing again. Grant hadn't been listening, so he wasn't completely sure, but it sounded as if they were evacuating Palamar. Geta stood tall and strong next to General Sinero, refusing to be intimidated by his sneers whenever she suggested something.

Grant didn't really understand why he needed to be a part of these meetings. He never had anything to offer, and even if he did, his uncle and cousins shot his input down faster than he could blink.

"If you do not evacuate, the Mezerans will destroy people."

"We will meet them head-on," Johan countered. "We'll take the armies and the dragons, and ambush them in the woods, Odenmal and Oszerack. We'll take back the cities."

"Why not do both?" Geta argued. "My queen has said your people can take refuge in Lysic until war ends, and we can 'take back cities.'"

Johan looked ready to argue, but couldn't come up with anything. "Father?"

General Sinero rubbed a hand over his beard. His Royal Guard uniform was pulled taut over his chest and biceps. He looked rather Godlike dressed in all white.

Grant rolled his eyes.

"I supposed it could work." He continued to rub his beard.

"Gods," Lord Sinero threw up his hands. "Anrick, you know it's a solid plan. You're only hesitating because she's a woman."

"And she's not Eltharian," Anrick said.

Grant rolled his eyes again.

"We can send the people in Palamar out on boats, and the ones in Rivland through the forest, over the border into Lysic," Lady Pedgram said.

"Yes, My Lady. That does seem like a good plan," Vilhem III said, bowing.

"Fine," General Sinero conceded. "After we clear out Palamar, we ride for Rivland." He closed his eyes and seemed to be praying. When he opened them again, he stared at each individual in the room. "If the castle falls, we fall."

Fire messages had been sent to the others in Rivland. They confirmed and planned to have the city evacuated by nightfall.

Grant's heart squeezed. He had read about the wars in history and never had they had to empty the entire kingdom to protect it. He felt very little hope for the outcome of this war.

All across the sandy beaches, dinghies were ferrying Eltharians to the Lysin ships that waited further out at sea. Dragons zipped through the air, carrying people to make the process faster.

"Please tell me you're getting on one of those ships," Lonis said as they helped an elderly woman into a rowboat.

"I'm not." Grant ran a hand through his hair, looking at the ship in the distance that held Ralsair and Milden. Ral had kicked and screamed, wanting to stay with her father and brothers, as Milden dragged her aboard. Grant hated telling them goodbye. "You get on the fucking ship."

"I've been training for this, Sin."

"I may not be a soldier," Grant said, wishing he could reach out and hug Lonis to him, but he knew the risks. The guard was watching. There were too many people around. "But I will die for this fucking kingdom. My heart beats Elthare blood, Lonnie." He picked up a small toddler and put the child in beside the old lady. "Besides, if you're not getting on the ship, then neither am I."

"You're so stubborn," Lonis said, but didn't press the issue further. There was a deep fear in his eyes every time he looked at Grant.

Further down the shoreline, Andalen was hugging Arlen and Nixema before they climbed on the back of a black dragon. Arlen was still upset with her. He didn't want to leave, but Andalen had to keep him safe. His fighting skills were pale in comparison to everyone else's.

"I need you to keep Nix safe."

People kept cutting them sour looks. All able men between the ages of seventeen and sixty were supposed to fight, but the Noble council had made an exception for Arlen. Those that were giving him looks didn't know that he had started to see things as warped and distorted at the age of fifteen in his right eye. They didn't know that he found it difficult to draw and paint like he used to years ago. They didn't know that he was starting to go completely blind in that eye, and it terrified him.

The Noble Council had not known until Andalen told them about his disorder that morning. Arlen had begged her not to share his secret, but she would do *anything* to keep him safe, even if that meant betraying his trust.

"I can't lose you two," Andalen said, clutching both of their hands.

"Ari, promise me you'll enjoy life. Promise me you'll fall in love again."

"Andi. Stop talking like you're going to die."

Nixema sobbed into the sleeve of her dress. The Lysin was patient as they said their goodbyes.

He allowed them their privacy, but Andalen could see the empathy playing out on his rugged features.

"Nix." She unclasped the necklace at her throat. The gold chain glittered in the sun, and the red pendant reflected on the sand. "I love you. I never told you that, but it's true. I love the way your fingers feel when you brush my hair. I love that you are strong and good. I love the way you say my name first thing in the morning." Andalen sniffed. She couldn't list everything she loved about nixema; there was no time. "If this is the end, I want you to be happy, Nix. We will find each other again in the Heavens. Remember that."

Nixema nodded, crying too hard to say anything. Andalen pressed the necklace into her palm, closing it over the chain and stone. She brought Nix's hand to her mouth and kissed her balled up fingers.

"My heart is yours, Nix. Forever."

"F-forever."

The dragon rider made a low humming sound in his throat, and the dragon took off towards Lysic. Arlen and Nixema screamed, holding on for dear life.

Andalen spun, tears burning her eyes. She found Grant and Lonis at her side. None of them said a word as the last of the Eltharians gathered into the ships and set sail for the neighboring kingdom.

Chapter Twenty-Five

Light spilled in through the cracks of the curtains. The white walls of the castle seemed to sparkle with multiple colors in the morning light. Roslen's red hair spilled over the black pillow, a river of lava on volcanic rock. Ikar reached over, brushing her cheek with the back of his fingers.

"Roz." Ikar's voice was soft as he nuzzled her neck. His hand traveled over her skin, under the covers and over her slight bump. "You can't have the baby before we marry. We can't have a bastard." He rubbed her belly as he spoke. "Many men have bastard children, and I refuse to be one."

"You haven't asked me to marry you," came her sweet, sleepy voice.

Ikar smiled into her neck. "Haven't I?"

She giggled. "No."

He pulled back, taking her face in his hands. She returned his smile as he bent and placed his lips to hers. He kissed her soft and sweet, exploring lips he had memorized like a well-loved book. Her hands came up, covering his hands on her cheeks.

"I love you," he whispered before taking her mouth again in a passionate kiss. She moaned, arching her back, rubbing her warmth against his thigh. He pulled his head back to look at her once more. "Marry me, Roz. Let's make our dreams a reality."

"I'm pretty sure I'm still dreaming," she countered. "Are you sure you're real?"

"Very real." He pecked her lips again. "You haven't answered my question, shall I take that as a 'no'?"

"Yes, Ikar. A million times, yes." Her hand slipped into his trousers. "I love you, Ikar."

"And I, you, my Roslen."

The door to the chamber opened. A servant dressed in pure white hustled forward with a basin. "My Lord, the others are arriving."

"You're interrupting my proposal," Ikar ground out. "Leave me to make love to my bride-to-be."

Roslen hit his shoulder. "Be nice."

She shimmied out of bed, uncaring of looking indecent in front of the servant. He averted his gaze, although Roslen was covered in a black gown. Ikar groaned and got out of the bed.

"You owe me," he told Roslen.

"We have all our lives for me to make it up to you."

"Not if I die during this fucking war."

Roz rolled her eyes. "You're not going to die, my love. I forbid it."

A female servant entered the room and ushered Roslen to the chamber down the hall, where she would be dressed and pampered. The male servant had already begun pulling Ikar's clothes from the wardrobe.

"Even in war, I'm still treated as if I can't dress myself."

"Some things should give us a sense of normalcy in these troubling times, don't you agree, My Lord?"

"The only thing troubling me is why we didn't open the castle to the refugees. It's big enough to house many of the people in Rivland, and yet, only the nobles and Roxell are inside its walls."

"That's the way it's always been, My Lord." The servant began helping Ikar into his clothes. "For hundreds of years, the temple has served as a refuge for those in need. It has served well for centuries as it has served well for the past ten days."

"The Temple isn't big enough to house all those people. What about the others?"

The servant frowned. "I'm not sure, My Lord."

"Did everyone make it out of the city?"

He had helped the morning before, loading people into wagons and horses, handing them food to prepare them for their trek through the woods, but Master Roxell had called the nobles away to try and convince Ikar to go with the evacuees.

Ikar had argued with Roslen for hours to go, but she was stubborn. It was one of the many reasons he loved her.

"I will not leave," she had huffed, "and you will not say another word about it."

"There are those who refuse to go," the servant replied, "but everyone else is gone. The last wagon left just before yesterday's sunset."

Ikar nodded as the man fixed the finishing touches on Ikar's belt and coat.

A loud roar shook Ikar out of his deep contemplation of whether he should buy Roslen a gift when the war was over to celebrate their engagement. It was customary that the husband present their bride with a gift on their wedding day, but would it be bad luck to give her one beforehand? He had just opened his mouth to ask Briar what he thought when the deep bellow had shook the sky.

A black shadow fell over the crowd on the castle grounds. The green dragon landed just before the trees in the orchard. Its wings tucked into its body, and it bowed forward to let its passengers off.

It's graceful for being such a large creature, Ikar thought idly.

Grant's curls were wild and windswept, but there was a smile on his face.

"Dominikov, dragon-riding is the only way to travel."

Ikar clapped his old friend on the back. He would never admit it out loud, but he was happy to see Grant. There was something nostalgic about seeing a childhood friend during troubling times.

Andalen looked green, and put her face between her knees. "That was awful."

"Worse than the ship?" Grant wondered.

"So much worse."

In rapid tones, the three of them began talking over each other. Ikar told them about Yvney and Alithane. Andalen shared her exchange with Nix and Arlen. Grant told them about finally telling Lonis he loved him.

Ikar still remembered the night Grant drunkenly told him and Roz that he was in love with his oldest friend. That had been two years ago.

"I'm happy you finally admitted your feelings," Ikar said, crossing his arms over his slender frame. "I was ready to intervene."

Grant rolled his eyes. "Yes, well, Roz had already tried--"

"Kel!" Andalen screamed, running towards a tall young man with light brown hair and pulling him into a tight hug. "I was so worried."

Everything seemed normal, and for a minute, Ikar could ignore the dragon, the sound of soldiers filing into position around the castle, and the looming threat of the Mezerans. He was among friends. There was no war. Everything was fine.

There was a whoosh in the air, and the candle the Wood Witch carried with her lit itself. She closed her eyes, chanting, and when she opened them, she stared into the flame as if it were speaking to her.

Her face visibly paled. "The Mezerans have taken Alithane. They're coming this way."

Chapter Twenty-Six

Grant hadn't anticipated this. He didn't think he would be separated from Andalen, Ikar and Lonis. He didn't think it would be him on the back of a dragon, clutching a Dragon Rider for dear life.

He didn't think he would be on the front lines.

"Is this first war?" Fedirij asked.

"How can you tell?"

"Your face is green."

Grant adjusted the grip on Fedirij's belt. "Thanks. It's my natural pallor."

Fedirij laughed. "In Lysic we're born for war."

"So I heard."

The trees around them had turned orange and yellow. Leaves littered the browning grass, and a fog rolled in from the sea. Grant had always loved autumn, but it was hard to love anything when you knew that somewhere in the trees the enemy was waiting.

Around him, Elthare and Lysic's best soldiers and men who have only held a sword once in their lives stood at the ready. The man next to him--only a few years older than Grant--shook with fear.

Some fifty-thousand men and women away stood Lonis.

Return to me, Sin. I'll be waiting.

The words from Lonis' letter kept repeating in his head. It served as his mantra to not die in this Godsdamned war.

A twig snapped in the distance.

"They come," Fedirij said.

Grant was too terrified to come up with a snappy comeback.

Mezerans broke through the trees. Thousands of them, hundreds of thousands. They walked shoulder to shoulder. Axe blades hitting together in a rhythmic, metallic clang.

"Prepare yourself!" Fedirij said, and then hummed.

His dragon, ShadowCloud, rose into the air. Grant gripped Fedirij tighter around the middle.

The Mezerans watched, as one by one, ten dragons took to the sky.

The trance broke, and they charged towards the Elthare and Lysin soldiers.

Gods, I'm going to die.

No. You will not. Mikhial's voice filled his mind. Somewhere below, his brother was fighting. Grant was slightly annoyed that Mikhial was using his powers instead of concentrating fully on the Mezerans. *You will fight, little brother.*

Get out of my head, Mik.

Then fucking fight!

"Get me closer!" Grant shouted to Fedirij.

The dragon hovered lower, and Grant readied his bow, launching arrow after arrow into the fray. He wasn't as good a shot as Andalen, but as long as he hit some Mezerans, he didn't think it mattered.

Fedirij made ShadowCloud rise higher into the sky. He hummed again, and the dragon opened its mouth, setting fire to the line of trees the Mezerans were still spilling from.

Grant scanned the ground. He needed to find Lonis.

"Closer!"

Fedirij complied, and Grant swept the field until he saw Lonis, fighting side by side with Ikar. They were surrounded by five Mezerans. Grant pulled his *padares* from the sheath on his back. He stood on the back of the dragon and jumped as Fedirij got close enough to the ground.

Grant rolled into the grass, slicing out with his weapon as a Mezeran tried to drive an axe through his skull. His *padaré* sliced through the man's thigh, severing the femoral artery. The man screamed, clutching his leg. He dropped his axe in the process. Grant placed one of his *padarés* back into its sheath and picked up the discarded axe, and ran towards the area where he saw Lonis and Ikar.

He kicked, slashed, dodged and spun out of harm's way. He remembered every bit of training Lonis had taught him over the years, and he didn't have to think when a Mezeran tried to slam his fist into Grant's face. He blocked the blow by crossing his arms, and then spun, bringing his arm down while twisting the Mezeran's arm up. A sickening crack filled the small space around them.

He was only twenty feet from Ikar and Lonis when something hit him from behind, and his head slammed into the ground.

Andalen was with the archers on an old wall that had once been part of a fort during the late 1600s. She loosed arrow after arrow into the melee, hitting each target she aimed for.

The tree line was on fire, and the Mezerans had slowed, but there were still more. They were trying to find a way around the flames, but to the left was a lake, and to the right there were the archers.

The Mezerans hesitated only a moment before they began to charge the fort.

"Father!" she yelled. Her father and others were on the ground, pushing the Mezerans back from reaching the archers.

Her father turned and led a small group to head the other Mezerans off. Andalen commanded the archers along that section to provide them cover.

She turned her attention back to the battlefield. Below her, the Mezerans were getting closer to the wall. They attacked with no remorse. Their eyes were lifeless but wild, almost like a diseased, crazed animal.

Andalen drew her sword. "Keep firing!"

She ran behind the archers to the stairs that led out to the grass. Her father swung his own blade, stabbing a female Mezeran through the heart.

He turned his head when he felt her approach. He and two others were the only ones left standing.

"Get back up there!" he yelled.

"You need help!"

"Andalen!"

A Mezeran cornered her against the stone wall, swinging a crude weapon with a blunt head. She ducked, and the weapon hit the stone. Large bits flaked off and landed in her hair. She stabbed her sword upwards, digging her blade under the man's ribs.

His eyes flew wide, and Andalen felt bile rise up in her throat.

She had killed plenty with her arrows. She had seen the points strike true, but there was something unnerving about seeing death up close. She felt her blade vibrate slightly as it sliced through him, warm blood trickled on her fingers.

"An--" her father's words were cut short.

A large weapon with a head that looked much like an anvil was stuck in his skull. His eyes flew wide, his mouth open as he had tried to say her name.

"FATHER!"

The Mezeran laughed as he removed his weapon with a sickening squelching sound from Lord Amadon's skull.

"War is no place for a little girl."

Andalen didn't respond. She hefted the sword Gellen had gifted to her years before, bringing it down in a wide arch. The Mezeran swung his anvil, breaking her sword in half.

Out of shock, she dropped the handle.

She looked up at the Mezeran's wild eyes and pulled two daggers from her belt. From overhead a rain of arrows showered down in front of her.

Chapter Twenty-Seven

Beautiful, messy chaos. There was no other way to describe a battle. It was beautiful in the unity of soldiers banding together to combat a common enemy. It was beautiful in the dance of ducking, diving, blocking and stabbing. Messy with the blood spraying from severed limbs and stab wounds, and the metallic tang of new death filled the air. Chaotic with screams and shouts ringing through the foggy morning.

Overhead, a dragon bellowed before setting fire to a row of Mezerans.

Ikar spun from a Mezeran's grip, his tunic ripping at the neck. He was graceful in his movements, fluid like water.

"Gods!" Grant shouted from somewhere near him. Ikar looked over in time to see several Mezerans fly through the air by an invisible force. "It's never-ending."

"Keep fighting," a soldier commanded, covered in blood and entrails. His white coat was more red than cream. "We're going to push them back towards the east."

Another dragon whipped through the air, lighting the grass only feet away from Ikar ablaze.

"Watch it!" he yelled up to the rider.

His protests were met with a war cry.

Ikar rolled his eyes and focused his attention on the several Mezerans that advanced. "Lonis!"

Lonis turned after killing the two attacking him, and ran to Ikar just as the six men and women approached, their eyes rolling and wild.

"Something's wrong with them," Lonis said.

"Like what?" Ikar asked, blocking a woman's fist and driving the hilt of his sword into her kneecap. She roared in pain. "Besides the fact that they are trying to kill us."

Lonis paused. "I don't know." He seemed distracted, and Ikar knew why. Not ten feet away, Grant was battling a Mezeran. He looked to be losing, but Lonis couldn't help. For every one Ikar killed, two more popped in place. He needed the extra pair of hands.

The Mezeran Grant was battling suddenly fell. The man's heart hovered in the air in front of Grant. Blood dripped from the ends of Grant's curly hair. He surged forward to help Ikar and Lonis, and the heart dropped into the grass.

As suddenly as he lurched forward, Grant came to a halt. He tilted his head to the side, the way dogs do when they hear a noise. His eyes flew wide.

"Mikhial."

"Go!" Lonis demanded, growling when a dagger cut his shoulder. He spun, driving his elbow into the man's nose. "Grant, go find your brother!"

Grant only hesitated for a moment, his eyes clashing with Lonis' before he turned and disappeared into the carnage.

Ikar was exhausted. He felt as if they had been there for hours. His muscles burned, and he felt sticky with sweat and other substances he would rather not think about.

He chanced a glance out to the open field. Bodies--Mezeran, Lysin, Eltharian--littered the grass. Thousands on each side still stood, and the clang of metal against metal vibrated in his ears.

He still had hope. He had to, or else the pessimism would drive him insane.

"Ikar." Lonis' voice was low, confused.

They had defeated the Mezerans in front of them, but Lonis' attention was turned away, to Ikar's left.

Yvney stood with a small group of Mezerans. He wore their clothes: fur-lined cloak and boots, and he held a crude, large war hammer in his hand. His smile was cruel. Ikar had seen many of his brother's smiles over the years, but he had never seen one like this. He seemed to be enjoying the killing, basking in the smell of blood in the air.

"IKAR!" Yvney bellowed, running forward.

As he got closer, Ikar could see the same wild, but lifeless look in Yvney's eyes as the other Mezerans.

The last words Yvney spoke to him echoed through his mind. *I never truly hated you.*

But hate was the only thing he saw in his brother now.

Ikar only had a second to bring his own weapon up to block his brother's blow. His arms vibrated with the force of the hammer knocking against the axe he had stolen from a fallen Mezeran.

"Yvney, please."

Lonis took one step forward to help Ikar, but the other Mezerans--Ikar now saw they were also prisoners from the Round Tower, he recognized the man who had called out to him during his visit--attacked, seeming to swallow Lonis like an army of ants overtaking left out food.

Yvney did not falter. He swung the hammer time and time again, and Ikar blocked each blow, but he was not sure how long he would be able to fight off his brother. His whole body shook with fatigue.

"Yvney."

Yvney roared. He paused in his attacks, but only long enough to change his features. Black hair turned orange, and pale skin turned warted and brown. He grew several more inches. In front of Ikar stood, no longer his brother, but a tall, husky ogre.

"Fuck."

The ogre swung, and Ikar blocked his blow, but with Yvney's new appearance came new strength. The attack made Ikar fall into the grass, and his ass twinged with pain.

"Yvney," he pleaded. He tried to reach into Yvney and find that part of him that was still Dominikov.

"Fight me, you fucking coward!" Yvney bellowed. "*Wachë!*"

Ikar froze. Never had Yvney called him *that*. Yvney had spent the early part of his teen years learning Lysin swear words, and he had called Ikar others, but never a *wachë*. It was the lowest insult in the Lysin language.

"Ikar!" Lonis' voice shook him from his shock.

The hammer came down again, driving into his forearm. There was a sickening crack. Ikar screamed in pain, but he had no time to nurse his injury. His brother had taken up Ikar's fallen axe and swung. With no other weapon near him, Ikar put his broken arm up as a means to defend himself.

Stupid, he chastised himself.

The blade connected, severing his hand from his wrist. Ikar screamed.

His hand flopped in the grass.

Several soldiers surrounded Ikar, pushing Yvney and the other prisoners back.

Tears streamed from Ikar's eyes as he cradled his bloody stump to his chest. Lonis was at his side in seconds, kneeling beside him, face covered in dirt and blood.

"Let me see."

Gently, Lonis took Ikar's arm in his hand, surveying the wound. Just above the stump was turning purple, bone protruding from the skin.

"We have to stop the bleeding."

"How?"

Lonis thrust his arm into the smoldering grass, not even inches from Ikar's head. He screamed.

"I'm sorry," Lonis said.

Around them, the Eltharian soldiers had created a barricade, giving Lonis time to see to Ikar's wound.

One of the soldiers had a large piece of cloth tied around the shield at their back, Lonis stole it, earning nothing more than a disgruntled look from the man.

"My wife gave me that."

"Well, now I need it," Ikar said. "I'm more injured than you."

The end of his arm was black and red, and the smell of burning flesh hung in the small space around them. Ikar laid back in the grass. A dragon flew overhead.

"Just leave me to die here."

"Stop being dramatic. You're not going to die. I promised Roz I would keep you alive."

"That woman has no faith."

Lonis smiled slightly. "She just loves you."

Ikar's eyes pinched as Lonis tied his wounded arm to his chest. "Have you seen Grant?"

Worry etched Lonis' features. "Not since he went to find Mikhial." He stood, offering to help Ikar to his feet. "The bind should hold. We'll see a doctor once this is over."

"If I don't die first."

"You're not going to die."

The soldiers made a path to let Lonis and Ikar back into the battle. Lonis stuck close to Ikar's side, defending him when Ikar couldn't defend himself.

Ikar searched the field for Yvney and found him not far away, driving a sword through the heart of a Lysin.

He's too far gone. Ikar did not know what the Mezerans had done to his brother, but the man before him was no longer Yvney.

"We're going to have to kill him," a soldier said, kicking a Mezeran down onto the grass as she tried to grab his coat. "He's not your brother anymore."

Even though Ikar thought the same, he tried to come up with a retort, another solution, but he had nothing. If Yvney knew this was what he had become, he would beg for Ikar to take his life.

"I'll do it."

"You're injured," Lonis said.

"Thank you. I'm highly aware that I am now sans hand." Ikar shifted his grip on the sword he held. He wasn't sure where he had even retrieved it from. "At least it wasn't my wanking hand."

Lonis ignored that comment. "I'm coming with you."

But Ikar shook his head. For the first time in twenty-two years, he truly felt his powers stirring in him. As if they had been lying dormant until this exact moment. Ikar closed his eyes and willed them to consume him.

Bones cracked. His body shifted. It was painful, but Ikar didn't scream.

When it was over, he towered over the others. Long black fur lined his arms.

"Holy shit," one of the soldiers said. "You're a bear."

Even as a bear, Ikar rolled his eyes.

He fell to all fours. His stump was already healing due to the magic in his veins, but it still stung to use it to limp across the field to his brother.

Yvney's eyes caught on him, and his cruel smile grew. "Brother, you finally found your powers."

Ikar swung his large arm, putting his weight on his front paw. Yvney's eyes went wide before he sailed through the air, body slamming into a large tree. He slumped to the ground, shaking his head from the daze, but he didn't get up.

Ikar shifted back to his human form, uncaring that he was naked. He knelt down, grabbing a dagger from the belt of a fallen Eltharian soldier.

Yveny's eyes met his. They were flickering between the wild Mezeran and the clarity of his brother. The clarity in his eyes told Ikar that Yvney was already dying.

When Yvney saw him approach, he smiled. His lips turned up in resolution. "Brother." Blood trickled from his lips. "I'm proud of you."

Ikar hesitated. If he tried to save Yvney's life now, would he go back to being the pain in the ass he always was? Or would he be lost to the Mezerans?

"Don't hesitate, Ikar. Kill me."

Ikar's hand shook. "Yvney." There was so much he wanted to say. Despite their dislike for one another, Ikar had looked up to him once, had loved him once. They were blood, bonded in ways that superseded the fights over the years, the dark words.

"It's okay, little brother. I would rather it be you."

Ikar drove the dagger into Yvney's heart. Tears leaked down his face. Yvney's eyes flew wide momentarily. Then his smile faltered as the last of his life flickered from his eyes.

"M-may Kurem lead you to the Gates."

Chapter Twenty-Eight

Kelmen stood at the front of the city walls. The soldiers expanded across the road, lining the tall stone structure for as far as the eye could see. Two dragons stood before them in the middle of the Main Road, their riders perched on top, ready for battle.

The sun was almost to the highest point in the sky.

"They're coming," his mother said.

He had tried to beg her to go into the castle with the other women, but she had scoffed.

"I was front and center during the Ogre Wars and the War with Soldare. I was in the room when the peace treaty between the three western kingdoms was signed. I will *not* sit out for this one."

Kelmen found it better not to argue with his mother.

A small smattering of Mezerans crossed the bridge over the Roaming River, spilling out before them. The man at the front was Emperor Lo-Bie Jabü, the ruler of the Mezerah. He was broad-chested and tall. He wore long emerald robes and a fur-lined cloak. His hair was black, and his tawny skin shimmered in the sun. At his side was his brother, Ai-Jael, and his nephew, Bahst-el.

No one spoke. Master Roxell broke from the line and stepped forward. "Lo-Bie, leave our kingdom at once."

General Sinero shook his head. He had planned to greet the Mezerans with arrows and swords, not words of warning.

The dragons shifted restlessly.

Emperor Jabü chuckled. "I have no intention of doing that, Roxell Vaslev."

"Enough of this," Johan Sinero surged forward, sword in hand.

Everything happened quickly. The Mezerans came forward, crying out a battle roar that seemed to shake the earth. The dragons took to the sky. Arrows flew overhead. His mother began chanting incantations at his side.

Kelmen's body tensed. *Run.* But he couldn't run. He had been drafted into this fight like every other man in Elthare.

Run.

He pulled the sword he had been given from his back.

Run.

And he did.

Toward the fray.

He was not a skilled fighter. He was only nineteen and had worked as a fisherman since the age of eleven, but he had quick hands. He knew how to wield a knife.

If being a fisherman had taught him anything, it was how to cut open something living.

But before his sword connected with the Mezeran, the man fell over. As if he was a wind-up toy that had lost power.

Kelmen groaned. *Mother.* He turned, and she flashed him a small smile.

She tried to keep the Mezerans away from him, but they were quicker than she could spew out spells and curses. One slipped through, and his axe sliced through Kel's calf. He fell into the dirt and screamed.

"Kel!" the Wood Witch screamed.

The air around Kelmen pulsed as he tried to stand, but he couldn't. The cut was too deep, and when he fell, he had sprained his ankle. The Mezerans gave him a wide berth. His mother had erected a shield around him that none could penetrate. Kelmen could do nothing but watch the battle from the dirt.

Blood seeped from the wound on his leg. It was too deep for the magic in his veins to heal it swiftly. It would take a day or two at the most.

Kel watched as Johan battled Bahst-el.

The pain in his leg was making him groggy. He felt ready to puke.

General Sinero blocked a blow from the Mezeran General.

Black blinked at the edges of Kel's vision.

The last thing he saw before he passed out was Master Roxell cutting off Emperor Jabü's head.

Grant was injured. Beyond injured. He was surprised he was still moving, still fighting. His pinky finger of his right hand was bent at an odd angle, and a sizable cut slit across his forehead and dripped blood down his face. A stab wound to his side left him gasping for breath.

Mikhial looked worse, but he was still standing as well. He was protecting Briar, who was unscathed, minus a large cut spanning the length of his chin to his shoulder.

Grant could feel the pain now. His adrenaline was fleeting. He sank to his knees.

"Come on, little brother!" Mikhial commanded.

"I can't do it anymore, Mik."

They had pushed the Mezerans back to the outskirts of Odenmal. Some were already fleeing back to the ships waiting in the sea.

Briar knelt in front of Grant, tugging him up by the hand. "Come on, Grant. We're winning."

By some miracle, they were winning. Thousands of men and women still stood, and more than half were either Eltharian or Lysin.

"Alright," Grant conceded. "I'm going to need a pint of ale and chocolate after this."

"I'll get you the big--" Briar's eyes flew wide, blood spilled from his mouth. He fell to his knees in front of Grant.

Grant's hands flew out to catch him. A dagger stuck through the back of Briar's skull. Behind him, a Mezeran smirked.

Grant jumped to his feet. Fury boiled inside of him. He pushed every single ounce of his power at the man. His smile slid from his face.

Grant held the man's feet above the ground, never wavering as he willed his power to crush the man's spine like a boa would its prey. The man screamed.

Grant watched the life bleed from his eyes.

He fell into a heap on the ground when Grant released him.

More and more Mezerans were falling back, running away into the streets of Odenmal. Ships were starting to sail back to the east.

Grant heaved. Bile burned his throat as it left his mouth, splashing to the ground.

Mikhial was at his side, rubbing between his shoulder blades. "Let it out, little brother."

Grant shook Mikhial's hands from his shoulder. "Don't touch me."

Mikhial looked hurt, but stood back. Soldiers and dragons gave chase to the retreating Mezerans, killing those that were too slow to make it back to the ships.

Thick and eerie silence fell. But the echoes of dying screams still rang in Grant's ears.

"I need to find the others."

Grant couldn't bring himself to look at Briar's corpse.

He stalked back through the woods, stepping over bodies that littered the forest floor. ShadowCloud was not far, arrows pierced his side. Fedirij lay a few feet away with an axe stuck through his chest.

Soldiers were going through, stabbing the Mezerans that still lived, but were too injured to get up, and helping allies to their feet.

A man was cut in half before Grant. He came to a stop. The top half of the man belonged to Garis Frell, one of his family's Guard.

"Grant!"

Grant turned at the sound of his name. Ikar, Lonis and his father limped toward him. They were injured as badly as anyone else. Lonis was covered in cuts and stab wounds, Ikar was missing a hand, and his father was missing a leg. He was holding onto Ikar and Lonis for support.

Grant wound his arms around his father's neck and sobbed into his chest.

"It's alright, my son. We won."

Grant pulled back, dashing at his tears. "Ikar," he started, emotion choking him. "Briar--"

"I know." Ikar hung his head. "I saw."

Grant turned to Lonis next. His left eye was swollen shut. "Lonnie."

He smiled, and Grant noticed one of his teeth had been knocked out. "We survived, Sin."

The four of them continued through the field, looking for familiar faces and helping those alive.

"We sent a fire message for a doctor," one of the soldiers said. "The Wood Witch said that a few hundred Mezerans slipped passed us and tried to take the castle."

Lord Sinero nodded. "Master Roxell?"

"Alive. He killed the Mezeran Emperor."

Grant left his father and the soldier, and followed Ikar and Lonis to the fort Andalen had been defending. There were no signs of life. All their archers and Lord Amadon were dead.

Under the body of a large Mezeran, they found Andalen. Her large brown eyes stared up at the afternoon sky. Her hand still clutched her family's dagger.

Grant's heart squeezed. He knelt at her side, brushing his fingers over her curly hair. "May Kurem lead you to the Gates, my friend."

Lonis and Ikar stood behind him, silent as he said a prayer to the Gods to guide Andalen safely through the Afterworld.

Chapter Twenty-Nine

Months after the battle, the setting sun turned the sky above the sea pink and orange. Grant had been sitting on Oszerack's dock for the latter part of the day, thinking about all that he had lost during the battle, the scars he still bore. A mouse skittered across the dock to his side.

"What are you doing here?" he asked the mouse.

It chittered.

Grant rolled his eyes. "Turn back. I can't have a conversation with you as a rodent."

He felt movement at his side, and a very naked Ikar sat beside him. "I'm going to get splinters in my ass."

"That's your problem, Dominikov." Grant swung his bare feet, his toes skimming the water. "What are you doing here?" he asked again.

"Master Roxell is up at your house. He wants to talk to us."

"Are you planning on putting on clothes before that?"

Ikar smiled slightly. "I was thinking I would show up naked. What do you think?"

"I think I am seeing too much of your cock."

Ikar laughed. "I talked to Lonis. You're leaving with him, aren't you?"

Grant nodded and threw a pebble into the sea. "Be happy, Dominikov. That means you're going to be king."

His mind briefly went to Khett. The former prince had survived his injuries but would no longer be able to speak. He woke nightly from horrible nightmares, and could only make it through the day after he had smoked a pound of Nestvor, and he and Lady Pedgram had left to live with her sister in the wilds of Rivland.

"This is not how I wanted to get the crown," Ikar answered soberly. "We were all supposed to survive, and everyone was supposed to cheer for me at the end." His voice cracked. "Briar was supposed to see my beautiful Freja grow. Khett's gone insane, and now you're leaving too."

Grant's mind flashed images of Briar, Andalen, Mr. Hesito's stiff hand holding a blood-stained picture of Lonis and his wife. "I can't stay here right now."

"I understand, Sinero."

They stood, and Grant gave Ikar his cloak to cover himself. They were silent as they walked back to the Sinero Estate. He led Ikar to his chambers to find some clothes before meeting Master Roxell and the remaining Noble Council in their Library.

Lady Monneaire and Lady Amadon were sitting close together on the couch. Lord Monneaire hovered by the fireplace. Lord Sinero, Arlen and Mikhial sat at a round table with Master Roxell. Lady and Lord Dominikov lounged in plush armchairs. A man Grant had never seen before leaned against the window.

"Ikar, Grant," Lord Sinero rose, gesturing to the unknown man. He looked to be sixteen or seventeen at the most. "This is Christophe Pedgram, Khett's cousin. He is now the head of the Pedgram house."

Grant and Ikar bowed their heads in recognition.

Master Roxell waved Ikar and Grant forward. He still looked as flawless as he did during the Trials, but a large scar ran the length of the left side of his skull.

"You two are the last remaining Champions of the 43rd King Trials. A Trial has been set up in three days' time to claim the winner."

"That won't be necessary," Grant said at the same time as Ikar said, "I have had enough fighting for a lifetime."

"It's tradition," Master Roxell pursed his lips. "Tell me, Lord Grantham, why won't it be necessary?"

"I forfeit my right to the crown. Ikar is king. I'm leaving for The Republic."

Master Roxell turned various shades of red. "This is outrageous!"

"This is my choice," Grant countered, unwilling to back down. "Ikar will be a better king than me."

"Dishonorable," Master Roxell muttered.

Lady Amadon stood, coming to the table. "Roxell, calm down. After everything we have been through, you're really going to call Grantham dishonorable? He fought bravely in the Ten Day Battle."

Master Roxell scoffed, but said nothing.

"Are you sure this is what you want, my son?" His father's voice was soft, barely audible in the quiet room.

"I'm sure, Pa." Grant stood. "Just give me the Deserter's Mark, and I'll be on my way."

"You're not getting Marked," Ikar said.

"He has to be Marked!" Master Roxell pushed back from the table, running an agitated hand through his blond hair. "If he abdicates the throne, he has to be Marked!"

Grant shuddered. He could still smell the burning flesh of Arlen's Marking, and could still see the look of despair in the other man's eyes when Master Roxell reiterated he would never be allowed to step foot in Elthare again. Arlen was no longer an Eltharian or an Amadon. He was a man with no home and no name. Though that future terrified Grant, he would accept it. He looked at Arlen, sitting in a velvet chair, the red angry Mark barely covered by his rolled up sleeves. They would be men without a home. Without status.

Would he be able to survive never seeing Elthare again?

For Lonnie I can endure anything.

Ikar walked around the table calmly, standing toe to toe with the Trials Master. "Grant fought for this kingdom, and you want to kick him out? Tell him he can never come back? You won when we wanted Arlen to remain part of this kingdom and not get Marked, but you will *not* win this time,

Vaslev. Grantham remains Eltharian. He will remain a Sinero until the day he takes his last breath. I am king now, and I say that Grant is *not* getting Marked."

"You're not king yet," Christophe said. "But I agree. We can forgo tradition for a hero of the Ten Day Battle. He may not have lost his mind like my cousin, but we all lost something during those days." Lord Christophe gazed at Arlen. "Sorry, chap. Seems ill mannered of us to talk about this in front of you."

Arlen waved a hand. "It's fine." He stood and left the room, the door slamming behind him.

Ikar raised an eyebrow at Khett's cousin. "I don't know who you are, but I'm glad you agree."

Christophe pushed up from the window and stood at the front of the room next to Ikar. "Does anyone object?"

No one argued, and Grant breathed easier.

Ikar came back around the table to clap Grant on the back. "You better stay for the coronation and come back for my wedding, or I'll hunt you down."

Grant laughed. "Wouldn't miss it."

Ikar shook with nerves as he waited in the small atrium just off the throne room. The robes he wore were made of black fabric with fur lining the neckline. Red swirls and snowdrops had been embroidered on the velvet in sparkly red thread. His hair was styled to be pushed back from his face, so his ears stood out more than usual.

On the other side of the door, he could hear the people of Elthare--his subjects--as they settled into their seats. Master Roxell's booming voice echoed through the throne room as he directed where people should go.

"Ladies and Gentlemen!" His voice traveled as the noise settled. "Welcome to the Coronation of our 43rd king. Today truly is historic. We have never had a Dominikov sit on the Elthare throne." He paused for applause and raucous cheering from where Ikar imagined the Althanens sat. "This happy occasion comes out of dark times for our beloved kingdom. Many fell during the Ten Day Battle, including four of our six Champions. Let's say a silent prayer for our fallen." The last of the sentence was met with a long bout of silence, then Master Roxell spoke again. "Our new king showed great heroics during the battle, and I believe he is the light we need after a dark, heavy storm. Ladies and gentlemen, the winner of the 43rd King's Trials, Lord Ikar of House Dominikov, first of his name."

Loud cheers met Ikar's ears as the door to the atrium opened, and he stepped out onto the dais. In front of him sat thousands of Eltharians; Palmans dressed in their colorful harem pants, their faces painted, and their hair wild. Oszerackians with vests and trousers. The Odemalians with their leather pants and tunics. The Rivs with their conservative high, stiff collars. And last, the group that cheered loudest of all--the Althanens with their thick cloaks and fur lined boots, stomping on the marble and Opal Stone floor. Each Eltharian had a Snowdrop pinned to the collar of their tunic, coat or dress.

Ikar turned towards Master Roxell, who held a scepter in one hand and a pillow holding the Dominikov crown in the other. The gold and rubies shimmered under the light of the sun streaming through the high windows around the room. Behind Master Roxell were Ikar's parents, both scarred and armed. Pride etched into the features of their rough faces. His mother held his daughter in her arms. Next to them were the royal families from Soldare and Lysic. None of them clapped, but Queen Selia was smiling. President Lishu from the Republic stood with his daughter, Jineya. The Kereshi and Kunai leaders had turned down the invitation to the event.

Ikar's feet felt like lead as he moved to stand in front of the throne. The Dominikov throne was framed with Opal Stone and steel carved to look like filigree with a red velvet cushion.

The Master handed Ikar the scepter, and the Temple Priest held out the Gods' Script for Ikar to place his right hand over. Master Roxell removed the crown from the pillow, holding it over Ikar's head.

The crowd fell silent, and the room built with tension as if it were holding a collective breath.

"Ikar Dominikov, do you vow to protect the kingdom and rule with a fair, but stern hand?"

"Aye, I do."

"Do you vow to be guiding light for the Eltharian people?"

"Aye."

"Should the time arise, do you vow to lead the Eltharian soldiers in battle?"

Ikar swallowed. "Aye. I have done it, and I will do it again."

Master Roxell's smiled. "May the Gods bless your reign. May your rule be long and prosperous." The Master sounded as if he were reciting the words from a text.

Master Roxell placed the crown on his head.

He lowered himself to the throne, looking over at his parents, still not accustomed to Yvney being absent. He turned to the crowd, catching Grant and Lonis, and then Roslen's eye. Ikar's mouth ticked up into a broad smile as he gazed at Roz. His daughter, Freja Briar Dominikov, rested happily in Roz's arms.

The moment would have been perfect if he could find Briar's face in the crowd. Or if Yvney stood with his parents, wallowing with envy.

I never truly hated you. The words continued to haunt him.

Ikar stood from his throne to address the people of Elthare. Silence fell over the crowd, and he cleared his throat.

"During the battle I had to watch people I had come to consider my friends die." His eyes met Grant's, and his friend gave him an encouraging smile. "As an homage to the people we lost, I have made the decision to build centers for those in need in every city. There will be four centers named after each of the Champions lost in battle." He paused, clearing the emotion from his throat. "The Oszerackian people have graciously allowed me to name the center that will be built in their city after someone I lost, my dear friend Briar Shaden. And I humbly thank them for their gratitude.

"May these centers remind us that even in the darkest times we are stronger together. Let us work together on rebuilding our kingdom, making it a stronger, brighter place for all to live."

Grant smiled at him, and Roslen cried as she clapped along with the rest of Elthare.

I hope I made you proud, Bri.

Ikar sighed and sank back onto the throne. He felt hopeful for the future, for new beginnings.

But he couldn't help feeling something lurking on the horizon.

Epilogue

Prince Hektor picked at his pristine cuticles as he waited for his father to stop fawning over the new king of Elthare.

King Ikar of house Dominikov. What a joke.

Throngs of people shuffled out of the throne room and into the great hall, where a feast had been set up to ring in the new king's reign. Hektor turned away from the people and walked in the opposite direction to the large wood and iron doors that led to the front of the castle.

Outside, the sun was beginning to set, painting the Opal Stone and marble gold and bronze. Hektor had to admit the effect was rather pretty and much more pleasing to look at than the tan bricks of Soldare.

"Are you not in the mood for a feast?" a soft voice came from behind him.

His sister, Princess Iliana, leaned against a marble pillar, smoothing out her dress. Her dark hair was gathered in an elaborately braided bun. He sneered at her.

"Leave me be, Iliana. Shouldn't you be drooling over the new king like father and Queen Selia?"

Iliana shrugged and looked out across the gardens to where the apple orchard began. "If Ozkur were still alive, he would love this sight."

Hektor stiffened at the mention of their deceased brother. "Do not mention Ozkur."

Her large eyes swung to him. "Why not? You wish to forget him?"

Hektor climbed the two steps until he reached Iliana, his face mere inches from hers. "More than I wish for anything."

Iliana smirked. "Well, maybe--"

"Ah," came their father's voice from the door, "here you two are. Iliana, head on to the feast. Hektor and I have matters to discuss."

King Pytir hobbled down the grand stairs, his bad leg nearly giving under the weight of his portly belly. Hektor leaned against a pole, waiting for his father to come to him.

"What is it, Father?"

Pytir lowered himself onto one of the iron benches along the front of the castle, rubbing his swollen, gout infested leg. "It's time I abdicated the throne, Hektor. It was meant to be your brother's, but after his untimely death--" Pytir trailed off, his throat croaked. The only time Hektor had ever seen his father show vulnerability was when he talked about Ozkur.

Hektor stiffened again at the mention of his brother. Would the bastard ever stop haunting him?

"You're giving up the crown?"

"I'm getting old, Hektor. It's time."

Hektor's smile broadened, cruel and wicked on his handsome face. *Soldare is mine at last.*

Khett paced the small room of his aunt's cottage. The entire house smelled of goats and wheat. He found himself constantly wrinkling his nose when the wind blew a certain way, and the stench became stronger. He never understood why his Aunt Naideen had given up the large manor near the forest in Rivland after his uncle died. Surely, she would have been more comfortable there.

The only positive thing about his aunt's cottage was that the building was away from the large city. It was away from the memories of Andalen, away from the castle he had grown up in. It was away from his traitorous cousin.

Khett could not find it in his heart to forgive Christophe for what he had done. Even if his meddling had saved Khett's life.

He never had a desire to be like Christophe. He had no desire to have his soul linked to someone else.

No, not someone. Some*thing* else.

He felt the darkness in him. The *thing* that had been tethered to his soul to keep him alive.

The *mondin*, an evil spirit from the Infernal Flames.

No one knew what Christophe and that witch had done. Khett feigned his insanity, locking himself away in his aunt's cottage. Even his mother, who only roomed down the hall, thought him mad with the grief of losing Andalen.

He had grieved Andalen. He missed her as he missed Fresia. As he missed Arlen. He wished he could find the woman he had been falling for and his old friend. He wished he could bring back the woman he had loved more than life.

Well, aren't you particularly melancholy today, the *mondin* hissed in Khett's mind. *I thought we were over this melodrama.*

Fuck off.

The *mondin* laughed, making Khett wince. *Can't fuck off, my dear human. You and I are one.*

Acknowledgments

A huge thank you to my beta readers, especially Dai and Jordan, who I went to every time I changed the smallest detail in the book. Your feedback was given with honesty and kindness, and you two are the sweetest beans I have ever met. Your help and input on *The King Trials* means the world to me.

Another enormous thanks to Rebeca and Charmaine, without the two of you my book would not be the visual and edited glorious *thing* that it is.

Thank you to Jenna Moreci. Your videos were a guiding light as I worked on my novel. Without you my world and characters would not be what they are today. And without you, I never would have met Dai and Jordan.

The biggest thanks goes to those that I hold the closest in my heart. My family and my bestest bud. Without your unwavering support I would not be here. Bob, thanks for listening to me ramble about my characters and world for hours on end, and helping work out kinks in the plot. I love you!

And lastly, thank you to the person reading this. Thank you for purchasing *The King Trials*. I hope you enjoyed what I created. This book, these characters, this world are all for you! Thank you.

About the Author

D.L. lives in the southwest where she has a great view of the Sandia Mountains, and an even better view of the enchanting sunsets. When she's not writing D.L. can be found reading, cuddling with her dog, drinking tea or shopping at thrift stores. *The King Trials* is not D.L.'s first novel, but it is the one she has been most excited to write about to date. You can find D.L. on Instagram @dl_sims_books, Twitter @DL_SIMS_BOOKS and on Facebook at D.L. Sims.

CPSIA information can be obtained
at www.ICGtesting.com
Printed in the USA
LVHW010721231219
641450LV00015B/611